KU-593-877

DARK SKIES

A DCI RYAN MYSTERY

LJ Ross

Copyright © LJ Ross 2017

The right of LJ Ross to be identified as the author of this work has been asserted in accordance with the Copyright, Designs and Patents Act 1988.

All rights reserved. No part of this publication may be reproduced, stored in or transmitted into any retrieval system, in any form, or by any means (electronic, mechanical, photocopying, recording or otherwise) without the prior written permission of the publisher. Any person who does any unauthorised act in relation to this publication may be liable to criminal prosecution and civil claims for damages.

This is a work of fiction. Names, characters, businesses, places, events and incidents are either the products of the author's imagination or used in a fictitious manner. Any resemblance to actual persons, living or dead, or actual events is purely coincidental.

Cover design copyright © LJ Ross

Other books by LJ Ross

Holy Island

Sycamore Gap

Heavenfield

Angel

High Force

Cragside

"Though this be madness, yet there is method in't."

—William Shakespeare

"Nothing exists except atoms and empty space;

everything else is just opinion."

—Democritus

PROLOGUE

Kielder Forest, 1981

The sky was papered with stars on the night Duncan Gray died. He watched them from the depths of a muddy crevice, his breathing a laboured gurgle as he began to drown in his own blood.

"We can't leave him like this!"

"Shut *up!*"

Duncan heard their voices drifting on the chilly air, over the mound of debris and rubble that had once been a stone farmhouse. The demolition area was supposedly 'out of bounds' but a bit of wire mesh fencing hadn't been enough to keep them away; not when they could forage around the dusty detritus, camp and smoke without fear of discovery.

Friends.

He began to choke, blood bubbles popping at the corner of his mouth. Their conversation grew distant and he imagined he was swimming underwater, floating, his body lapping on gentle waves as death prepared to consume him.

"But it was an accident! We can tell them it was an accident. You didn't mean to do it, d-did you?"

There was an infinitesimal pause.

"No, of course not."

"Well, then, if we hurry, we might be able to get help—"

"It's too late, Roly. He's dead."

"I can still hear him—"

"He'll be dead soon enough," the other snapped, with an air of impatience. "You know what'll happen if we tell anybody. They'll say it was our fault and put us both away."

"But I haven't done anything—"

1

"You helped dump his body, didn't you? You pushed him into that hole and his blood is on your hands."

Roly looked down and began to sob loud, self-pitying tears.

"*Shut up!* Nobody needs to find out, especially not the coppers. You just need to keep your big mouth shut."

"They might believe us…"

But the seed of doubt had been planted and they both knew it.

"Look, there's nothing we can do for him now. Do you want to ruin my life—and yours—because Duncan fell over his own big feet?"

"Did he really fall?"

Roly's tear-clogged voice was hopeful, betraying an eagerness to reject the awful truth of what had happened and replace it with an alternate version where Duncan had somehow been responsible for his own death.

"He was off his head, okay? He was desperate to get his hands on the stuff we found. I told him we could share it between the three of us but Dunc wanted to keep it all for himself. He was running back to the village, stealing it while we were setting up the tents. I was trying to take it back, that's all, and he tripped and smashed himself up."

It was a lie, but that hardly mattered now. The heavy piece of rock used to crack Duncan's skull lay discarded somewhere amongst the rubble, covered in blood and hair, but they'd never find it, just as they wouldn't find the penknife he'd used to finish the job.

Maybe it wouldn't be a bad idea to use it on Roly as well.

Too risky.

"Nobody knows we're down here and if we hurry back, they won't notice either of us was ever gone. This whole area will be under water soon enough."

Their voices became a distant buzz as Duncan struggled and the stars blurred, just for a moment. He blinked, the muscles in his face twitching, his body convulsing in a final effort to survive. He thought he heard someone crying; blubbering, childlike tears that jarred with the silent valley. There were more words, harshly spoken and peppered with threats. Finally, a short, deafening silence before the first heavy stone landed on his leg, fracturing the bone.

He felt nothing.

More stones followed as they worked quickly to bury him beneath the soggy ground and Duncan watched from a motionless shell, his face a pale mask against the dirt.

"Sorry, Dunc," he thought he heard Roly say.

The stars dimmed a final time and then there was nothing but a black, empty void as the world slipped away.

* * *

Christmas 1984, three years later

They sat side by side on the dewy grass overlooking the new reservoir, surrounded by the familiar faces of friends and neighbours who had turned out to watch the Aurora Borealis set the night sky aflame. They were not disappointed, for the Northern Lights rose in a kaleidoscope of colour, more beautiful than anything they had ever seen.

Around them, the villagers gathered in clusters, their voices muffled behind heavy winter coats and scarves. Steam rose from flasks of hot tea and, every so often, there came the sound of uproarious laughter. Someone had brought a portable radio and it hummed the crackling melody of Band Aid's newly-crowned Christmas Number One.

The pair said nothing but continued to watch the rippling lights reflected on the lake, thinking of what lay hidden far beneath its surface.

"They've stopped looking now," Roly whispered.

"I know."

"Do you think that's it, then? Can we—can we pretend it never happened?"

"No, we can't. Everything is different now."

They cast their eyes up to the heavens and felt something click softly into place; some hitherto unknown part of themselves that had been missing. There was no need to pretend, no need to feel ashamed of what had been the defining moment of their lives and what set them apart from the common herd.

"You don't understand, Roly. We're special, now. Superhuman, or something like that."

"What d' you mean?"

"I dunno…" It was hard to describe the incredible, overwhelming feeling of power. "Just, different. Above all the rest."

The sky flared in shades of green and blue, scattering light over the rippling water. Three years had passed and there had been no repercussions after Duncan's death; especially now that the rumours had started about him running away from home. In another six months, he'd be nothing more than a distant memory.

Nobody could touch them now, not ever.

CHAPTER 1

Kielder Reservoir, Friday 30ᵗʰ September 2016

Thirty-two years later

Mist curled across the silvery expanse of water, rolling its way towards the shoreline and through the dense forest that lined the reservoir and stretched back as far as the eye could see. The sun cast bright shards of light over the quiet morning and there was no sound to be heard except the gentle lapping of water against shingle.

Lisa Hope stood on a long wooden jetty dressed in full diving gear, surveying the placid water with a dubious expression.

"It looks really, *really* cold."

"You'll hardly feel it, once you get going," came the cheerful response from their diving instructor, who continued to check the air tanks from the deck of his small motorboat.

A reassuring arm curled around her waist.

"Having second thoughts?"

She sighed, remembering Oliver had used that same persuasive tone to convince her to give up her Saturday mornings to attend a scuba diving course at Kielder Water. *It'll be just like the Red Sea, only much closer to home*, he'd said. *We can earn our certificates together*, he'd said.

She heaved a long sigh, which clouded on the frosty air.

"Well, so long as we're here…"

"That's the spirit!" Oliver gave his girlfriend a quick smacking kiss. "Besides, people say there are forgotten villages lurking down there, filled with all kinds of treasure. Isn't that right, Freddie?"

The diving instructor fiddled with the zip on his wetsuit. The idea of ghostly villages lurking beneath the surface like a poor man's Atlantis was a draw for the tourists, but everybody knew the old

5

buildings and smallholdings had been demolished to make way for the new reservoir back in the early eighties.

He supposed that's what they called Progress.

Still, it wouldn't hurt to keep the legend alive, if it meant they'd recommend the diving course to a few of their city friends.

"Oh, aye," he said, clearing his throat. "There's an old church down there and, if you swim to a certain spot, they say you can still hear the bells ringing."

He'd never heard any such thing but it was the best he could come up with at short notice.

"Really?" Oliver's eyes gleamed. "C'mon, Lisa, let's go and see for ourselves."

A spark of excitement had overtaken their fear of hypothermia for the time being and Freddie helped them aboard *The Daydream*, checked their gear one last time and flicked the engine into life.

* * *

The icy cold water had been a shock to the system but it was nothing to compare with the shock awaiting them as they dived deeper into the bowels of the reservoir.

Freddie led them in a fan formation, thrusting downward with the kind of grace that was borne of long experience, leaving a stream of bubbles in his wake. The couple followed, eyes widening as a shoal of fish darted through the reeds and skittered around them, adjusting to the fall in temperature while they concentrated on keeping their breathing slow and even to conserve oxygen.

They followed his brisk hand signal and glided left through the murky water until they came to a clearing where the land dipped towards the basin of the reservoir at its deepest point. The water was clearer here, revealing the enormity of their surroundings, and they felt a momentary panic at the sheer size of it.

What if something went wrong?

Sensing their unease, Freddie gave them an "OK" signal and bobbed his head in the direction of what looked like a collection of tumbled-down stones. Its shadowed outline was barely visible without the natural light of the shallows and he tapped the small torch attached to the hood of his diving suit, waiting until they followed his example. Diving deeper, they found themselves amongst the rubble of a large farmhouse. Part of its walls remained intact, marking the territory of what had once been a kitchen or a living room and Freddie pointed out the dusty outline of a tin can and the glint of a silver fork. It was mesmerising, the silent underwater landscape with its eerie remnants of the past, and the three divers drifted apart as they explored its secrets, the light from their torches flickering as they went.

After a few minutes, Freddie rounded them up and tapped his watch, giving the thumbs-up signal to indicate it was time to start making their way back to the surface. Lisa nodded and pushed away from a nearby stone, crying out in a sharp burst of bubbles as the stone dislodged, bringing with it an avalanche of silt. She kicked frantically upward to escape the cloud of brown dust that engulfed her, disorientating and blotting out the light from her torch so it was impossible to know for sure whether she was heading in the right direction.

Her breathing became erratic and fear took a stranglehold. Her arms flailed as she forgot her training and succumbed to blind panic, striking out for the surface with clumsy movements.

Something brushed against her leg and Lisa tried to shake it off. She turned to look back through the gloom and, as the muddy water dissipated, she caught sight of what had risen from the reservoir floor.

It was an arm, outstretched and crooked, its skin covered in a thick layer of peat that was crumbling into a mist under the pressure of the water. Her eyes widened in terror as the body of an adolescent boy twisted into view, his face shockingly preserved except for gaping black holes where his eyes should have been.

Lisa screamed and then she was falling, down and down into the darkness towards his outstretched arms.

* * *

Doctor Anna Taylor battled with the gearstick on a temperamental old university minibus and told herself that this was definitely, *positively*, the last time she would volunteer to lead a weekend residential course. As a light drizzle began to settle against the windscreen, she thought fondly of the private honeymoon villa she'd occupied for the past three weeks, tanning herself in a tropical paradise with her new husband. They'd spent long, lazy days doing very little except enjoying each other's company and making extravagant plans about leaving their respective jobs to run a Tiki bar or something equally flamboyant. Sadly, as with all good things, the honeymoon had come to an end and was replaced with the promise of a long weekend spent in an area that boasted one of the highest statistical averages for rainfall in the whole country.

Anna flicked a glance in the rear-view mirror at the motley collection of postgraduate history students slumped in their seats and wondered what the next few days at Kielder would hold. The journey west from Newcastle upon Tyne had been scenic, leading them through rolling countryside and along the 'military road' running parallel to Hadrian's Wall towards the western edge of the county of Northumberland. The road wound up and down the valley, across sparse plains where hefted sheep grazed, until a vast forest loomed on the horizon. The scale of it never failed to impress, reminding her of Canada or perhaps Alaska, the trees towering on all sides in a patchwork of rich green and brown. The area might not boast an exotic climate but she had to admit that whatever it lacked in temperature, it certainly made up for in breathtaking natural beauty.

The minibus wheezed its way along the main road through the trees and Anna slowed to look out for the exit that would lead to the holiday lodges they'd rented near the banks of the reservoir. Spotting it, she directed the protesting vehicle along another winding road until the water came into view, glittering steel-grey in the morning light. Next to it was a collection of low-roofed, eco-friendly buildings that housed a visitor's centre with an inn, a gift shop and conference facilities, as well as a couple of water sports kiosks, the Birds of Prey Centre and a boathouse next to a long wooden jetty. There were a few small boats moored alongside it, including the passenger ferry that carried people to various stopping points on the lake. Anna parked the minibus in the visitor's car park, stretched the aching muscles in her neck and prepared to unload her human cargo.

"Alright—wakey, wakey! We're here!"

They had barely set foot on the tarmac before the commotion began.

A man dressed in a black wetsuit leapt from the deck of a small motorboat and ran halfway along the jetty, bare feet slapping against the decking. He bellowed towards one of the kiosks, waving his arms wildly to attract attention.

"*Mitch! I've got an emergency!*"

Immediately, a fit-looking man of around fifty and dressed in a company-logo polo shirt ran out of the kiosk carrying a white canvas bag emblazoned with a green cross. He was met by two or three other locals who ran out of the inn to see what all the fuss was about.

Anna slipped her mobile phone out of her pocket, intending to call the emergency services, but was frustrated to find she had no signal.

"Stay here!" she called out to her students, without much success. An edict from a history professor held no weight against morbid curiosity and they began edging forward to see what had caused the ruckus.

Anna felt honour-bound to offer up her services as a first aider, so she jogged towards the water's edge and slipped through the gathering crowd of onlookers.

"Has anybody called 999?"

She spoke to a woman somewhere in her late forties, wearing classic country garb and a concerned expression.

"An ambulance is on its way but Mitch is already down there with Freddie, doing what he can."

Anna nodded and fell quiet, waiting with bated breath to see if his efforts would do any good. A little way off, she could see the swift rise and fall of a man's shoulders performing CPR on the still, unresponsive figure of a young blonde woman whose body lay inert on the deck of the motorboat. The boat's captain stood a few feet away, his wiry arm gripped tightly around a younger man who was ashen with shock, his eyes trained on the woman lying at his feet. Across the tense silence, they could hear the rasping breath of the first aider as he worked hard to keep the woman alive.

"Come on," he muttered roughly.

One, two, three, four, five.

"Come *on!*"

"She's not going to make it!" Oliver's voice cracked, and Freddie's arm gripped more tightly around his shoulders.

"There, lad," he said, with more conviction than he felt. "She'll pull round, you'll see."

After another endless moment of taut silence, there came the sound of an enormous splutter as Lisa Hope expelled water from her lungs and gasped for life.

"Oh, thank God," Anna murmured, and relief rocketed through her system.

She blew out a long breath and looked down to find her hand clasped tightly by the woman standing beside her, whose eyes were closed as she mumbled softly-spoken words of prayer.

Anna gave her fingers a squeeze and held on for a moment longer, for there was worse to come.

CHAPTER 2

Detective Chief Inspector Maxwell Finlay-Ryan entered the new headquarters of the Northumbria Police Constabulary with a spring in his step. He supposed he could have waited until Monday before returning to work but, since Anna was away on a residential weekend with her students, he might as well surprise his team and see whether the wheels of justice had fallen off the proverbial wagon while he'd been away on his honeymoon.

Ryan strode through the wide reception area and grinned at the shocked expression of the duty sergeant at the front desk, who had probably never seen a senior officer sporting a tan—or a smile, for that matter. He gave her a jaunty wave and let himself through the secure double doors leading to the main office area that housed the Criminal Investigation Department.

He jogged up a single flight of stairs and bounded onto the first floor, whistling under his breath as he passed along a wide central corridor in an unimaginative shade of taupe. The smell of fresh paint had dissipated since the new building had opened and it was starting to develop a 'lived in' feel, with undertones of chicken casserole and stale sweat, not to mention the scent of drains wafting from the general direction of the gents toilets.

However, when Ryan entered the open-plan office shared by staff assigned to the Major Incident Team, the place was like a ghost town. Desks were suspiciously empty and there was none of the usual half-drunk coffee cups, crisp packets and other paraphernalia he would expect to find littering the room by the end of the working week. A telephone rang plaintively across the room and he frowned at it, black brows drawing together.

"Where the hell is everyone?"

So much for his dramatic entrance.

Ryan dumped a plastic carrier bag of novelty souvenirs on his desk, then turned and headed back out into the corridor, poking his head into the neighbouring offices but finding them equally deserted. By a process of elimination, he made his way to the conference suite on the second floor, situated beside the executive offices belonging to upper echelons of the police hierarchy. When he reached the largest conference room, bold black lettering declared a 'MEETING IN PROGRESS' and Ryan pushed through the door to find it brimming with police staff, from the humblest administrator all the way up to the Chief Constable. At the front, the constabulary's newest member of staff, Detective Chief Superintendent Jennifer Lucas, addressed the room.

Ryan's jovial mood evaporated immediately at the sight of his new boss and he leaned back against the wall, arms folded, to listen to her inaugural speech.

The audience was rapt, he thought scathingly, hanging on her every word.

And why not?

They knew nothing about their glorious new superintendent; nothing of her manipulative character or desire for control at any cost. It had been his misfortune to learn those things many years ago, when he had been a much younger man working at the Met in London. Naivety and misguided pity had prevented him from making a formal complaint at the time and now it was too late to rectify that mistake. It would be his word against that of a more senior officer, just like it had been all those years before.

Still, he supposed a lot of water had passed under the bridge. Lucas had given no indication that she harboured a grudge or that she had followed him to Northumberland with any other intention than to progress her career. He had spent a long time trying hard to forget any memories of their former relationship and he could only hope she had done the same.

Perhaps they could work together amicably enough, with a little effort on both sides.

But his eyes narrowed as her clear, well-rounded voice carried across the room.

"I want to assure you all that I will be your biggest ally, whenever you need me. I won't sacrifice you to the bigwigs when things get tough or play the blame game when things don't go to plan. In return, I expect your loyalty and diligence as we work together towards a better, brighter Criminal Investigation Department."

There were murmurs of assent and a spattering of applause.

Sycophants, he thought.

Lucas scanned their faces with satisfaction and registered a degree of shock as she spotted Ryan's tall figure at the back of the room, watching her with an unreadable expression that could have signified contempt or boredom. She gave him a tight smile, acknowledging that she'd been caught out. The meeting had been planned in his absence, in the full knowledge that he was not due to return to the office until Monday. No doubt he understood her motivations and resented her for trying to exclude him. There were many in CID who would have preferred to see Ryan as their new superintendent but, since he'd turned the job down, they'd have to make do with her instead. She intended to make very sure that they knew who called the shots, right from the start.

As for Ryan, he'd come home to a New Order and the sooner he came to terms with it, the better.

If he didn't…well, it wouldn't be the first time she'd brought him to heel, would it?

Her smile widened.

"The department has taken quite a hammering, in recent times," she continued smoothly. "I need hardly mention the actions of my predecessor"—she referred to DCS Gregson, who was now ensconced behind bars at Her Majesty's pleasure, thanks to Ryan and his team—

"nor the times when impulsive decision-making rather than solid policing has brought the Service into disrepute."

Ryan recognised the oblique reference to his sergeant's disciplinary action a few months ago, not to mention the times when he'd been forced to step outside the bounds of strict procedure to get the job done, and his jaw tightened.

"But from now on, things are going to change. We're going to instil public confidence and gain back the ground that's been lost." She spread her hands in an open gesture. "Let's do it together."

She stepped away to allow Chief Constable Morrison to move forward, clapping her approval like a circus seal.

"I want to formally welcome DCS Lucas and to thank her for those inspiring words, which I'm sure we can all agree with and get behind, one hundred per cent. We're in the business of law and order, so let's start on home turf…"

Ryan could stand no more. He pushed away from the wall and out of the room, uncaring of who might see. He would not stay and listen to a lot of crowd-pleasing nonsense which had, ever-so-subtly, shoved a knife in the back of his team of detectives. They were dedicated men and women who had committed themselves to seeking justice for victims of the most serious crimes one human being could inflict upon another.

And now, Lucas wanted to undermine everything they had done, to bolster her own public persona?

It was sickening.

Ryan cast a fulminating glare back over his shoulder and was almost outside when he heard the unmistakeable heavy tread of his sergeant's feet against the carpet-tiled floor.

"Oi! Hold your horses!"

A frantic hustle along the corridors of CID and out into the staff car park had left Detective Sergeant Frank Phillips out of breath but pride prevented him from saying as much. Instead, he sucked crisp autumn air into his lungs as he recovered and cast a wary eye over the stony-faced man standing beside him.

"What was all that about? You took off like the hounds of hell were yappin' at your heels."

Ryan shoved his hands in his pockets.

"I've heard enough propaganda to last me a lifetime," he said shortly. "It turns my stomach to hear all that bumf about public opinion. The public would have a much worse opinion if we failed to catch the bad guys, and that's a fact."

Phillips pulled an expressive face.

"Aye, but the Supers always like to pretend they're giving the Sermon on the Mount when they first start out. It's expected."

"It's bullshit."

Phillips scratched his chin to hide a smile.

"I guess it's the wrong time to mention that your speedy departure was noted by the Powers That Be?"

Ryan gave him an eloquent look.

"Aye, I thought as much."

Phillips hastily changed the subject.

"Looks like you've got that post-honeymoon glow," he offered, gesturing a broad hand towards Ryan's tanned forearms. "But you're not in Bora Bora any more, son. You'll catch a cold if you don't put a coat on."

"Thanks, Mum," came the rejoinder.

Just then, Ryan's mobile phone began to shrill, serving as a timely reminder that his first duty was to the victims of crime. When he saw that the caller was Anna, his face softened.

"Missing me already?"

But his smile soon faded into professional interest and, when he ended the call a few minutes later, he turned back to Phillips.

"Fancy a drive into the country?"

Phillips' eyebrows raised into his receding hairline.

"Have we got a live one?"

"Just the opposite, Frank. We've got a dead one, trapped beneath a few billion gallons of water."

* * *

The first thing Ryan and Phillips noticed when they arrived at the small tourist development known as 'Kielder Waterside' was not the sweeping landscape but the unnatural *hush*. People had begun to whisper about what Lisa Hope had seen in the depths of the water but now they fell silent and stood in huddles outside the visitor's centre watching the police divers, who were suited up and ready to begin their grisly task, cadaver dogs stretched out on the ground beside them.

Ryan swung into the car park and was distracted briefly by the sight of Anna's old banger of a minibus, parked forlornly a few bays along. There was no sign of his wife but he guessed she was settling her students into their accommodation—that is, if she wasn't calling a local mechanic to have that rust-bucket towed away.

"I'll eat my hat if those dogs can sniff out a body in the middle of all that water," Phillips declared, as they slammed out of the car.

"I've seen them do it before," Ryan said. "It's incredible what they can smell."

Phillips was dubious.

"A dead body isn't a T-bone steak."

"A pint says those dogs will take them to the right spot," Ryan replied, very casually.

Phillips knew a sucker-bet when he heard one but decided to take the risk anyway.

"Aye, you're on."

Ryan flashed a grin, then his face fell back into serious lines as they crossed the tarmac to meet the sergeant in charge of the small team of police divers attached to the Underwater Search and Marine Unit. There were several divers, each sporting a 'dry' suit to guard their skin against poisonous or dangerous substances in the water, although the reservoir was so clear it almost rendered the precaution unnecessary. A brief conversation confirmed what they already knew: a local diving instructor had taken a couple down earlier that morning as part of an advanced diving course. The witness, Lisa Hope, had the misfortune of unsettling a small mountain of earth on the reservoir bed and had become panicked and disorientated, dislodging her air supply and inhaling a large quantity of water, but not before she saw the body of a young man.

"Did she say anything else about the state of the body?" Ryan queried.

The sergeant shook her head.

"Lisa Hope has been transferred to hospital for observation and one of the local constables is with her. They'll take a full statement as soon as she's been given the all-clear."

Ryan nodded. To determine whether it was a case for CID he needed to recover the body. That was a matter for the Marine Unit and, as far as specialist teams went, he knew there was none better.

"There was one other thing," the sergeant added as an afterthought. "She said the body looked stained."

"*Stained?*" Phillips repeated.

"That's what she said—might have been all the dust surrounding it." The sergeant shrugged and made a low whistling signal to one of the dogs, whose nose lifted from the floor. "We'll find out, soon enough."

They looked out across the water and watched a late-season osprey swoop low over the water, which rippled gently on the morning breeze.

"Safe   diving,"   Ryan   murmured.

CHAPTER 3

They didn't have to wait long.

Freddie Milburn provided a good approximation of where his motorboat had dropped anchor that morning and after an hour of careful sniffing by the cadaver dogs, the divers were able to narrow down a search area. An inflatable buoy marked the spot and a line ran from there to the police boat, where four divers remained while one went down to begin a coordinated search in expanding circles. When that didn't immediately yield results, they moved into a necklace formation, working their way through the sludge on the bed of the reservoir until they found what they were looking for.

Back on dry land, Ryan received the news via radio and felt an all-too-familiar tug of sadness for the dead and those they left behind.

"Unfortunately, it looks like you owe me a pint," he murmured to Phillips, who stood at his shoulder.

"Aye, I think we'll need one," Phillips said quietly. "I've got the mortuary on standby."

Ryan nodded, shading his eyes against the glare of the sun as he watched the divers re-emerge and in no time, the boat began its return journey to the shore. Ryan instructed a couple of local police constables to keep the crowd well back from the water's edge, where a cohort of local onlookers remained. He took a moment to scan their faces, finding them a curious mix of young and old, men and women who worked at the marina or in neighbouring developments that had sprung up at intervals around the waterside. If there had been foul play, it wouldn't take long for news to spread in a sparsely populated area like Kielder, even across thousands of acres of wood and sky.

"Guv?"

Ryan followed the direction of Phillips' gaze. A plastic tunnel had been erected at the end of the jetty to preserve a degree of dignity, while professionals from the coroner's office wheeled a squeaky metal gurney along the wooden slats to transfer the body.

They waited beside a plain, private ambulance vehicle parked nearby and prepared to witness the unpleasant evidence of Nature's handiwork. It would not be the first time either man had seen a body abused by air and water, and they made a conscious effort to divest themselves of emotion as the gurney approached. But when Ryan donned a nitrile glove and reached across to unzip the heavy black body bag, he almost fell back in shock.

The mummified face of a boy in his late teens stared up at him, the skin wasted and weathered to a deep shade of terracotta brown. At the side of his matted head there was an obvious gash, which had crusted into a deep groove and was unbelievably well preserved.

But surely that wasn't possible.

"Frank?"

Ryan gestured for his sergeant, who hung back until his stomach finished performing slow somersaults, then manfully stepped forward.

"Well, that's a first," Phillips managed, peering closely at the shrivelled figure in its rubbery shroud. A wave of sympathy came next, for the young man whose face was still recognisable, even down to the fledgling stubble growing against his chin.

"I've never seen a body so well preserved," Ryan muttered, and took a photograph to compare with Missing Persons. "Did you notice the head injury?"

Phillips eyed the deep cut in the skull and cleared his throat again.

"Aye, that'd do it."

They committed what was left of the boy's face to memory, then Ryan resealed the body bag and stepped back.

"What do you reckon?" Phillips said. "Should we hand him over to Missing Persons?"

Ryan thought of budgets and resources, then again of the boy's face that was forever frozen in time. *What was his name?* How old had he been and how did he die? A person rarely sustained a head injury like that if they'd merely fallen or drowned in the water. More likely, the injury happened on dry land, which begged the question of how he'd found his way underwater.

At the very least, it was suspicious.

"No," he decided. "We're not handing him over. Somebody must be missing him and we need to find out who that somebody is. Until then, he's one of ours."

* * *

Angela Gray scrubbed an invisible speck of dirt from the sales counter inside the gift shop, her cloth turning in rhythmic circles against the glass until it shone. The whole place was immaculate, from its polished wooden floor to its rigorously-maintained shelves filled with knick-knacks, toys and books of all shapes and size. At her back, large windows boasted panoramic views of the reservoir which was coming alive as the sun crept higher into the sky towards midday.

But she wouldn't look.

She knew there were police divers down by the waterfront. She'd seen them arrive a couple of hours ago with a smattering of local police in their noisy squad cars. The sound of the sirens rang in her ears, interrupting the peace of her surroundings, reminding her of all the other times they'd come calling, telling her they'd found a body that might be Duncan. They refused to accept what she had been *forced* to accept—it was a constant intrusion, a wound that would never heal so long as the police continued to pester her with their well-intentioned house calls over the long, empty years.

Hadn't she told them, time and again?

Duncan had run away.

He hadn't wanted to stay in a quiet place like Kielder, that was all. Her boy had been ambitious, with dreams of travelling the world. What was there to keep him here? Lord knew, there'd been precious little money to spend on fancy holidays abroad after John had been made redundant.

Her son had upped and left—that was all there was to it.

Sometimes, she allowed herself to imagine how Duncan might look now. He'd be handsome, she was sure of that, with his floppy ash-blond hair and green eyes. He probably lived somewhere very exciting, like New York. Or maybe he was in Africa, helping to save endangered animals. He'd always been so caring.

A tear leaked from her eye and she swiped it away quickly, her arm working faster and faster, scrubbing harder at the glass.

Other times, she wondered whether Duncan suffered from amnesia. There might have been an awful accident that prevented him from getting in touch all these years. She'd watched documentaries about it on television.

There's a smudge.

Angela paused for a moment to look critically at the glass, tutted, then began all over again.

Busy hands, she thought. Busy hands distracted her from the busy thoughts crowding her mind. People said she should retire, that she was too old to carry on working as she did. Maybe they were right but what else was there to do?

If she stayed at home, there'd be too much time to think.

Angela blew an errant hair from her eyes and caught sight of herself in the gleaming counter. The face was blurry but she saw a woman pushing seventy with a thatch of wiry grey hair, not fashioned in any particular style. She'd given up trying to fight the passage of time and, in many ways, she welcomed it. There were no grandchildren to entertain and no big, messy dinners on Sundays. No babies to croon over, with their soft hair and tiny hands.

Sometimes, she thought she heard his voice calling her name.

"Mum! Did you wash my jeans?"

She smiled and shook her head, one hand straying to rest against her cushioned belly, where once a baby had grown.

No sense in wishing for things that were out of reach and always would   be.

CHAPTER 4

After exchanging a few words with the local police and thanking the Marine Unit for their efficient work, Ryan put a call through to Jeff Pinter, the senior pathologist attached to Northumbria CID. Even to a layperson, it was clear that the body they'd recovered from the water had been down there for some time and a specialist would be required to assist with any post-mortem examination. To that end, he approved the additional funds to engage Doctor Ann Millington, a forensic anthropologist based out of Edinburgh whose unique skills had been invaluable to them in the past.

After putting those wheels in motion, Ryan slipped his phone into the back pocket of his jeans and turned in a wide circle to locate his sergeant, who was by now chatting amiably with some of the locals in a picnic area on the far side of a grassy verge overlooking the reservoir. He took a moment to admire Phillips' easy, trademark style and decided to leave him to work his magic while he went in search of Freddie Milburn.

Ryan found the diving instructor inside his kiosk, talking in hushed tones with another middle-aged man who had the same healthy, outdoorsy look as his friend. They wore bright blue all-weather jackets bearing their company's logo and cut-off khaki shorts, displaying a frank disregard for the biting September wind rolling in from the lake.

He rapped a knuckle on the open door and watched them turn in surprise.

"Freddie Milburn?" he enquired, reaching for his warrant card. "I'm Detective Chief Inspector Ryan. Do you have a minute?"

The two men exchanged a glance.

"I'll give you some privacy," the taller one began.

"Do you work for the company?" Ryan's voice stopped him.

"I—yes, I'm Mitchell Fenwick—Mitch." He held out a hand, which Ryan shook briefly. "Freddie and I co-own the company. I was the first aider when they brought Lisa in this morning," he added. "Got a hell of a fright, I can tell you."

"Her, or you?"

Mitch's laugh was strained.

"Both of us, I s'pose. We haven't had an emergency like that in a good long while and, to be honest, I was a bit worried I might have forgotten the procedure."

"You did a grand job," Freddie put in. "She's going to be alright because of you."

"Yeah," Mitch ran an agitated hand through a mop of thick dark hair and, were it not for the deep laughter lines around his eyes and the odd grey hair, Ryan might have pegged him for a much younger man. "If you'll let me know when she's up to having visitors, I was thinking of heading along to the hospital to see for myself."

"I'm sure that can be arranged," Ryan replied.

Fenwick nodded his thanks.

"Could have been one of my own girls," he said quietly. "But there's no sense in thinking of what might have been, not when you've found some other poor soul who was lost down there."

Ryan bobbed his head in the direction of the water.

"What do you make of it?"

Mitch and Freddie let out a sort of synchronised murmur and shook their heads in a manner Ryan had come to understand was part and parcel of interviewing witnesses from the North East. In this neck of the woods, the pageantry was part of the process.

"You've got two hundred and fifty square miles of forest out there," Mitch began, jerking a thumb over his shoulder to reinforce the point. "Some tourists stay in the holiday lodges so they can hike around or go sailing, maybe visit the observatory and see the stars. Others, they like to keep themselves to themselves, take a tent and go off the beaten track to get lost in nature and all that. Makes them feel better about going home to their desk jobs in the real world."

"Had a few get lost in the woods," Freddie added, and his friend nodded sagely. "The forest rangers searched high and low, had the 4x4s out looking for them, helicopters and all that. Mostly, they find those who want to be found."

Ryan understood what he meant. It was a sad fact that some of the missing didn't want to be found. But the boy they'd recovered from the lake had a severe head wound, the kind he could not have inflicted upon himself, and that was a different matter entirely.

"How about teenagers?" he prodded. "Any been reported missing, lately?"

Freddie leaned back against the edge of a little wooden desk stacked with leaflets and paperwork. On the wall behind him was an enormous cork board covered in photos taken of Freddie and Mitch smiling alongside an assortment of diving partners Ryan presumed were former students.

"There was that French lad, back in July," he offered.

"Nah, they found him pretty quick," Mitch interjected. "Suffering from exposure but mostly alright."

The two men scratched their heads and blew out another synchronised breath.

"Sorry, I can't think of anyone recently. Nobody local, anyhow."

Ryan shrugged off the wistful hope of an easy identification and resigned himself to a long conversation with his counterparts in the Missing Persons department.

He turned to Freddie and asked one final question.

"Did you see the body while you were down there?"

The man tugged at the zip on his jacket, burying himself deeper into the folds of the jersey lining to stave off a sudden chill.

"Aye, I saw it…*him*. Lisa lost her mouthpiece and took in a lot of water, so I didn't have time to worry about it because I needed to get her back up to the surface. But it looked as if he was asleep, you know? Peaceful, like he was just resting."

"Yes," Ryan said.

Freddie compressed his lips and looked away, out of the window and into the distance, before turning back to meet Ryan's eyes.

"D' you think it was an accident? Like, maybe, he fell somehow?"

Ryan's eyes turned flat.

"Our enquiries are ongoing," he replied. "But we are treating his death as suspicious until further notice."

He went over a few more questions, retracing the ground already covered by the local constables when they had taken preliminary statements earlier in the day, before stepping back out into the nippy air. The little passenger ferry was just departing the jetty to make its journey across the water to Kielder Village, on the north-western tip of the reservoir, and Ryan watched its progress for a couple of minutes while his mind wandered.

Secrets, he thought.

There were secrets to uncover in this little corner of the world, he could feel it.

* * *

Anna spotted him immediately, a tall, solitary figure standing at the waterside with his hands thrust deep inside the pockets of the waterproof jacket she'd bought him. The wind ruffled his black hair away from a striking profile that was hard and unsmiling, and she could almost hear the thoughts whirring through his mind as he considered his investigation. It might have been intimidating, if she didn't know him so well.

When her walking boots crunched across the ground, Ryan's head whipped around, grey eyes instantly alert.

"Hello, stranger," she said.

Ryan flashed one of the brief, blinding smiles he reserved especially for her.

"Hello, Doctor Taylor," he murmured. "Or should I call you Doctor Ryan?"

He bent his head to bestow a kiss.

"I'll answer to either," she said, then gave him a pained look. "You know, one of these days, I'll go to work and come home again without being part of a police investigation."

"But not today, it seems."

She looked over his shoulder towards the reservoir.

"Lisa Hope was right, then? There was a body?"

Ryan nodded.

"Yes. He looks adolescent but could be early-twenties, I suppose."

She thought of the small group of history students who were happily settled at the Inn tucking into a late lunch. They were Masters level, mostly twenty-one or twenty-two, fully grown adults. All the same, she was responsible for their welfare and if life had taught her anything, it was to expect the unexpected.

"Do you think I should cancel this trip? If the area is unsafe…"

Ryan considered the question but shook his head.

"I can't discuss any details, but I can tell you the boy didn't die recently. I don't have reason to believe there's any immediate danger; for one thing, we don't know *how* the kid died. We'll know more after the post-mortem."

Privately, Anna thought that if he truly believed there was nothing to worry about, Ryan would have handed the case over by now.

"Whoever he is, you'll do your best for him. You always do," was all she said.

Ryan looked faintly embarrassed.

"I'll try. That's all any of us can do."

Anna rested her hand against his chest and rubbed the invisible ache festering there. She knew he was thinking of others he hadn't been able to save; crimes he hadn't solved, murders he couldn't have prevented. He carried the memory of them on his shoulders and it was a heavy burden to bear. Now they'd decided to spend their lives together, she hoped she might be able to help lighten the load.

For now, she asked the question that was uppermost in her mind.

"Did you—ah, did you see your new boss this morning?"

There was no casual, nonchalant way of asking and it came out in an awkward rush of words.

"I saw her," he replied, and his tone conveyed a wealth of meaning. "Giving a speech to the masses about how the department has been up shit creek without a paddle—before her timely arrival, that is. Lucas organised an all-staff meeting for a time when she thought I'd be away from the office. Unfortunately for her, I decided to surprise them," he tagged on.

Anna's heart sank. Years ago, Ryan had moved away from London to escape a woman whose behaviour had become erratic and volatile. Jennifer Lucas had been his superior officer at the time and their personal relationship had been discreet. When things became unbearable, there had been little recourse except to make a clean break of it. Now, Lucas had followed Ryan north, invading the new life he had built, and it remained to be seen whether they could work together given all that had passed before. One thing was clear: Ryan didn't trust his new superintendent and, frankly, neither did she.

"You haven't had a chance to clear the air a bit?"

Ryan scrubbed a hand over his face.

"What would I say? *Hey, Jen, long time, no see?*"

His voice dripped sarcasm but, beneath it, she caught a thread of unease.

"You have to try speaking to Morrison again," she said, urgently, but Ryan shook his head.

"The Chief Constable made it abundantly clear she's not interested in ancient history. Morrison doesn't understand what happened and, since I didn't make a formal complaint..." He trailed off, thinking of what a monumental error that had been.

"Lucas has an impeccable work record," he continued. "She's respected, and Morrison wants her to swoop into the department and overhaul it, so we can all bask in the reflected glow of her popularity with the people who matter."

"And you're thinking of her husband—and children, if she has any," Anna concluded, softly. Ryan's compassion might be cloaked in steel but it was there all the same.

He gave a brief nod.

"I don't know who it might hurt if I start raking up the past. For all I know, she might have kids now and they don't deserve to have their mother dragged through the mud if she's a changed person. So, for as long as Lucas does the job she's paid to do without causing trouble, I'll set it aside," he said, but then his voice grew cold. "But if she tries to tear down everything we stand for, everything we've worked so hard to do—"

"She couldn't," Anna interjected. "Nobody has the power to do that."

Ryan looked down into his wife's soft, dark eyes and wondered what it would be like to believe so wholly and completely in the better side of human nature. After all she had been through and all she had lost, Anna still believed people were fundamentally good and that it was within their power to change. He wondered whether he'd lost that idealism somewhere along the way, but listening to her unshakeable faith in people made him want to grasp at the threads of it.

"I love you," he said simply.

"Same goes, Chief Inspector. Now, are you planning on doing any work today? Taxpayer's money and all that."

"I wondered how long it would take before you started nagging me in a wifely fashion."

Anna gave him a toothy smile.

"Darling, I've been doing it since Day One, you were just too love-struck to notice."

"'Love-struck'? I'm a grown man," he argued.

"Whatever you say, dear."

CHAPTER 5

The running machine echoed loudly in the empty basement gym at Northumbria Police Headquarters but Detective Inspector Denise MacKenzie couldn't hear it above the sound of her own laboured breathing and the music pounding in her ears. There were no frills and no view except an empty concrete wall, but that was just how she liked it.

No distractions.

Her muscles ached and sweat ran in rivulets down her back and across her forehead, seeping into her eyes, but there was no question of slowing down or stopping. Not yet.

Just a bit further…

Every muscle ached, and she could feel the old wound in her leg beginning to protest, reminding her of why she needed to push herself harder, faster, until she regained her strength.

Not so long ago, she'd been the prisoner of a madman who almost killed her. He hadn't succeeded but *The Hacker* had still left his mark, branding her leg with a six-inch scar to remind her of where his knife had torn through muscle and flesh. But the scars were more than skin-deep; they went all the way to her very core, and she fought each day to help them heal.

The music shifted, and she picked up her feet to sprint into the crescendo.

From her position in the doorway, Jennifer Lucas cast a thoughtful eye over Denise MacKenzie. She was aware of what had happened earlier in the year—the whole country knew about it—and couldn't fail to be impressed by the determination etched into every line of the woman's body. It would have been easy for her to take more time off work to lick her wounds and ruminate on what had happened but, instead, she was down here in the police gym pushing herself to the limit.

Perhaps she would be a useful person to know.

MacKenzie's pace slowed to a jog, then to a walk, until the machine stopped completely, and she tugged the headphones from her ears. Almost immediately, she was aware of a sensation of being watched and turned to find the new superintendent lounging in the doorway. Unlike herself, Lucas was sleek and polished in a tailored grey suit, her dark, expertly dyed hair styled into a neat bob around an attractive face dominated by a pair of baby-blue eyes. She knew that Lucas was somewhere in her late forties but, at first glance, she might have passed for ten years younger.

"Ma'am," she said stiffly, feeling irritated by the scrutiny. "Am I needed upstairs?"

It was her designated lunch hour but she could shower and change quickly enough.

"No, no," Lucas said, with a wave of her hand. "Nothing that won't keep. I wanted to have a word with you about…well, a private matter."

MacKenzie stepped off the treadmill and kept her face neutral.

"Oh? I'm not sure I'm the best person to speak to about private matters. Perhaps, if you talk to HR?"

Lucas wasn't put off.

"It's just, as a fellow woman, I wanted to ask how you've found working with DCI Ryan."

MacKenzie's face betrayed nothing and she looked her superior dead in the eye.

"That's easy. Working with Ryan has been a privilege. He's been more than just a boss, he's been a mentor and a friend."

"Well, I'm glad to hear that," Lucas said briskly. "But…well, it just strikes me as odd that a woman of your obvious capabilities hasn't been promoted to higher rank and I can't help wondering whether that is a symptom of bad management or bad judgment."

MacKenzie gave her an empty smile.

"From the very first, DCI Ryan has encouraged my progression through the ranks and, if I ever express a desire to move higher up the ladder, I have no doubt he would support my application because there isn't a sexist bone in his body. He doesn't care, so long as you do the job and do it well. Now, if there's nothing else, I'd like to go and clean up."

With that, she brushed past Lucas and headed towards the locker room but, instead of reaching for a towel, she rummaged around for her mobile phone and pushed 'speed-dial'.

After a second, Phillips answered.

"Frank? Is Ryan with you?"

Phillips looked across at the man in question, who sat in the driver's seat as they prepared to depart Kielder and head back to the city.

"Mm-hmm," he said. "Is anything the matter?"

MacKenzie craned her neck towards the open doorway and lowered her voice.

"I think we've got a fox running loose in the hen house."

* * *

As it turned out, MacKenzie's instincts were not wrong.

DCS Lucas wasted no time in implementing her New Order and when Ryan and Phillips returned to CID Headquarters they felt a different energy in the air, one they didn't recognise or feel part of. But there was no time to worry about it before the superintendent's mousy personal assistant informed Ryan he was expected in the superintendent's office immediately.

"That doesn't sound promising," Phillips muttered, collapsing into his ergonomic desk chair.

"She probably wants an update or to talk about resourcing," Ryan said. "That's reasonable."

Phillips folded his lips and thought of what MacKenzie had told him.

"Aye, well, you know where I am if you need anything," he said gruffly.

Ryan nodded his thanks and turned in the direction of the executive suite, where he was ushered quickly into a large corner office that was now Lucas's domain.

The first thing he noticed was not the woman herself but the extreme minimalism of her workspace. The industrial beige wall colour splashed around the rest of the police building had been obliterated by lashings of white paint to give the space a stark, clinical feel. There was not a picture on the wall nor a photograph in sight. There were no plants or bookshelves to create a homely atmosphere or give anything away about Lucas's personality. The only adornments were a large, expensive-looking antique desk in dark mahogany and matching desk chair, a row of concealed filing units—also painted white—and two standard-issue visitor's chairs covered in black foam.

Ryan's gaze swept the room and then focused on the woman who watched him like a spider.

"I never did like trinkets," she said, reading his thoughts. "Please, come in and take a seat."

She gestured to one of the visitor's chairs and didn't wait for him to take up her invitation before rising to open one of the concealed cabinets which, it turned out, contained a coffee machine.

"Care for a cappuccino? Ah, no, I remember—you prefer stronger coffee." She threw her remarks over her shoulder, in a kind of casually intimate way that made his stomach turn.

"No thanks."

Lucas returned to her desk with a delicate china cup and saucer and settled herself, seemingly unperturbed by the fact he had chosen to remain standing several feet away. She took a tiny sip from her cup, then set it down carefully beside her notepad, which was placed directly in front of her and perpendicular to a silver-plated fountain pen embossed with her initials. Ryan remembered it was a habit he had first observed years ago and had failed to associate as one of the symptoms of her obsessive compulsion.

Her voice cut through his reverie.

"You're looking well," she observed, noting the tan and general aura of contentment.

Shame it wouldn't last.

"You've been having quite a ball up here, haven't you, Max?"

His body froze at the sound of his first name rolling off her tongue, as if she had the right.

"Ryan," he corrected.

"Oh yes, I'd heard you're going by your surname, now."

He said nothing. After all, she was part of the reason why he preferred to leave behind the man he had once been.

She took another sip from her cup and continued in the same, maddening tone of voice.

"While you were away frolicking on a beach, I spent a lot of time reading over the paperwork on cases closed recently in CID. It made for *very* interesting reading, I don't mind telling you."

"I'm glad the misfortune of others amuses you."

Once again, she continued as if she hadn't heard him.

"The fact is, you don't seem to be aware of what your job entails."

He laughed shortly.

"Really? How strange. Here I was thinking I'd been running a successful team of detectives. Perhaps you'll enlighten me as to how I've been missing the mark."

"Gladly," she said, flipping open a notepad with one long fingernail. "For starters, your role is to coordinate the work of a team of constables, sergeants, inspectors and civilian staff. That does not include you scampering around the countryside like a wannabe action hero."

He swallowed back the angry retort on the tip of his tongue and focused on facts.

"Every statistical report during my tenure as chief inspector has recorded an upward trend in closed cases," he replied. "Internal surveys have recorded very high levels of staff satisfaction as to workload, progression and management style."

"Well, they'd hardly complain about the fact their boss was never in the office to breathe down their necks," she shot back.

"You'd know all about that, wouldn't you?" he ground out.

"Careful, Ryan," she said softly. "Your temper is showing."

He was incredulous.

"Are you seriously trying to suggest that the team I manage has been anything other than highly successful?"

"That's exactly what I'm suggesting," she said. "You follow instinct rather than hard evidence, putting the lives of other people at risk."

His body revolted at the suggestion that he would ever, *could* ever, put the people he considered family at risk.

"Every detective in CID knows their job comes with a certain level of risk," he threw back, vibrating with anger. "There have been times when I've tried to protect them, but they don't want to be mollycoddled; they want to learn their trade, which is something they can't do if I'm wrapping them in cotton wool. As for relying on *instinct*, you're living in a dream world."

He took a step closer, urging her to listen.

"Look, I get the same feel for people as any experienced detective who's been in the game long enough, but that doesn't mean I rely on instinct over hard evidence." He cocked his head, mockingly. "Do you think I go up against murderers and madmen just for kicks? No. I do it because it stops them hurting the people on the street, the people who don't know what kind of monsters lurk outside their front door."

"How laudable," she cooed. "I'm sure you have the media eating out of your hand, dishing out speeches like that."

He shook his head.

"Oh, I'm not finished yet," she continued, standing up to walk around to the front of her desk so that the scent of her heavy perfume assaulted his nostrils. It was the same fragrance she'd worn all those years ago and the sensory memory was an uncomfortable trigger to the past.

"A little birdy tells me that your girlfriend—oh, I beg your pardon, your *wife*—often comes along to spectate at crime scenes. How *romantic*, and how wholly inappropriate."

Ryan willed himself to remain calm in the face of her provocation.

"When we met, Doctor Anna Taylor was engaged by DCS Gregson as a police consultant on a case in which her own sister was eventually murdered and where she was also targeted."

"In other words, she was a material witness," Lucas put in.

"No, not in the beginning. According to proper protocols and due to the unique geography of the crime scene on Holy Island, it was necessary to designate a residential property as the incident room during that investigation. It wasn't possible to avoid contact."

"Contact? Is that what you call it?" She let out an ugly laugh. "How about the rest? Do you expect me to believe there has been a legitimate reason why she's been present in these offices or at a crime scene in subsequent cases?"

Ryan looked at her for a long moment, trying to read what lurked behind her eyes. He wondered if Lucas knew she was prodding an open wound, laying bare the guilt he carried each day.

Of course she knew.

His voice was curiously flat when he spoke again.

"Thanks to my unwanted association with *The Hacker* and my failure to apprehend the remaining members of The Circle cult immediately, Anna had the great misfortune of being a potential target over the past two years. Just by knowing me, her life was endangered. Therefore, it was not possible for her to avoid contact with this department. But if you're suggesting that I'd compromise an active investigation by embroiling my wife in the work that I do, that is nothing more than grubby slander which I demand you retract."

Lucas folded her arms, enjoying herself.

"Aha, now the breeding comes out," she mused. "Nothing much ruffles you, does it, Ryan? I seem to remember a time when I could get under your skin."

He looked down his nose from a superior height of six or seven inches.

"If you have nothing more to say, I think I'll head along to the Chief Constable's office to make her aware of exactly what I *do* remember and, in particular, the incredible hypocrisy of being lectured about professional boundaries by you, of all people."

He turned to leave.

"Oh, I don't think you'll do that," Lucas said, very quietly.

Something in her voice stopped him in his tracks and he waited to hear what ace she had up her sleeve.

"Like I said, Ryan, I've been doing some checking. It always struck me as very odd that ballistics couldn't identify who fired the shot that disabled *The Hacker*. I see from the files that you found that rather odd, too."

"There was no shot fired."

"You don't believe that any more than I do."

He said nothing, but a sick dread began to spread in his gut.

What had she found?

"The investigation ruled out MacKenzie and Phillips," she continued, ticking them off her fingers. "It ruled out the tactical team and you weren't carrying a weapon at the time. But when I look at the statements taken from officers on the ground, who else do I find listed as being present? None other than Doctor Anna Taylor, right there, in the thick of it all."

A dawning suspicion hit Ryan squarely in the face and he wondered why it hadn't struck him before. Had it been Anna, his wife, who had disabled the man who would have killed him that night?

Where would she find a weapon?

His police revolver, which he kept in a locked box at home, the combination for which was her birthday digits.

His face remained impassive as possibilities roamed his mind and when he spoke again, his voice was cool.

"What are you implying?"

"Oh, I think we both know that your wife took matters into her own hands. No doubt to save the man she loves," Lucas said. "Problem is, she had no right to discharge a weapon and, if she used your police issue, you are culpable."

"Forensics found no evidence of a gunshot wound anywhere on *The Hacker's* body."

"And yet, in your own statement given last April, you clearly say you heard at least one gunshot."

"I was recovering from a severe trauma," he said. "I had just been water-boarded at the top of a dangerous waterfall. God Almighty could have spoken to me, a choir of angels could have sung, and I wouldn't have heard a damn thing. Obviously, I didn't hear a gunshot, since there was no evidence of one having been fired."

Lucas tapped a finger against her lips. He was a cool one, she'd give him that.

"It is within my power to order an internal investigation and refer it to the Independent Police Complaints Commission. I can find the proof."

"Then find it," he bit out. "Until then, I'll be making my own complaint—to the Chief Constable."

She let out a soft, tinkling laugh.

"Oh, but Sandra agrees with me—and my proposed course of action."

Ryan frowned.

"Which is?"

"There's going to be a shake-up," she explained, moving back around to sit at her desk, signalling that the meeting was almost closed as far as she was concerned. "Effective immediately, I'm re-allocating your team. Phillips will handle affairs at Kielder, alongside his other active cases, and he can take Melanie Yates with him," she said, referring to the young police constable Ryan had recruited and was in the process of training to become a detective. "MacKenzie will be assigned to cold cases while you will remain here, at the office, where you belong."

A muscle ticked at the side of his jaw, then he thought of his other protégé and wondered what fate she had in store for him.

"And Jack Lowerson? What menial duty do you plan to assign to him?"

She merely pressed the buzzer on her phone and her personal assistant appeared like an apparition in the doorway.

"Priya, I'd like you to come in and take some notes for me, please."

With adrenaline pumping through his veins, Ryan stalked from the room and went in search of the Chief Constable.

* * *

At Kielder, the police had completed their usual checks and returned to their stations, but the whispers continued long after their departure, spreading like wildfire through the small settlements and villages scattered around the banks of the reservoir. They seemed to crawl from the woodwork, people who normally thrived on being so far removed from ordinary civilisation in their secluded patch of the world. They were drawn to gossip like moths to the flame, unwittingly flapping their lips closer and closer to the truth of who had risen from the water like a ghostly apparition.

But Duncan Gray was no ghost.

He was dead and gone, years ago. It was best to remember that and not the memory of his pale face staring up from the hollowed-out pit of earth where they'd left him to die, nor the awful memory of betrayal and its acrid taste that never quite went away. Over the years, it had been possible to forget sometimes; even to enjoy the trees and sky, to swim and sail on the water. On a clear day such as this, it had been possible. With every passing year, the truth became distant and faded, like an old black-and-white film whose imagery became grainy until it was distorted out of all recognition.

But now, Duncan was back.

He had never really gone.

CHAPTER 6

Ryan found Chief Constable Morrison in the staff canteen, picking at a bowl of pasta carbonara. She was seated at a table in the corner, fork in one hand as her other hand cradled an e-reader while she made the most of her break. Her sandy-blonde head was bent with her body angled away from the door and consequently she didn't see Ryan's approach.

"Ma'am? I'd like a word, please."

Morrison nearly dropped her fork.

"It's my lunch break, Ryan. Can't it wait?"

"No, I'm sorry. I think I've waited far too long already."

Her brows furrowed and she jerked her chin towards the free chair opposite, but he shook his head.

"I'd rather go somewhere private."

Her lips firmed.

"If this concerns Superintendent Lucas—"

"It does."

Now she let her fork clatter back into the bowl and reached for a napkin, wiping her hands and mouth with short, irritated movements.

"I thought we'd settled this, once and for all. The two of you had a personal relationship many years ago, while you were both at the Met. Long enough, I should have thought, to let bygones be bygones. Frankly, I would never have expected you to behave in such an unprofessional way."

Her words struck like angry little knives and, if Ryan had thought he would find the compassion of a friend, he realised he'd been sadly mistaken.

He lifted his chin and waited for her to collect her things and stomp from the room, in the direction of her office. Once they were behind closed doors, Morrison dumped her bag, shouldered out of her blazer and faced him with impatience.

"Well? Let's have it," she commanded.

Now it came to it, Ryan found he didn't know where to start. As a notoriously private person, how could he begin to detail the events that had once nearly broken him? How could he relive the memory of what a young fool he had been?

Besides, he thought of Lucas's threat to re-open the *Hacker* investigation and it gave him pause.

"I'm not here to complain about the past," he said eventually. "What I have to say very much concerns the present."

"How so?"

"Look, I understand that you want a new superintendent—*any* superintendent—to blow in here like a whirlwind, wave their magic wand and sprinkle fairy dust over all of us so that the brass will smile, nod, and give us a bunch of cash," he said. "But life doesn't work that way. It's demoralising to take a hard-working team and break it up just for the sake of it."

Morrison opened her mouth to protest but he held up a hand.

"Just hear me out. Please," he added.

Her mouth shut again, and he took a deep breath, thinking carefully about what he could and could not say. He hadn't forgotten Lucas's threat against Anna and, until he'd spoken with her himself, his hands were tied.

"I'm talking about methods and motivation. It wasn't the department's fault that we uncovered a cult on Holy Island, but we put them down in the end, as quickly as we could. Just like it wasn't your fault, or mine, that Lucas's predecessor turned out to be part of it." He thought of their former DCS, Arthur Gregson, and his heart hardened. "We didn't ask for any of it, or the shadow that it cast on all of us, but we dealt with it as best we could and saved countless lives in the process. You know how many other cases we've closed, on top of all that. It's got to be worth something."

Morrison listened, admiring the idealism shining through his words; his belief in the system and in the wheels of justice that they both fought to maintain, in their different ways.

She sighed and rubbed at the tension beginning to spread across the base of her skull. She had always been a fair woman, or tried to be. But they were under attack from all sides. The department needed fresh blood who not only looked and sounded the part but acted it too. If she'd had her way in the first place, it would have been Ryan performing that special duty and not Jennifer Lucas.

But if wishes were horses, beggars would ride.

"I've spoken to DCS Lucas," she said. "All she's suggesting is a trial period where the teams are reorganised to clear some of the inactive cases that are still circulating in the press. Surely you'd welcome that? I'd have thought you'd also welcome some time spent in the office, rather than having to work the beat, as it were?"

No, he thought. He could think of nothing worse. But she made it all sound so damn reasonable, as if Lucas's only motivation was to act in the best interests of CID.

What a joke.

"The fact is, Lucas is your superior and I'm not about to step in and undermine her authority at a time when she needs to establish her credentials with the rest of the staff. You should know that."

Yes, he did know it, but he had hoped for a miracle.

"I want you to lead by example and get behind her," Morrison told him sternly. "Whatever grudges you might hold against each other, I need you to pull together and work in the best interests of the department."

"Yes, ma'am," he said, in a voice entirely devoid of emotion.

For long minutes after Ryan left, Morrison stared at the door and wondered why she felt so uneasy. They had been through a lot together and she trusted his judgement. Ryan might be high-handed at times and he could be downright cold-blooded when it came to tracking down criminals, but he had an infallible nose for the business of policing and was universally respected in the constabulary.

Yet she had dismissed his concerns out of hand.

She hoped to God she'd been right.

* * *

"Run that by me one more time?"

Phillips stood beneath the plastic canopy outside the back entrance of police headquarters with his stocky feet planted and his shoulders hunched, reminding Ryan of an angry bull preparing to charge into an unsuspecting china shop. Beside him, MacKenzie leaned against a pebble-dashed pillar with a murderous expression on her face that was vastly more terrifying. The youngest members of his immediate team, Lowerson and Yates, stared at him with twin expressions of shock.

"But...why would she do that?" Lowerson asked, puffing rhythmically on a menthol e-cigarette. "The team works fine as it is."

He glanced across at Melanie Yates, whose company he was most interested in cultivating.

"Lucas wants me to work the *cold cases?*" MacKenzie burst out, and her Irish accent was more pronounced in the heat of anger. "We already have a dedicated team for that. I didn't spend twenty years working my way up the ladder just to sit in the archive room."

Ryan couldn't have agreed more, but he had to maintain a professional front.

"Like I said, they're re-allocating resources. Lucas wants somebody to take over the management of that team and you have the experience—"

"Don't give me any of that old blarney," MacKenzie cut in, with a swipe of her hand. "We both know that this is about Lucas flexing her muscles and my experience has bugger all to do with it."

Ryan couldn't argue with that but Morrison had made it abundantly clear his job was to lead.

"Whatever her motivations, that's the edict and we have to deal with it. Yates? You'll be working with Phillips from now on; he'll be your new mentor during your training."

PC Melanie Yates set aside her disappointment that she wouldn't be working with Ryan day-to-day and gave Phillips a smile because, as far as mentors went, they didn't come much better. Meanwhile, Lowerson took another long drag of his e-cigarette and watched his hopes of getting to know her better go up in a cloud of billowing smoke.

"Looks like you've drawn the short straw," Phillips joked, with a fatherly wink, and Ryan was grateful to him for helping to keep things light.

He turned back to Lowerson.

"Jack? I'm not entirely sure what Lucas has in store for you, but she wants you to report to her office first thing tomorrow morning."

It was on the tip of Ryan's tongue to tell him to be on his guard, to protect himself against foes from within, but that would necessitate a full-blown discussion he wasn't ready to have. Besides, hadn't he made the mistake of trying to mollycoddle Jack once before? It had been an unwelcome intrusion and he'd been roundly ticked off for it.

"What will you be doing?" Lowerson asked the burning question.

Ryan pulled an expressive face.

"I'll be chained to my desk engaged in the highly important business of resource and case management," he drawled. "What else?"

"This is bollocks!" Phillips could contain himself no longer. "You need to be out there, not stuck inside crunching numbers—"

"It's decided," Ryan said flatly.

Phillips started to speak again, then stopped himself. He'd save his breath and have a word with Morrison about it, first chance he got. He might not be the Commissioner or some other pillar of the community, but his word still meant something around here and he'd known Sandra Morrison since their first days on the Force. The least she could do was listen.

"We'll get the job done," MacKenzie murmured.

Ryan looked at each of them and felt something dip in his stomach; as if a door were being closed to the past and their future was now uncertain.

When they disbanded, Ryan put a hand on Phillips' arm to hold him back.

"Frank?"

Phillips detected an unusual tone in Ryan's voice.

"Aye, lad?"

Ryan looked out at the staff car park and watched uniformed and non-uniformed staff arrive in time for the start of a new shift. On the far side of the tarmac, the infamous Pie Van was doing a roaring trade as local workers flocked from neighbouring offices to buy all manner of cholesterol-heavy snacks to see them through the afternoon.

His eyes registered it all but his mind was far away, re-living the events of a night that would stay with him forever.

"Did you know it was Anna who took the shot?"

Phillips' silence gave Ryan all the answer he needed before his gravelly voice confirmed it.

"I knew she saved your life," he said. "Any one of us would have done the same but it's thanks to Anna that you're standing here, talking to me now."

Ryan felt a lump rise in his throat.

"She never told me," he managed. "Neither did you."

Phillips looked across at the man who was his superior, at least on paper, and the best damn friend he could ask for. They'd butted heads in the early days, finding their feet. But now, they were like family, and family spoke the truth to one another.

"Anna respects your integrity and so do I," Phillips said. "She didn't tell you because she didn't want you to be compromised at work. There'd be hell to pay if the press got wind of it."

"Does anyone else know?"

Phillips tugged at his lower lip and decided it was best to make a clean breast of it.

"MacKenzie guessed it first," he said, and a smile touched the corner of Ryan's mouth.

"Nothing gets past Denise," he murmured.

"Nothing worth knowing, anyhow," Phillips agreed.

Ryan let out a long breath and stuck his hands inside the pockets of his jeans.

"Lucas knows. She's threatening to make an internal referral to the IPCC."

There was a small pause while Phillips considered the implications of that.

"She knows, or she suspects?"

"Alright, she suspects."

"Suspicion isn't the same as fact," Phillips pronounced, and gave Ryan a bolstering slap on the back. "Nobody was harmed, except an inhuman maniac who would have killed you, given half the chance. There isn't an officer in the land who wouldn't have done the same thing Anna did that night. She's one in a million, that one. Hold on to her, lad, and hold her tight."

Ryan gave him another lopsided smile and wondered what he'd done to deserve such friendship.

"Thanks, Frank."

But when the doors clicked shut behind him a few moments later, Ryan stood for a while longer and felt the ground begin to quake beneath   his   feet.

CHAPTER 7

While Ryan re-acquainted himself with his desk, Phillips took up the baton and went about the business of introducing Yates to one of the less glamorous locations on a murder detective's map.

The mortuary at the Royal Victoria Infirmary was the province of Doctor Jeffrey Pinter, the chief pathologist attached to Northumbria CID. He was a fastidious and often infuriating man in his early fifties, but they forgave his little foibles because he was far and away the best in his field. Pinter could be relied upon to pinpoint a post-mortem interval to within a couple of hours and to find even the smallest indicators of foul play on a body that had been subjected to the worst abuse that man could imagine. Unfortunately, Pinter resembled one of the dead he cared for, owing to a combination of genetics and long-term Vitamin D deficiency from a life spent largely indoors.

When Phillips and Yates trudged along the long, stiflingly hot basement corridor with its row of industrial air conditioners and buzzed through the security doors into the mortuary, the first thing they heard was Rod Stewart blasting through the speaker system. The sound of it carried across the freezing airspace and Phillips jiggled his hips in time to the music as he pulled on a visitor's lab coat.

"Howay, let's see what Jeff's got for us."

They hurried past a row of metal gurneys, all empty except one, where a single mortuary technician stood poised to complete a neat 'Y' incision. It was degrading for a man of Phillips' experience to admit that he still felt queasy at the thought of seeing a cadaver, but an old leopard doesn't change its spots and it was better for all concerned that he worked with his stomach, rather than against it. Glancing across at Yates, he was mollified to discover that, for once, he was not alone. He just hoped they could hold it together until their task was complete.

Pinter turned from his discussion with a tall, blonde woman of around thirty.

"Frank! Good to see you." He extended a bony hand and Phillips hesitated for a fraction of a second, always fearful of where it had been.

"Aye, good to see you too, Jeff." Phillips angled his body to introduce Yates. "I don't think you've met my trainee? PC Melanie Yates, this is Doctor Jeff Pinter."

Yates found her fingers engulfed in a friendly grip.

"No Ryan, today?" Pinter queried.

Phillips cast around for something non-committal to say.

"He's held up at the office with…this and that," he finished lamely. "We'll be taking care of business in the meantime."

If he sensed an undercurrent, Pinter decided not to pursue it any further.

"You might remember Doctor Ann Millington," he said, turning to the studious-looking young woman to his left. "She's come down from Edinburgh to help us with the body you found at Kielder this morning."

"Aye, I do," Phillips recognised the forensic anthropologist from the last time she'd helped them to date and assess a body found hidden deep inside Hadrian's Wall. "Thanks for coming on board."

"I was fascinated when I heard what you'd found," she said. "I wish I could say I hurried down here on the first available train as an act of pure altruism but there was a healthy dollop of professional interest. We don't find these 'bog bodies' very often but, when we do, it's a real coup."

"Bog bodies?" Yates queried.

Millington nodded.

"If the conditions are right, a body can be mummified naturally for extraordinary amounts of time; even thousands of years. The body you found this morning bears all the markers of having been preserved in a similar way. Pretty exciting," she remarked.

Phillips supposed that was true but, as far as he was concerned, 'the body' was a young lad who had been missing for God only knew how long. He'd had a life ahead of him, and probably a family who cared.

"Have you had a chance to look him over?" Phillips asked.

"I've made a start and I can give you some very general observations. Why don't we go and take a look?"

Before they could protest, Millington turned in the direction of a small corridor off the main workspace, leading to a series of smaller examination rooms and offices. She unlocked one of them and flicked on the bright strobe light hanging overhead.

There, in the centre, was a shrouded figure.

"Obviously, air will accelerate decomposition and so we've spent some time this morning trying to ensure the body remains preserved."

Yates wrinkled her nose at the pungent scent of noxious chemicals permeating the air and, when the paper sheet was turned back, she was faced with something she had not expected. She had seen one or two dead bodies and it hadn't been anything to write home about, but this was different. The teenage boy—at least, he looked like a teenager—was shrunken, the skin stained terracotta brown and shrivelled, as if his insides had been sucked out. His features were still recognisable; the outline of nose, chin and mouth and the hair plastered against his head. He might have been sleeping, cocooned for years in death.

"It's incredible," she found herself saying.

"Mm, in purely scientific terms, I have to confess I was mildly disappointed to find he's only been *in situ* for around thirty years," Millington remarked, with a degree of clinical objectivity that might have been distasteful in other circumstances. "In fact, I doubt you'll need my services much except to confirm what you already know."

Phillips frowned.

"How's that?"

"His clothing," she explained, moving across to a computer station where she brought up a series of images they'd taken earlier. "It was fairly well preserved, like the rest of him. He was still wearing the Levi 501s he died in, as well as the t-shirt and jacket. He lost a shoe somewhere along the way, but he was wearing the other trainer—an Adidas Gazelle, size nine."

She stepped back to allow them to flick through the images on-screen.

"We've swabbed the clothing for analysis and sent them across to Faulkner's team," she told them. "You never know what they might be able to find."

"Looks like seventies, maybe early-eighties fashion," Yates guessed.

"Sounds about right. Better still, we found a bus pass inside the pocket of his jeans," Pinter replied. "Laminated plastic, with a start date of January 1981, expiring in December of the same year. Unfortunately, no name printed."

"That's brilliant," Phillips said, and enjoyed a brief daydream about closing the case before nightfall. "That'll really help us narrow down the field when we look at Missing Persons."

"The bus pass was issued as a 'youth' pass, for ages up to sixteen. It's hard without the bone structure to work with, but factoring in his size and facial features, I'd estimate he was between the ages of fourteen and sixteen when he died. I've already requested dental records," Millington said. "Hopefully, they won't take too long to come back and we'll have a more definitive answer."

Phillips began to think he'd be home in time to watch *Game of Thrones*.

"We've already spoken to Missing Persons," Yates said. "Hopefully, the dental records will help us there. But how did he die?"

"Badly," Pinter said, scratching the side of his long nose. "Blunt trauma to the cranium, here," he indicated a spot on the boy's skull with a retractable pointer. "After that, massive internal haemorrhage and asphyxiation by drowning, or cardiac arrest, most likely. Impossible to say for sure at this stage but that's an educated guess."

"Drowning? But the reservoir didn't exist in 1981," Yates argued.

"He didn't drown in the water," Pinter explained, and a trace of compassion entered his voice as he looked down at the wasted remains of what had once been a living, breathing person. "He would have drowned in his own blood."

There was a short silence as a mark of respect to the dead, then Phillips asked the next question.

"Could it have been self-inflicted? Did he fall on a rock?"

"Highly unlikely," Pinter said decisively. "I would say the blow came from behind, in a downward motion from the right, judging by the angle of the wound. The force necessary to cause that degree of trauma wouldn't have been caused by a simple fall, unless he fell from a great height. Then there's the small matter of the gashes to his chest," Pinter said, with a degree of smugness, as if he'd been saving that little coup de grâce.

He pointed to four or five shallow wounds dotted around the boy's torso.

"These injuries resemble what I'd expect to see from a knife, probably a small-to-medium blade of around three or four inches."

"Like a penknife?" Yates suggested.

"Yes, or a small chopping knife, something smooth with a sharp point rather than serrated."

"I might have passed off the head injury as an accident but I'm betting he didn't stab himself in the chest several times for good measure," Phillips declared, matter-of-factly. "What I don't understand is, how did he get into this state? How did he stay down there for so long without decomposing?"

"This level of natural preservation only happens in very specific conditions," Millington explained. "It's a natural phenomenon of bodies encased in peat because of its unique biochemical composition; the water content is highly acidic, the temperatures are usually low and there's a lack of oxygen which combines to preserve the skin—but it's tanned to a deep brown colour, as you can see."

"How about his bones and internal organs?" Yates wondered.

Millington gave a slight shake of her head.

"That really depends on the *type* of bog. In this case, most of the bones haven't survived because the acid content in the peat has dissolved the calcium phosphate, whereas his internal organs have survived remarkably well, along with the skin. Patches of land and substrata around Kielder are rife with sphagnum moss, which plays a major role in creating the right pH levels in the peat."

"It's like vinegar," Pinter said, bluntly. "Bog acid has a similar pH level, so it preserves the skin and soft tissue just like pickled vegetables."

Phillips pulled a face.

"Howay, man, Jeff. I just had my lunch."

"Sorry, just trying to help…"

"Aye, that's what you always say," Phillips complained, thinking of the pickled gherkin he'd enjoyed on a bacon cheeseburger at lunchtime. "How about bacteria? Wouldn't it get into the peat and decay the body?"

Again, Millington shook her head.

"That's what makes the peat conditions so unique. They're almost completely anaerobic. Research has shown that if a body is conserved during the coldest months, that works even better."

"What about this lad?" Phillips cast his eye over the boy again. "What time of year would you say he was buried?"

"Given the fact he had injuries that would attract scavengers, it's more likely to have been a cold month," Millington postulated. "Anything warmer and he wouldn't have been so well kept."

"Which means early or later part of 1981, if we assume the bus pass is an accurate indicator," Yates concluded. "Couldn't have been later, because they started filling the new reservoir after then and the whole area was closed to the public."

Phillips nodded, thinking through the next steps.

"Must have been buried pretty deep all these years," he mused. "Otherwise, the water from the lake would have let in pockets of air."

"Yes, I'd agree with that," Millington said. "It's likely that the natural ebb and flow of the water gradually dislodged the layers of peat and stone, causing his body to rise."

"This is going to be big news when the press find out," Pinter thought aloud.

"Let's keep it under our hats for now," Phillips said briskly, and gave the two clinicians a warning look. "He must have been reported missing back in '81 and whoever's responsible for cracking his head was probably hoping that Nature would do the rest. When the reservoir filled, they must've thought they were in the clear."

"They were wrong," Yates said, and the light of battle shone in her eyes.

"Aye," Phillips murmured, and surprised everybody—including himself—by stepping closer to the boy's body, where he looked down at the remains with a kind of tenderness. "Don't worry, son, we'll make sure you find your way home."

CHAPTER 8

"**B**loody buggering hell!"

DI MacKenzie stared at the list of supposedly 'urgent' cold case files on her computer screen and swore viciously.

"Ma'am?"

A timid-looking detective constable occupying the cubicle next to hers popped his head over the parapet and gave her a worried look.

"Is everything alright?"

She ran frustrated hands through her mane of red hair and then held them up, palms outward, to signal the coast was now clear.

But when he ducked down again, she looked back at the list and recognised some of the names from her years in CID. The memory of those cases and the long months spent tracking a killer, or a rapist, brought the same depressing sense of failure and loss that every detective experienced when they'd been unable to solve a crime. When she was working on active cases, it helped to overcome that lingering feeling of disappointment and, she admitted, it was easy to forget the faces of those they had been unable to help.

MacKenzie clicked open the first one on the list.

Hannah Adams.

The image of a young woman of around twenty with a pretty, smiling face popped onto the computer screen. She'd gone missing back in 2010 and her body had been found in a shallow grave not long afterwards, bearing marks of sexual abuse. MacKenzie remembered how the department had rallied to find her killer; how they'd searched, analysed, questioned and finally, desperately, begged the public to help them, but all to no avail.

Hannah wasn't the only one.

Northumbria CID had a strong track record, one they could be proud of, but that didn't mean they were infallible. Some cases slipped through the net, ones where a perpetrator was either smart enough or lucky enough not to get caught, or where CID hadn't been equipped with the resources to find them.

MacKenzie scanned witness statements and case summaries, supporting documents and forensic evidence. The worst of it was, they had DNA on file that probably belonged to Hannah's killer but no match to any existing offender on the national database. Nearly sixty-six million people lived in the United Kingdom last time she'd checked, three million of whom were permanently based in the North East. Not great odds for catching a killer without a stroke of luck, and that didn't count the possibility of transients, or tourists.

She drummed her fingers against the desktop and then brought up the landing page for the police DNA database, the National DNA Database and European Nucleotide Archive, thinking it wouldn't hurt to run another check just in case things had changed. There were automatic alerts in place that constantly checked old evidence samples against new DNA listings, but some instinct led her to key in the manual check.

But a few moments later, her computer gave a jingling alert.

No match.

With a heavy sigh, MacKenzie glanced again at Hannah's smiling face and then moved on to the next.

* * *

As night fell and washed the sky in shades of deep midnight blue, Anna stayed up for a while chatting over the events of the day with her postgraduate students. However, when the discussion moved away from local history and turned to important questions of the age such as which act had performed better on *The X-Factor,* she realised she was out of her depth and decided to give up the pretence. She said goodnight to the small group of twenty-somethings and left them to chew the fat over bottles of cheap beer with the sure and certain knowledge they would be skinny-dipping in the Swedish-style hot tubs that came with every lodge the moment she left.

Anna smiled as they called out inebriated farewells and promised her they would be up bright and early to explore the next historical landmark on their itinerary the following morning. With a chuckle, she stepped onto the narrow asphalt road leading to her own lodge a couple of doors down.

Then she simply stared.

It was incredible.

Stars covered the night sky in a swathe of diamonds, winking in the heavens above where Anna stood, enraptured. The temperature had dropped and the air was icy cold but she lingered because, at times like these, she understood why people believed that an omnipotent being had created such splendour. She stood there with her neck craned upward and watched a shooting star blaze a trail across the sky, burning through the atmosphere in one final, beautiful act of defiance.

When the cold penetrated through the layers of her clothing, Anna turned away and crunched across the gravel, following a line of solar-powered lights in the direction of her lodge.

Then she came to a complete halt.

She didn't know what had alerted her to the presence of another, but the extreme darkness of the surrounding trees heightened her senses and magnified every whisper of wind through the leaves, every creak and moan.

Her body went on full alert.

Fear crawled across her skin and she began to shiver. During the day, the area had seemed so full of people wandering back and forth towards the visitor's complex. Now, the place was deserted but for the odd yellow light shining at intervals along the roadside from the row of lodges.

Her breath came out in short gusts as she geared herself up to run.

Now, her mind whispered. *Do it now!*

She could scream. The area was so quiet, her voice would sound like a banshee and people would hear.

If she just turned and ran…

"Anna?"

The scream welled up and died in her throat when a tall, dark figure materialised on the shadowy road ahead.

"*Ryan*? For goodness' sake, do you have to creep about like that? You nearly gave me a heart attack!"

But she smiled and hurried along the road to meet him.

"I didn't know you were coming to stay," she said. "I wouldn't have spent so long with the others if I'd known you were waiting around."

Ryan tugged her against him in a hard embrace, wrapping his arms around her slim body.

"Hey," her voice was muffled against his coat. "Is everything alright?"

Ryan rubbed his chin across the top of her head.

"Let's go inside," he suggested. "It's getting cold out here."

* * *

A short while later, they were seated side by side on the leather sofa in front of a hearty log-burner which crackled in the living room of Anna's holiday lodge.

"I wish you'd told me," Ryan said again, and she rested her head against his shoulder.

"You might have felt compelled to report it. I don't care for my own sake but I didn't want your reputation to be damaged. Not after everything we'd already been through."

He nodded, understanding the choice she had made.

"I'm sorry I didn't tell you," she added softly.

"I'm sorry I wasn't able to thank you properly for what you did."

Anna gave him a startled look.

"What? You don't need to thank me—"

"Oh, yes, I do. Discharging a weapon is upsetting at the best of times, on a licensed gun range and with specialist firearms training. Discharging a revolver that isn't your own, to save the person you love whilst running the risk of killing someone? I can't imagine what that must have cost you."

Anna looked down at their hands, linked together in her lap.

"Yes, you can," she said softly. "You did the same thing for me, not so long ago."

His fingers tightened and Anna plucked up the courage to ask something she hadn't dared ask before.

"Ryan, was I the one who killed him? *The Hacker*?"

He hugged her close to his body, thinking of how she must have been wondering and worrying these past months.

"No, you didn't. The inquest found no evidence of a gunshot wound and if you'd hit him squarely, there would have been. You might have skimmed his shoulder," he admitted. "But his skin was so badly torn from the fall, the post-mortem was inconclusive. One thing was certain: it was the fall from High Force waterfall that killed him, not you."

"Oh," she said, feeling both relieved and oddly disappointed. "Turns out I'm not as much of a crack shot as I thought."

Ryan huffed out a laugh and turned to face her.

"Did anybody ever tell you, you're a force to be reckoned with?"

In that moment, he forgot about his troubles with Lucas and the worries awaiting him at work the next day and thought only of the woman sitting beside him with dark eyes that shone in the firelight.

"You never told me these places come with hot tubs," he said.

"I thought a southern boy like you would find it far too cold for your constitution."

"How about we go skinny-dipping and you can be the judge?"

She waited a beat.

"You're on."

* * *

Sleep would not come.

The long hours of the night crawled by and the *tick-tock* of the chamber clock fell like a death knell on the mantelpiece. Shadows passed across the walls of the bedroom, seeming to morph into the shape of a person.

Not just any person.

As the first light of dawn began to shine through the windowpanes, the shadows formed the shape of a boy who was not yet a man, his gangly limbs trailing closer and closer to the person lying huddled on the bed in the foetal position.

"No, no, no."

It was not possible.

It was not possible.

It was only a nightmare.

But ever since the police found his body, Duncan's face had begun to appear; blurred, snatched glimpses in a windowpane or in the mirror, before he disappeared again like the rippling water where he'd lain.

Why now?

Why had he waited so long to rise again and destroy everything that had been built, so carefully, for thirty-three years?

A new day dawned, casting blazing rays of ochre light across the room. But the shadows lingered, clinging to the person who lay shaking and sweating against the bedclothes while sanity slipped slowly away.

CHAPTER 9

Guy Sullivan was still drunk.

It was the only possible explanation for why he was up at the crack of dawn, taking a bracing walk through the trees without a map or any clue where he was going. Unable to sleep, he had taken the executive decision to seek out a pharmacist or a 24-7 supermarket that could dispense Alka-Seltzer, ibuprofen or some other magical drug that could make hangovers disappear. However, as he continued his pilgrimage through the trees, he realised he had failed to consider three very important things.

Firstly, the need for appropriate footwear. In his drunken state, he had donned canvas shoes rather than water-resistant walking boots and his feet were now soaking wet.

Secondly, the nearest pharmacy or supermarket was at least five miles away, in any direction.

Thirdly—and most mortifying of all—there was a gift shop less than fifty yards from their lodge which sold a small selection of essentials including things like headache and indigestion tablets, so he could have just waited in the cosy lodge until it opened.

Now, disgruntled and humiliated, Guy continued to wind his way through the trees, brushing past low-lying branches of towering Sitka spruce until he stumbled upon the worn track of a public bridleway.

"Follow the yellow brick road," he murmured.

The air was heavy and claustrophobic as the pathway meandered through overgrown thickets, further and further away from civilisation. He could hear the tinkling sound of water somewhere nearby and wrongly assumed it was the reservoir, so he continued walking in the wrong direction. Having failed to consult a map, Guy was blissfully unaware of his predicament as he continued to forge ahead with a combination of youthful complacency and desperation brought on by an excess of cheap plonk.

Why, oh, why hadn't he gone to bed?

Of course, he knew the reason, and her name was Isabella. Gorgeous, half-Italian and specialising in pre-Christian religious history, she was a constant distraction and he'd stayed up half the night hanging on every dulcet word she'd said.

And where had it got him?

Nowhere.

Guy raked an impatient hand through his floppy fringe of blonde hair and tried to gauge his position. He couldn't see the reservoir and there were no sounds of life other than the low drone of insects buzzing in the undergrowth and his own feet squelching in their sodden insoles.

"Shit," he muttered, feeling suddenly afraid. There were no signs or markings and he wouldn't have the first clue about how to 'read the land' or whatever the hell they called it.

He pulled out his mobile phone and tried again to find a GPS signal, but the entire area was a black hole and the battery was running dangerously low.

Guy turned a full circle and then looked up at the sky, screwing his eyes up against the sun.

Was that east or west?

Panic was starting to bubble on the edges of his mind when he heard a rustle on the bridleway ahead. His young face broke into a wide grin as he turned to see who had come to save him.

* * *

"Duncan?"

He was standing further along the bridleway smiling in that silly, puppyish way he always did. He was even wearing the same stonewash Levi's and his blonde hair was still too long, flopping into his eyes.

"You can't be here. You're *dead*," Roly whispered.

Guy Sullivan walked the short distance along the path towards the person who watched his approach with wide, frightened eyes.

"Sorry, I didn't hear—"

The first blow took him by surprise, connecting hard with his left temple, and he stumbled backwards, dazed.

"Leave me alone!" Roly hissed. "Leave me alone!"

Guy held out a defensive arm but his faculties were already weakened and the adrenaline hadn't kicked in yet, that crucial 'fight or flight' instinct that might have saved him. Instead, there was no time to think before the next blow came down, then again, harder and harder until blood began to pour into his eyes.

"Wait! Stop…" he slurred.

He waved his arms frantically to stave off further blows and then turned blindly to run, but his movements were sluggish and he stumbled, falling hard against the uneven ground. His fingers gripped the mossy earth to find purchase and the toes of his shoes slipped against the damp path as he scrambled to get up, but there was no time.

Another blow came from behind, bouncing off his skull at first and then cracking through the bone until his body jerked once, twice, then stilled while blood pulsed away into the grass beneath him.

The blows rained down for several minutes after Guy Sullivan died and they didn't stop until his face was utterly unrecognisable, nothing more than a mass of bloodied flesh and cartilage, as if he had never existed at all.

* * *

Just before eight, Kielder Waterside began to awaken. Ryan watched a couple of small fishing boats head out onto the water from the deck of Anna's eco-lodge and thought of how the discovery of a teenage boy's body had scarcely broken the stride of this remote community. It was their way of coping, he supposed. They continued living and going about their ordinary routines to keep their hands and their minds occupied.

"I'd better go and see if the postgrads are awake," Anna said from the doorway, where she sipped from a steaming mug of coffee. "They seemed to be going for it last night, so I don't know what state they'll be in this morning."

"Nothing you can do about that," Ryan remarked, turning back to face her. "They're all over twenty-one."

"Yeah, except we're supposed to be doing a full day's hiking today. It'll be a real hoot dragging them up and over hillsides to look at Roman ruins."

"Guess that's their look-out," he said with a grin. "They'll have to drink a few litres of water and be brave."

Anna laughed and stepped out onto the deck beside him.

"I've seen you the morning after a couple of pints with Frank," she said, poking an accusatory finger against his chest.

Before he could come up with a pithy response, Ryan spotted one of Anna's students jogging along the woodland lane towards them.

"Uh-oh," he murmured.

Anna hurried to open the front door and a dark-haired girl stepped inside with an air of urgency.

"I'm sorry to disturb you, Doctor Taylor, but…oh!"

The words died on her lips as Ryan stepped back through the patio doors to join them and Anna told herself to be patient in the face of raging hormones.

"Isabella?" she said firmly. "What's the matter?"

The girl snapped back to attention and her face creased into lines of worry.

"It's Guy," she said. "He—we all had a few too many last night and he was in pretty bad shape. I thought he'd gone to bed to sleep it off but when I went to wake him up this morning, he wasn't in his room. We've been down to look around the main complex to see if he's anywhere around there, but the place is practically empty and there's no sign of him."

Over the girl's head, Anna exchanged a look with Ryan.

"Alright, Isabella, I don't want you to worry. Guy has probably gone for a stroll and has forgotten to tell anybody. Have you tried ringing his mobile?"

The girl nodded, and her fingers began twisting the material of her thick jumper.

"It goes straight to voicemail because there's no signal around here. I had to use the phone at the lodge to call him," she explained.

Anna's heart began to pound but her face betrayed nothing of her turmoil.

"Okay, what I want you to do is go back and stay with the others while I make some enquiries."

"What's Guy's phone number?" Ryan interjected.

Isabella flushed and stammered out the digits, which he keyed into his own phone contacts.

"Alright, do as Doctor Taylor says and stay in your lodge, for now. We'll make enquiries."

The girl let herself out and Ryan reached for the landline to put a call through to the tech support team, back at CID Headquarters.

"Steve? Yeah, it's Ryan... Good, thanks. Look, can you run a search for me? No, it's not on the system yet but we've got a potential missing person up at Kielder. It could save us a lot of time." There was a small pause. "Thanks, I owe you one."

Ryan read out the number and ended the call, then looked across to where Anna was perched on the edge of the sofa.

"He's going to contact the telephone companies now and try to triangulate Guy's position, or at least his phone. In the meantime, we need to alert the local police and Forestry Commission."

He paused to check his watch and found it was edging past eight o'clock. He was expected in the office by nine at the latest and he was already going to be late, since it was an easy fifty-mile drive back into the city centre.

Then again, a young man had gone missing less than twenty-four hours after they'd fished another one out of the reservoir.

"I'll make the calls," he said, and prepared to face the wrath of his new superintendent.

* * *

DC Jack Lowerson surveyed himself in the dingy mirror inside the gents toilets, checking everything was where it should be ahead of his meeting with the superintendent. He'd worn his best suit—a slim-fitting, shiny Air Force blue number—and a bold red tie because he liked the colour. He didn't have Ryan's stature to be able to pull off smart-casual, nor Phillips' longevity to get away with wearing whatever he liked, so he made the best of what he had.

And what did he have, really?

Lowerson looked hard at his reflection, trying to see himself as others might. He was a man of thirty-one who looked several years younger despite his best efforts to inject a bit of gravitas with the addition of a designer beard that was more of a patchy goatee. He ran a hand over the fluffy hair, wishing he'd shaved it off, then patted his quiff, smoothing down the gel that held it rigidly in place while his thoughts inevitably wandered.

The fact was, he'd been single for longer than he cared to remember and, with every passing day, his confidence ebbed. He'd tried all the dating sites and apps, had spent countless Friday nights and most of his bank balance hopping around wine bars in the city on the off-chance he'd meet someone special and, when that failed, he had even succumbed to the obligatory round of blind dates arranged by his mother. His mates told him he should enjoy his freedom because these were the 'glory days', but it was becoming harder to enjoy a no-strings, hedonistic night out without worrying about the inherent dangers of that lifestyle; an overactive imagination being one of the major side-effects of his line of work. Besides, he was honest enough to admit he wanted some permanence in his life, not a meaningless, transient relationship. He wanted love, companionship and a bit of a spark. Consequently, most nights he ended up sharing the sofa with the TV remote and Marbles, his cat.

He wanted someone to walk hand in hand with and talk to at the end of the day.

That wasn't too much to ask, was it?

Above all else, he was tired of looking through the window with his nose pressed up against the glass, watching Ryan with Anna, or Phillips with MacKenzie. It wasn't that he begrudged them their happiness, it was only that he would like to find a little of his own.

Snatching up a paper towel, he dried his hands and screwed up the paper with more aggression than was strictly necessary.

For a while, he'd thought there might be something with Melanie Yates. He'd been plucking up the courage to ask her out, ever since the last time she'd turned him down, in fact. But there was only so much rejection a man could take and he wasn't sure he could stand another polite 'I'm busy, thanks', at least not until he'd had sufficient time to recover from the last setback.

Besides, much to his irritation, Melanie only had eyes for Ryan.

No surprises there, he thought sourly. Even though the man was recently married, his appeal hadn't dimmed and it was a constant and supreme effort not to hate his friend for simply being who he was. After all, Ryan didn't seem to be aware of his effect on the women— and some men, too—who were drawn to the kind of easy confidence projected, and most people spent their lives trying to emulate.

People like me, he admitted.

Pushing his personal woes aside, Lowerson headed back out into the long corridor that would lead him to DCS Lucas's corner office. CID Headquarters was quiet and mostly empty except for weekend shift-workers like himself and, apparently, the new superintendent. His heart began to hammer as he approached the door at the end and he injected what he hoped was a manly tone to his voice when he reached her personal assistant, who sat in a cubicle outside.

"Go straight in," the woman told him. "She's expecting you."

Lowerson knocked and, when he pushed open the door, was momentarily blinded by the sun streaming through the windows. He turned and found himself pinned by a pair of bright blue eyes.

"Good morning," she said.

Lowerson flushed and was instantly embarrassed by his own reaction. It wasn't as if he'd never seen a woman before, it's just that she wasn't what he had been expecting. For a start, he'd expected a much older person. He'd missed the staff meeting the previous day and hadn't been prepared to meet an attractive brunette who looked as if she'd just stepped off the pages of a glossy magazine.

"Good morning, ma'am."

"Come and make yourself comfortable, Jack," she said. "You don't mind if I call you Jack, do you?"

"No, of course not."

"Good. Thank you for being so punctual," she said. "I appreciate punctuality in my staff."

She rested her chin on her hand and looked at him across the desk, her laser-blue gaze assessing.

"You're probably wondering what you've done wrong," she said, with a tigerish smile.

Lowerson laughed nervously.

"I—well, yes."

"The answer is nothing. Nothing at all," she said. "I called a meeting because I've been looking over your work record and I'm impressed, Jack. In fact, I'm surprised the topic of promotion hasn't been raised with you before now. How long have you been a detective constable—three years?"

Lowerson dragged his jaw off the floor and forced his lips to move.

"Yes, ma'am, a little over three years."

"That's what I thought. Seems a long time for a person of your capabilities to be stuck in the same position, wouldn't you say?"

Lowerson didn't know what to say. He'd always thought his progression through the ranks had been quick but, if his superior thought otherwise, he wasn't going to argue.

"Take Ryan," she said, presuming correctly that Lowerson used Ryan as a benchmark for all things. "He's moved up the ladder at lightning speed and there's no reason you shouldn't do the same. Unless—"

She stopped abruptly.

"Unless?" he prodded.

Lucas lifted a slim shoulder and let it fall again.

"I was only wondering aloud," she told him. "In my experience, I've sometimes found that senior detectives seek to repress younger, more talented members of their team out of a sense of rivalry. I'd hate to see you falling prey to that."

His hackles rose.

"I'm sure that isn't the case here, ma'am," he said quickly. "DCI Ryan has always been fair with me. If anything, he's gone above and beyond to make sure I've been included in the most high-profile investigations."

"But weren't you the victim of an unprovoked attack during an investigation on Holy Island? I understood you were put in that position following a direct order from Ryan. I'm surprised you were left out to dry like that."

Lowerson swallowed, remembering the dark days when he'd come out of a coma having lost six months of his life.

"That wasn't his fault."

Lucas rose from her chair and moved around to the front of her desk, leaning backwards a fraction so that her suit jacket stretched, just a little.

By virtue of being alive and red-blooded, Lowerson couldn't help but notice. He dragged his eyes away and focused determinedly on her face, which was infinitely more dangerous.

"I'm offering you an opportunity, Jack," she said softly. "I need somebody trustworthy to help me get to grips with the department and to be my right-hand man while I clean things up. In return, I'll promote you to the rank of sergeant."

Lowerson was silent for a full ten seconds.

"I don't understand," he said eventually. "I need to take my sergeant's exams, go through the training pathway—"

"And you will," she told him. "Except, rather than working for Ryan, you'll be working for me."

His Adam's apple bobbed.

"Can I think about it?"

"Of course," she said, with a breezy smile. "As long as I have your answer by the end of the day."

CHAPTER 10

"You should be ashamed of yourselves."

Phillips and Yates exchanged a look of confusion as they stood on the doorstep of Angela Gray's 1950s terrace in the village of Kielder, a short drive away from the waterside complex where she owned a gift shop and where they had just informed her that her son had been found.

Phillips recovered first, putting it down to a mother's natural rejection of the worst possible news. It was often the case that the parents of missing children entered a long-term state of denial that prevented them from accepting the truth when it finally came knocking on their door.

"Mrs Gray, please listen—"

"I have nothing more to say to you," she said, gripping the edge of the UPVC door so hard her knuckles glowed white. "I have a shop to run and I'm already late opening, thanks to you."

She made a show of checking her watch but she could barely focus on the dials. Angrily, she looked between them again, willing them to be wrong.

"I've told you people time after time, *it isn't Duncan*. Why won't you believe me?"

Across the street, people began to trickle out of their houses to watch the fresh drama playing out on their doorstep. Phillips noticed they were beginning to attract an audience and detested that part of human nature which led people to relish the misfortune of their neighbours.

"Mrs Gray, why don't we discuss this inside where you'll be more comfortable?"

"There's nothing to discuss," she spat, with unconcealed venom. "Don't you have any sense of decency? Every time a body is found, you come knocking at my door telling me to prepare myself because it could be him. Well, why don't you save your energy and find out who that poor soul really is? Stop harassing me, making me think—making me *believe*…"

Her voice started to break and Yates took an involuntary step forward, but one look from Angela stopped her.

"If you come around here making false claims again, I'll make a complaint. I'll write to my MP. Don't think I won't."

"Mrs Gray, these aren't false claims and we're not here to tell you that the body *might* be Duncan. We're telling you that it *is* Duncan. A post-mortem has revealed a positive match with the dental records held on file belonging to your son. We're terribly sorry."

She shook her head back and forth repeatedly, closing her eyes so that she did not have to see the truth written all over Phillips' face.

"You're wrong," she whispered.

Phillips continued to hold her gaze, speaking quietly and calmly.

"We're not wrong, Angela. The search is over."

For a long, suspended moment, Angela stared at him. Then her body crumpled. She doubled over at the waist and clung to the door for support as she made a low, keening sound redolent of an animal in torment.

"Come on, now," Phillips murmured. "Let's go inside."

The fight drained from her body leaving her limp and, this time, she allowed them to lead her inside the house where Duncan had lived; along the hallway where he'd stored his bike and into the small living room where they'd once sat together as a family, laughing, playing board games or watching telly. She sank onto the old sofa with its plastic arm coverings and felt the last vestiges of hope drain from her body. All these years, she'd told herself he was alive somewhere and just unwilling or unable to come home. So long as she'd believed he was alive, there was always a chance.

Not now.

Not ever again.

Tears began to fall, running into the network of fine lines on either side of her eyes, dripping from her chin onto the material of the plain white blouse she wore for work.

"Angela?"

Dazed, she looked up into a pair of kind brown eyes belonging to the young female detective whose name she'd forgotten.

Yates sank onto the edge of the sofa beside her.

"Mrs Gray, is there anybody we can contact for you? Your husband, perhaps?"

"He's gone."

John had left years ago. The strain of losing a child and her refusal—she could see that now—her refusal to acknowledge even the *possibility* of Duncan being dead, had been too much for him to bear. He was living with a woman a few miles away, now. Sometimes, she saw them in the supermarket or at the post office.

"How? How…?"

Angela's ragged voice tore through the silence and they didn't need to ask what she meant. The family always wanted to know *how* and *why*, even when it caused them nothing but torment.

"We don't know exactly how he died," Phillips told her. "But I have to tell you we are treating Duncan's death as murder."

Her eyes closed and more silent tears made tracks down her face. There was another long pause as she digested the information, processed the horror and, finally, welcomed the rage that burned through her body when she thought of how her boy had suffered.

Angela's eyes opened again and they were bone dry when they turned on Phillips.

"Who killed him?"

He perched on the other side of the sofa, so he and Yates flanked her on both sides in a display of unity.

"I don't know, Angela, but we're going to find out."

"How can I help? I want to help. And I want to see him, to see Duncan—to tell him—"*To tell him how much his mother loved him.*

"We'll arrange it, as soon as possible."

"It's time he came home," she murmured, thinking of how close he had been to her all these years and she'd never known.

* * *

It was almost eleven o'clock by the time Phillips and Yates finally left Angela Gray to her grief and prepared to make the long journey back to the city. They were forestalled as they wound their way through the trees when they encountered a couple of local squad cars heading in the opposite direction towards Kielder Waterside, followed by a small convoy of high-spec 4x4s used by the Mountain Rescue team.

Phillips made an executive decision, performed a quick U-turn in the road and followed them back to the little complex that was swarming with police and forest rangers for the second day in a row.

"I thought Ryan was supposed to be back at CID?" Yates remarked as they exited the car. Phillips followed the line of her gaze to where the man stood briefing a group of local police and started to get a creeping feeling that something was very badly wrong.

"Howay," he said. "Let's go and find out what's happening."

Ryan spotted them immediately and stepped away from the small crowd of police to head them off.

"We've got a twenty-two-year-old missing male," he said, without preamble. "His name's Guy Sullivan and he's one of Anna's postgraduate students. So far as we know, he went missing some time after four o'clock this morning, which is the last time he was seen before his friends went to bed after a heavy night. Nobody knows where he went after that, only that he wasn't in the lodge when they woke up. They did a search of the vicinity and tried calling his mobile several times, waited a while, then raised the alarm with Anna just before eight o'clock. I happened to be there," he explained, never more conscious of the fact that he was working on borrowed time.

Right on cue, the phone in his pocket began to vibrate, signalling that he had stepped into a rare hotspot of mobile reception. A quick glance told him there were several missed calls and a voicemail message, all from the office.

He slipped it back into his pocket.

"As far as we know, this could be as simple as a young bloke wandering off into the forest and getting lost. But…" Ryan shook his head and looked across to where Anna stood beside the remaining group of students, trying to reassure them.

"But?"

"I don't know, Frank. Something about it feels off, coming so soon after the body we found yesterday."

"Could be coincidence," Yates offered, and watched two heads swivel in her direction.

"Do you want to say it, or shall I?" Ryan asked Phillips.

"You do the honours."

Ryan inclined his head.

"Yates, in this business, we don't believe in coincidences."

She nodded and made a mental note to cultivate a more suspicious outlook.

"Look, I have to get back to the city," Ryan continued, and was surprised the words didn't stick in his throat. "Anna and her students are pretty worried but they're holding up. The tech team are trying to triangulate Guy's position through the telephone companies but that could take hours or even days, considering it's the weekend. There's a search co-ordinator from the police organising a search with a rep from the Forestry Commission."

Ryan stopped mid-spiel, suddenly remembering that Phillips and Yates had been driving in the area and that could only mean one thing.

"Who was he?"

Phillips heaved a sigh.

"Duncan Gray, born and raised in Kielder. He went missing back in October 1981 along with a rucksack, some clothes and a few odds and ends. We told his mother this morning."

"How old?"

"Sixteen."

Ryan looked out across the water, not envying them their task but at the same time feeling robbed of a duty he felt he owed to the young man he'd made a silent promise to avenge.

But it was not his investigation any longer and that duty belonged to someone else now.

"Let me know how things progress," he said abruptly, before striding back to his car.

With one final, sweeping glance at the water and sky, Ryan turned away and prepared to face whatever awaited him back at the office.

* * *

"What have you done?"

They stood and watched the police swarm the area like ants as they began to search for the student who had died for no reason other than because he resembled the boy Duncan Gray had been.

"I didn't mean to do it," Roly whispered. "I panicked, I—"

"It was incredibly stupid, and you've endangered us both."

"I—but I thought it was *him*!"

Thankfully, the picnic area was only half-full and nobody seemed to have heard that little outburst. It was clear to see the madness in Roly's eyes, if you looked hard enough. Over the years, sanity had obviously eroded until the discovery of Duncan's body had opened the floodgates to full-blown paranoia.

The problem was, how to manage it?

"How could it possibly have been him? Duncan's dead; he had his accident years ago, don't you remember?"

"Yes. Yes, I remember."

But Roly's eyes skittered away, scanning the faces of the men and boys, just to be sure. A decision needed to be made, quickly.

"We can't be seen together. Don't call my number again; if they look at your phone records, they'll find it. I'll get a burner and get a message to you with the new number so you can contact me if you need to."

"Okay. Okay," Roly repeated. "You won't leave me alone, will you?"

It was pitiable to see such weakness, to see the fear that was so potent.

"I'll be in touch."

CHAPTER 11

"**S**he wants to see you, right away."

As Ryan had predicted, Lucas was waiting for him as soon as he returned to the office just before noon. He didn't bother to respond to the edict delivered by her personal assistant but turned and walked directly to the enormous vending machine in the corridor. A man was entitled to one last meal before facing a threat of unknown proportions and he chose to have a black coffee and a Kit Kat.

Five minutes later, he entered the superintendent's office.

Lucas did not immediately acknowledge his presence but continued to read a stack of papers sitting neatly in front of her. Years ago, he might have found her deliberate silence intimidating, but not now.

Finally, she closed the folder, rose, walked to a filing cabinet to return it to its proper place, returned to her chair and sat down again.

Only then did she look across to where Ryan stood in the middle of the room, feet planted, looking very much at ease. Anger flowed like lava, strong and hot; almost too much for her to control. It had always been that way with him, right from the very beginning, and she resented her own weakness bitterly. There had always been a terrible need to try to curb him; to control him and harness the energy. It had become an obsession, a dark, unnatural thing she thought she had banished from her life. It had taken years of work to regain the balance she had once lost and it was now within her grasp to see him pay for what he had once reduced her to.

Lucas's hands began to shake and she clasped them tightly in her lap.

"I see you've deigned to come in to work, after all," she said. "I thought I had made myself very clear yesterday, when I told you that your place was here at the office."

"You did."

"And yet you defied an order from your superior officer and went outside the bounds of your responsibilities. Again."

"On the contrary, I acted according to my primary duty as a police officer, to report an incident and ensure the matter was acted upon. Once I was satisfied correct procedures were in place, I stepped aside."

"You wouldn't have been in that position in the first place, if—"

Lucas stopped herself just in time but Ryan's eyes narrowed dangerously.

"If…*what*, exactly? If I hadn't been with my wife—where I belong?"

Her hands began to shake again and she dug her nails into the palms of her hands to try to stop it.

"If you had been committed to your role here at CID."

"You mean, if I had committed myself to being here at all times, at your beck and call," he threw back, then laughed. "You're delusional."

She thrust upwards, all semblance of control gone.

"One word from me and you'll be out on your ear."

Ryan felt his phone begin to vibrate and made a point of checking the caller, giving her time to calm down. The moment he saw it was Phillips, he knew what they had found.

His eyes were bleak and hard when they turned back to face her.

"I'm returning to Kielder, where I should have been since yesterday morning," he said.

"If you walk out of that door, you'll be out of a job."

With unhurried movements, he strolled closer to where she stood with her hands braced against the desk.

"Go ahead," he said softly, calling her bluff. "You can pull me up on a disciplinary and watch the office revolt against it, watch Morrison dismiss it and undermine your authority, and watch the local press back me to the hilt. Or, you can accept that I know how to run my department, that I know how to motivate my staff, and you can save face by pretending we came to that conclusion together. Either way, we both know you have no intention of sacking me."

"Oh? And why is that?" she asked in a brittle voice. "Because you're so bloody good at your job?"

Their eyes locked.

"I wish that were the reason, but no. You aren't going to sack me because you came up here to destroy me and you want me to be on hand to watch you doing it, to witness you breaking things apart, bit by bit. You want me to understand what you're doing, and why, but I'm not going to give you the satisfaction."

He nodded as the truth of it flickered in her eyes.

"Do what you like, Jen, but know this: you're not dealing with a naïve boy any more. You're dealing with a grown man. Whatever you rain down on me, I'll return tenfold this time, and I don't give a damn who you choose to hide behind."

There was an electric silence as they measured each other.

"Is that a threat?"

"It's a fact."

"You have no idea what I'm capable of," she whispered.

"I know exactly what you're capable of and your games stopped having any effect on me over a decade ago."

With that, he turned and left the room, clicking the door softly shut behind him.

* * *

Lowerson caught up with Ryan as he made his way towards the staff car park, dark thoughts circling his mind and lending him an air of general discontent that would have put off a lesser man.

"Boss! Do you have a minute?"

Ryan paused outside the driver's door and consulted his watch. He'd already wasted enough time facing off with Lucas and he was conscious that the first few hours of a murder investigation were the most important of all.

"We've found another body up at Kielder, Jack, so a minute is about all I have. What's up?"

"Another one? Like the one before?"

"This one's as fresh as they come," Ryan muttered, jiggling the car keys in his hand while he waited for Lowerson to come to the point.

"I thought you were chained to your desk?"

"Not any more," Ryan said, with satisfaction.

"Right. Well, I won't hold you up. I wanted to let you know how my meeting with DCS Lucas went."

Ryan's face became completely shuttered. Wasn't it possible to have a conversation without the woman's name turning up like a bad penny?

"And?"

Lowerson swallowed, detecting the sudden drop in temperature.

"She wants me to come and work with her, in exchange for a promotion to sergeant. She, ah, she seems to think I've been held back."

Ryan's face gave nothing away but it was as if he'd just received a sucker-punch to the stomach.

"Oh? And what do you think about that?"

"Obviously, I told her it's rubbish. You've been the one pushing me on, right from the start."

Ryan let out the breath he'd been holding.

"I'm glad to hear it. So, if that's settled—"

"Do you think I should take up her offer, though? I might not agree with her reasoning, but it's still an opportunity, isn't it?"

No, Ryan thought. It's a snare, designed specifically for lonely young men without enough life experience to see it.

"Look, Jack, I can't talk now. I need to get back up to Kielder. But if you'll give me a few hours, we'll sit down properly and discuss it.

If you want to progress, let's talk about how to make it happen using the right channels."

"The offer is open until the end of the day," Lowerson interjected. "I need to give her an answer before you go."

For Ryan, it was the straw that broke the camel's back.

"Then tell her the answer is *no*! For God's sake, Jack, can't you see? Jennifer Lucas is toxic. She'll use you up, turn your life upside down and you won't even realise she's doing it until there's nothing left. It's who she is, it's what she does, and it has nothing to do with wanting to promote you."

Lowerson stood in stunned silence and then an angry flush spread across his neck because, unwittingly, Ryan had touched a raw nerve.

"So you think no woman could take me seriously."

Ryan lifted a frustrated hand in appeal.

"What? No, that's not what I meant. But surely you realise Lucas is trying to manipulate you so she can break the team apart?"

Lowerson barked out a laugh.

"Oh, I forgot. You're the Almighty Ryan. Everything has to be about *you*."

He could hear the bitterness in his own voice and wished he could claw the words back but it was too late; they had taken flight and could not be unspoken.

"What the hell are you talking about?" Ryan flung at him. "I think of you as—" He almost said, *a brother.* "You're one of the best there is, Jack, and I've done everything I can to help you. I thought you were happy working with me."

Lowerson wondered what had come over him. With every word, he was pushing his friend further away but he couldn't seem to stop the acid rolling off his tongue. Professional and personal frustrations poured out in one long tirade until he rammed home the final nail in the coffin.

"D' you know what? I'm tired of listening to people telling me how bloody lucky I am to work with you. The truth is, I'll never be my own man as long as I'm living in your shadow."

There was a thrumming silence.

Ryan regarded Lowerson as if he were a stranger. It was like history repeating itself, he thought, with friend turning against friend as Lucas flitted around pouring poison in the ears of anybody who would listen. How he wished he could allow Jack to step inside his mind and see the memories he harboured there, but it was already too late.

"In that case, I wish you every success in your new position."

* * *

Lucas watched the altercation from her office window, which happened to overlook the staff car park. She read the body language of each man and thought it was incredible, really, what one could learn from a textbook or two on behavioural psychology. Add a few years' experience into the mix and it was like shooting fish in a barrel.

Clearly, her assessment of Ryan's relationship with Lowerson had been on the mark. She knew he had never been able to resist playing the big brother, taking a younger chick under his wing and nurturing it until it was ready to fly on its own. Ryan's problem was that he couldn't see himself through other people's eyes. To Jack Lowerson, he was a living, breathing, bona fide hero; but he also reminded him of everything he didn't yet have, and petty jealousies could easily turn love into hate, given the right conditions.

Thankfully, hate was an emotion she readily understood and could easily exploit.

Down on the tarmac below, she watched Lowerson jab an angry finger into Ryan's chest and thought he had been the easiest convert yet.

When Ryan climbed into the driver's seat of his car, Lowerson stood for a while longer and, if she wasn't mistaken, his shoulders were shaking. A minute later, he turned back inside the building with a determined look on his face.

Taking that as her cue, Lucas sauntered back to her desk and spoke to her assistant.

"Priya? When DC Lowerson comes up, let him straight in."

"Yes, ma'am."

* * *

Ryan drove on autopilot, braking and accelerating whenever necessary as much of the landscape passed by in a blur. The argument with Lowerson spun around his mind like a broken record and he blamed himself for failing to handle the situation better. He should never have lost his temper. He should have known Jack was vulnerable; an easy target for a predator like Lucas. Worse still, he should have realised how much he had contributed to the younger man's resentment. There was a saying somewhere, wasn't there, about people climbing mountains because they were there? Perhaps, in this case, simply by being who he was, he had drawn Lowerson's own life into stark contrast and failed to realise it.

But what was the alternative? To pretend to be somebody else, a man who was cowed by those who sought to undermine and create division?

He could never be less than he was, not even to soothe Lowerson's ego.

He should have warned Jack. He should have seen it coming. He should have known.

Ryan turned the radio up loud to blot out the sound of his own thoughts and concentrated on the grim task that awaited him at the other end of the road.

CHAPTER 12

Guy Sullivan lay where he had fallen, face-up on a stretch of remote public bridleway running alongside Adderburn, around three miles west of his lodge at Kielder Waterside. It was picturesque, the kind of place where you could walk for miles without ever seeing another living soul. The journey might have taken an experienced walker a couple of hours on foot but, factoring in his inexperience, they estimated it had taken Guy at least three to walk from the front door of the lodge to the rough patch of earth where he eventually died.

What had motivated him to wander off in the early hours of the morning?

Had he intended to meet someone?

These were the thoughts circulating around their collective mind as Ryan, Phillips and Yates stood a few feet away from the remains of what had once been a person. The man's face had been reduced to little more than mashed flesh and bone, a feast for the flies that were already beginning to swarm, and each of them knew it was a sight that would remain imprinted in their memory for years to come.

"Good God," Phillips muttered, holding the back of his hand across his mouth to repel the ripe scent of death carrying across the early-afternoon air.

"God had nothing to do with this," Ryan said, darkly.

"I-I can't—"

Yates found she was unable to speak and Ryan gave her a level, searching look. She was the most junior member of his team and it was his duty to help her to come to terms with moments like these.

"Are you alright?"

Melanie dragged her eyes away from the body and he could see that her face had taken on the kind of fixed expression he recognised as a symptom of shock.

"Take a couple of minutes," he ordered. "Focus on your breathing and get some air."

"No, I can stay," she argued, but her eyes were glassy, her pupils dilated.

In answer, Ryan took her arm in a gentle grip and steered her firmly away from the body so she was forced to keep pace. He didn't stop until they reached the edge of the burn, where light bounced off the water and the sound of it babbling through the trees was a balm to their senses.

"Sit down for a few minutes and clear your head," he urged.

Yates plonked herself down onto the mossy grass, feeling as wobbly as a fawn and utterly humiliated.

"You know, you're not the first or the last to be affected by a scene like that. Reacting normally doesn't make you weak, it makes you human. I've done the same thing myself," Ryan told her.

"I doubt it."

He cast his mind back to a time, not so long ago, when he'd keeled over like a felled redwood.

"No word of a lie. Phillips and Lowerson practically had to carry me out of there."

His chest tightened at the mention of Lowerson's name but he kept a smile fixed on his face.

"And if you think that's bad, you should have seen Frank over the years."

Finally, that brought a tentative smile to her face.

"I thought I was cut out for this," she confessed. "Maybe I was wrong."

"That's crap," he waved it away. "I've seen you work a scene like that before, more than once, and you held it together. Sometimes, it just depends on the circumstances, the body…the day of the week. Who the hell knows? Some days are easier than others, so don't beat yourself up about it."

Yates opened her mouth to protest, then snapped it shut again because he was right. Sometimes, it was just a bad day.

"I'll take a minute," she agreed, and realised she was feeling better already.

Satisfied that she wasn't about to collapse, Ryan made his way back to the scene where he found Tom Faulkner, the senior crime scene investigator attached to CID, crouching down beside the body. A couple of other CSIs were brushing the undergrowth in a perimeter around the body.

"What happened here, Tom?"

Faulkner's polypropylene suit rustled as he rose to his feet. His face was almost completely covered by the hood, with a hairnet and face mask on top of that, but beneath the layers they knew he was an average man in his forties with wispy, mid-brown hair and a propensity for knitted jumpers and thick-rimmed glasses. He raised a gloved finger to prop them back onto his nose and then made his way across to where Ryan and Phillips stood on the sidelines.

"The back of his head is almost completely caved in," Faulkner said. "That would have been enough to kill him, but that's not the half of it. Somebody really went to town on his face. We're looking at multiple lacerations and contusions, some slashing blows. You can barely identify his facial features."

Ryan wondered how he would be able to tell Guy Sullivan's family. That was an unfortunate bridge he would have to cross when he came to it.

"Did you find a murder weapon?"

"There was a rock discarded on the ground not far away, covered in blood and brain matter. I've bagged it up for analysis."

"What kind of animal does this?" Phillips asked, reaching inside the pocket of his jacket for a stick of nicotine gum. At times like these, the old habit made him wish for a tab, just to take the edge off.

Faulkner turned to look again at the whole scene, which was cordoned off from the public by a radius of a quarter-mile. The killer had to make his escape in one direction or another and they never knew what evidence might be left behind.

"That's your department," he said, with a helpless shrug. "But I can tell you the ground was damp earlier this morning, which works in our favour. We've been able to trace the path Guy took to get here," he pointed along the bridleway heading south-west. "About a hundred feet in that direction, there's a yellow marker which shows the point at which he joined the bridleway. Before then, he was in the woodland, probably weaving through the trees as he lost his bearings."

"It's possible he arranged to meet someone here," Phillips suggested.

"The local police are taking statements from his fellow students. We'll look at his text messages and call history to see if we uncover anything helpful there. If he planned to meet someone, it will probably be in his digital history. You never know, there might be a trail of helpful breadcrumbs leading back to the killer," Ryan said.

"Aye, and pigs might fly," Phillips grumbled. "Where's the nearest house from here, anyway?"

He unfolded a dog-eared map from the inner pocket of his jacket and the three men huddled around to look.

"We're here," Ryan said, pointing to a dashed line on the map marking the public bridleway where they stood. "If you walk through the trees in a north-easterly direction, you'd come to the burn and, beyond that, the reservoir."

Phillips turned to face that direction to get his bearings.

"If you follow the bridleway along that way," Faulkner turned to indicate a westerly direction, "you come to a few cottages and a track that leads back up to the main road. We found tracks leading here from that direction."

"You think the killer came from the direction of those houses?"

"I can't say for certain," Faulkner cautioned. "The tracks are fresh and, although I wouldn't like to say conclusively, I'd put my money on them belonging to the killer. They stop at the scene here, then double back on themselves at a longer stride, which suggests the perp ran away afterwards. Unfortunately, they trail off further down the pathway and we're still trying to trace them through the undergrowth. Whoever those footprints belong to might have headed south through the trees to pick up the main road if they parked a car there; they might have gone north towards the burn, or west towards those houses. We've taken some casts of the footprints and sampled the soil, so I guess we'll see what we see."

"Any blood trails?" Phillips asked.

Faulkner turned to look back at the floor where Guy lay, then gave Phillips a meaningful look.

"Plenty."

"In that case, the killer should be covered in it," Ryan put in. "That kind of blood spatter is hard to hide."

"Yeah, but look around you," Faulkner argued. "The place is deserted. This whole area is so enormous, it's possible to come and go without being seen, especially in the early hours of the morning. It's obvious from the state of the pathway that it doesn't see much traffic."

"Unless, of course, you happen to live nearby," Ryan mused. "That'd be convenient, wouldn't it Frank?"

"Awfully convenient," Phillips agreed.

Ryan waited a beat.

"What do you say we go and pay a few friendly house calls?"

"I'd say it's good to have you back."

"Naw, you'll make me blush."

"That'd be a first."

* * *

Yates met Ryan and Phillips on the pathway and they covered the remaining distance on foot towards the isolated hamlet of cottages located half a mile further west of the burn. They were careful to walk off the main bridleway and continued to wear plastic shoe coverings until they emerged from the forested area and out into direct sunlight, where they transferred them into evidence bags. Overhead, the sun had begun its slow descent and there was not a cloud in the sky.

"I love days like these," Phillips said, turning his face up. "Nice bit of breeze on the air, a bit of sun an' all. Blows away the cobwebs."

"You've turned soft since you got engaged," Ryan told him. "I hope MacKenzie knows what she's letting herself in for."

"Women love a man with a sensitive side," Phillips said, in dignified tones. "What do you reckon, Mel?"

Yates chuckled.

"Oh, no, I'm not getting dragged into one of your little macho tête-à-têtes."

"Y' hear that?" Phillips said to Ryan. "I think she's got us pegged."

"Doesn't take much."

They rounded a corner and came to a small clearing where a cluster of three stone cottages nestled like something from the pages of a Hans Christian Anderson fairy tale. They were each of a similar size but only one seemed to be occupied, judging from the truck parked on the edge of the track beside it, so they headed towards that one first. As they approached, a dog began to bark against one of the interior windows.

"Good doggy," Phillips muttered.

There was an almighty bellow and the dog instantly stopped. A moment later, the door swung open and a man filled the doorway, blotting out the light from the passageway beyond. They judged him to be somewhere in his late forties or early fifties, with close-shaven hair and a jaw so firm it could have been cut from marble.

"Who're you?"

His voice boomed out into the clearing and ricocheted around the trees.

"We're from Northumbria CID," Ryan said, pulling out his warrant card. "Can I have your name? We'd like to ask you a few routine questions following an incident earlier this morning."

"Oh, aye, I bet you do," he said belligerently, and Phillips gave him a keen look.

"Easy lad," he warned, although the man was probably only a handful of years younger than himself. "We're only doing the rounds, gathering information."

"Gather all the information you like," he said, butting out his chin. "I'm telling you, I had nowt to do with keying that woman's car and I'm getting sick and bloody tired of having to say it!"

There was a short pause.

"I think there's been a misunderstanding," Ryan said. "We're here in connection with a murder."

The man's face registered shock.

"Oh, aye? Right. You'd better come in, then."

He turned and heaved his considerable bulk along the passageway towards a small living room, where the phantom dog lay with its tail tucked between its legs. Their eyes tracked the floor and adjoining rooms for traces of anything suspicious, such as blood or the stench of bleach, but found nothing other than a single pair of discarded wellies flecked with dried mud and nothing else.

"Thank you for being so co-operative," Ryan said, as they entered the living room.

"S' alreet," the man replied. "I've got nowt to hide."

Ryan smiled thinly.

"Can I have your name, please?"

"Craig Hunter."

While Ryan took down a few particulars, Phillips and Yates scanned the room, finding very little to discover. There was a two-seater PVC-leather sofa and matching armchair facing a large, flat screen television mounted on the wall above a fireplace that was obviously still in use. Perhaps incongruously, there was a large bookcase in one alcove, stuffed with books of all genres. A magazine rack was also full of old papers and magazines and, to Yates' distaste, she noted a couple of porno mags peppering the broadsheets.

When she looked up, Hunter was watching her intently as he petted the dog who had come to settle itself at his feet.

"What's all this about, then?"

"A man was found dead this morning, not far from here," Ryan said, diverting Hunter's attention away from Yates. "We're eager to know if you saw or heard anything in the early hours, particularly between four and seven a.m.?"

Was it their imagination or did the man's eyes turn shrewd?

"Naht," he said clearly. "I was tucked up in bed all night."

"I see. May I ask what you do for a living, Mr Hunter?"

"Aye, y' can ask, it's no secret. I'm what you might call a 'Jack of All Trades'. I do a bit of handyman work, odd-jobs here and there, bit of painting and decorating if the mood strikes and a bit of gardening and clearing, if I can be arsed."

"Do you have a fixed employer?"

"I do a bit for the equestrian centre, over the way," he told them. "But I go where the jobs take me."

Ryan nodded and made a note.

"Were you at work this morning?"

"Aye, I did an early-morning shift with the horses. Mucking out and whatnot, since they're always short a hand or two."

"What time did your shift begin?"

Hunter gave them a knowing look.

"Should I be asking for a solicitor?"

"Only if you feel you need one," Ryan replied, smooth as you like.

Hunter considered the three of them, then shrugged his enormous shoulders.

"Makes no difference to me," he said. "I started work at Hot Trots just after seven."

"*Hot Trots?*" Phillips thought he must have misheard.

"Aye, bloody stupid name," Hunter said, with an unexpected burst of laughter. "Woman who runs it is batty as a box of frogs."

"And her name would be?"

"Kate Robson," he supplied. "You can ask her and she'll tell you I was there on the dot of seven this morning."

"Can you tell us who occupies the other two cottages?" Ryan asked.

Hunter absentmindedly scratched his crotch while he thought.

"Nobody lives in the cottage opposite," he told them. "Been empty at least two years, far as I know. There's talk about renovating it and turning it into another bloody holiday cottage. The one to the right is already owned by some city bugger who comes up in the summer and rents it out the rest of the year."

"Thank you for your time, Mr Hunter."

* * *

The dog barked again as they filed out of the cramped little cottage and, by mutual accord, they said nothing until they had walked well out of earshot. Ryan made a discreet note of Hunter's registration plate and they stopped at each of the nearby cottages to check nobody was at home. Finding them empty and the doors securely locked, they continued along the track that would lead them up to the main road, where their cars were parked alongside the vehicles belonging to the CSIs and local police who guarded the perimeter of the crime scene.

Once they'd put an adequate distance between themselves and the clearing, Phillips broke the silence.

"I still can't get over the name of that equestrian centre."

"Clearly, the owner admires the work of Charlie Sheen," Ryan replied, as if it were an everyday occurrence. "But to drag ourselves back to the point, what did you think of Mr Hunter?"

"He likes power play," Yates said thoughtfully. "He kept the dog beside him throughout, holding onto its collar, even though he could have put it in a different room so he wouldn't have to. I think he enjoyed knowing he could unleash it."

"Agreed. Anything else?"

"He enjoys making people—especially women—feel uncomfortable. He was eyeballing me quite blatantly in there, despite the fact you were both on hand, and that tells me he's complacent. Added to which, I don't believe him when he says he saw nothing this morning. He's lying. He saw something or heard something. I'm sure of it."

"Also agreed," Ryan said. "Are you after my job, Yates?"

She grinned.

"Not yet, sir. Did I miss anything?"

"You forgot to mention the part where you handled his behaviour with professionalism. Well done."

"Aye, he's a creep, that one," Phillips chimed in. "And what was that business to do with keying a woman's car?"

"Mm," Ryan said. "Shouldn't be too hard to find out, if we stop into the nearest drinking hole. The pub is the apex of all local gossip and Phillips still owes me a pint."

Frank made a rumbling sound of agreement.

"Well, if it's all in a day's work," Yates joked. "Do you think he's the man we're looking for?"

"Guy Sullivan was young, easily six foot with an athletic build. Even so, a bloke like Hunter could overpower him without too much bother," Phillips said. "He's built like a brick shithouse."

"Unless somebody took Sullivan by surprise," Ryan suggested. "Physical strength helps, but I've seen plenty of feeble-looking killers over the years."

They walked a little further along the winding track and, when the main road came back into view, Ryan turned to them with a thoughtful expression.

"Doesn't it strike you as odd that Hunter never asked about the dead man? There was no polite query, no expression of concern, not even idle curiosity."

Phillips rubbed the side of his chin, where the shadow of a five o'clock beard was starting to show.

"You think it's important?"

"I think it's highly unusual," Ryan replied. "And that tells me it's significant. Could it be that Hunter didn't ask us anything because he knew the answers already?"

"He definitely looked nervous," Yates said.

"He lives on the doorstep of a crime scene that is completely isolated, so he could have been nervous because he knows he would be first on our list of house calls. If we find Hunter has a sheet, he'll be worrying that we'll automatically look at him for the murder," Ryan said.

"He didn't exactly look like the cuddly type," Phillips was bound to say.

"No, but keying a car is a long way from committing murder."

"So what do we do?" Yates asked the pair of them.

Ryan cast his eyes over the darkened forest then up at the big, cloudless sky overhead.

"This is where the chase begins. Without knowing it, Guy Sullivan's killer has left pieces of himself behind. We'll trace them and start closing the net."

Phillips rubbed his hands together, partly to stave off the chill but mostly in anticipation of the hunt.

"I'll let the local officers know we'll be setting up an Incident Room nearby, location to be confirmed. First briefing at five o'clock which gives us"—Ryan paused to glance at his watch—"three hours."

A sudden wind whipped through the trees and curled around their small huddle, nipping against their skin. Ryan turned his face up to enjoy the sensation, feeling glad to be alive. Then he thought of Guy

Sullivan and of how that young man would never again know the simple joy of feeling the wind against his face.

"I want traffic cordons in place as soon as possible," he said decisively. "We may already be too late, but there's only one main road in and out of this whole area and a couple of smaller B-roads. Easy enough to record who enters and leaves the Kielder area, especially since there's no train station to complicate things."

Phillips made a sound of agreement.

"We'll see to it. I'll look out any CCTV on the roads or local businesses while I'm at it," he said.

"Yates? I'd like you to supervise the house-to-house," Ryan said, and almost smiled at the panic he read in her eyes. "Speak to the local sergeant and see how far they've got with gathering statements. Push out in a radius from the crime scene, in expanding circles so you don't miss any campers or cottages."

"I—yes, sir."

"One other thing, Yates. Ask the remaining students for their consent to take a DNA sample."

"They might not agree," she argued.

"A man has been murdered," Ryan growled. "It's reasonable enough to ask the people in the immediate area to rule themselves out. After all, they've got nothing to hide—have they? If anyone objects, I want to know about it."

With that, he turned and went in search of Craig Hunter's employer.

CHAPTER 13

Ryan drove a couple of miles further west along the main road through the forest and then took a left turn along a well-tended private track leading up to the main gates of *Hot Trots Equestrian Centre*, located halfway between the Kielder Waterside development and Kielder Village to the north.

The road cut upward through the trees until the land plateaued and Ryan's car emerged onto higher ground with far-reaching views of the valley below. There were small markers at the side of the road warning a maximum speed of five miles per hour, and Ryan crawled along the single track until the farmhouse came into view. It was large and stone-built, like many of the old Victorian properties in the area, surrounded by smaller outbuildings and a long stable block separated by a courtyard from the house. However, there had clearly been some serious investment in the facilities since the nineteenth century because now an additional stable block stood beside an enormous indoor gymkhana. Lining either side of the road were fields full of healthy-looking horses and ponies and all but the hardiest breeds wore stylish tartan turn-out coats to protect them from the cold weather.

Ryan had to admit it was a pretty sight to behold.

He drove through a set of pillared stone gates and into an area used for visitor's parking. The unmistakable odour of horse manure hit him squarely in the face as he exited the car and he was momentarily transported back to his childhood spent in the countryside in Devon, where he'd grown up riding horses. Unfortunately, it was not an essential skill for a murder detective in the North East and it had been several years since he'd sat astride anything other than the scooter he'd rented to pootle around the tropics with Anna.

Even then, she'd been the one doing the driving.

He walked into the courtyard and rapped a knuckle on the back door of the farmhouse, assuming correctly that the bulk of business took place via that route, but there was no answer. Finding the courtyard stables empty apart from a gentle-looking mare whose neck he paused to rub, Ryan continued towards the newer stable block.

"Excuse me? I'm looking for Kate Robson."

A young stable hand of fifteen or sixteen popped his head over one of the doors and peered curiously at the tall, raven-haired man with serious eyes.

"Are y' looking to go for a hack?"

Ryan smiled.

"Not today, although it's fine weather for it. Can you tell me where I'd find Kate?"

"Aye, she's over in the lower field doing a lesson. D' you want to wait somewhere until she's finished and I'll let her know you're here?"

Ryan shook his head.

"Thanks, but I'll wander down and watch the rest of the lesson, if that's alright."

The boy shrugged.

"It's down that way."

* * *

Ryan's first sighting of the owner of *Hot Trots* reminded him that people did not always conform to stereotype. After Craig Hunter's less than flattering description, he'd expected to find a woman with eccentric clothing and a demeanour to match. Instead, Kate Robson might have stepped from the pages of a Jilly Cooper novel and was as well-groomed as the horses she tended.

Her voice carried across the field as she called out to the small group of novice riders trotting in a wide circle and Ryan stopped to rest his arms against the fence beside a few other men and women who were probably the parents of the children who lolloped across the grass on horseback.

"Archie! Try to find your rhythm…that's right, work with the horse and keep your back straight!"

Ten minutes later, the lesson wound up and she began to lead the first rider back towards the stables.

"Ms Robson? My name is DCI Ryan, I'm from Northumbria CID. Could I have a moment of your time?"

Her brow furrowed at the sight of his warrant card.

"I—yes, of course. Let me finish up here and I'll meet you back at the house, okay?"

Ryan nodded and followed the procession, admiring the condition of the Welsh cob ambling to his left. Keeping horses could be a hard, expensive business and those who made it their profession usually tended to think of it as a vocation.

The cob nuzzled the back of his head, taking him by surprise, and when Ryan turned to look into its mischievous brown eyes he could understand the motivation.

"Watch it, beautiful," he murmured, reaching across to rub its neck.

Ryan left the horses to their stables and made his way back to the main farmhouse. Soon after, he heard Robson's footsteps crossing the cobbled courtyard stones.

"Sorry to keep you waiting," she said briskly.

Ryan followed her into the farmhouse and waited as she tugged off her boots.

"Should I…?" He gestured to his own shoes and she cast a critical eye over them, before shaking her head.

"No, you're not too bad," she said with a smile. "Come on in."

She made directly for the kettle in the cavernous kitchen, setting it to boil with one hand whilst waving towards one of the oak chairs surrounding a table in the centre of the room with the other.

"Take a seat. Can I offer you some coffee or tea? I'm parched."

"No, thank you."

She selected a mug from a wooden tree.

"You said you were from CID? I'm not very knowledgeable about the police hierarchy but I thought officers of CID dealt with serious crimes?"

"We do," he said, and drew back a chair. "I'm afraid my visit here concerns an incident earlier this morning. A person was found dead near Adderburn."

"Less than three miles away," she said, turning back to look at him. "I'm very sorry to hear it. Who was he? I mean, do I know him?"

Ryan's eyes sharpened. After all, he hadn't mentioned the gender of the person they'd found.

"I'm afraid I can't share those details with you at present. I can tell you he was a young man, not from the area."

She came across and slid into a chair, setting her mug on the table. The afternoon sunshine fell through the large sash window and he judged that Kate Robson was somewhere in her late forties and had chosen to age gracefully. She was slim, with a kind of wiry energy to her movements, and he realised with a degree of shock that she reminded him of his own mother, give or take a few years in between.

"How awful," she murmured, cupping her fingers around the mug as if to draw strength from it. "Was it drug-related?"

"What makes you think that?"

She heaved a sigh.

"People say urban areas have the worst drug culture but I think it's just as bad in the countryside. I've seen kids—young kids, who grew up here—going off the rails on heroin. And those dealers? Scum of the earth, if you ask me."

Personally, he couldn't have agreed more, but that was hardly the issue.

"It's a good suggestion," Ryan said. "I'll certainly bear it in mind."

"I'm terribly sad for his family but I'm not sure how I can help you, chief inspector."

Ryan leaned back in his chair.

"At this stage, we're asking routine questions to see if anybody saw or heard anything of interest, particularly between the hours of four and seven this morning."

She took a gulp of her tea and let the liquid warm her from the inside out.

"Well, I was fast asleep in bed until around five-thirty, when I usually get up for the day. Since then, I've been here or at the stables. My days are all mapped out," she explained. "I had a private lesson from six—"

"That's early," he remarked.

"You're telling me," she smiled, showing a set of perfect white teeth. "But this particular client runs very much on his own schedule."

"Do you mind telling me his name?"

"Oh, sure, it's Nathan Armstrong. He lives in Kielder for half of the year and spends the rest of his time jet-setting around the world."

"Oh? What's his business?"

"He writes thrillers," she told him. "Can't say I've read any of them," she confessed, with a conspiratorial smile. "But he's nice enough. A bit quiet, mind. Keeps himself to himself."

Ryan made a polite sound in his throat and decided to let her do the talking. It was amazing what could be learned if you talked less and listened more, especially in his line of work.

"Anyway, Nathan comes in for an early lesson every Saturday morning while he's in the area. I had to be up to get the horses ready for him arriving, so I'm afraid I didn't see much else."

"Do you manage this place alone?"

Ryan flicked a glance towards her fingers but there was no sign of a wedding ring.

"Oh, goodness, no!" She let out what he might have described as a middle-class snort. "This place is far too large for me to handle alone. My father died in 2003 and left everything to me. I've done my best to modernise things but, when it comes to horses, you can't beat a solid pair of hands. I have three full-time stable hands and one regular part-timer, alongside quite a few volunteers who come along and muck in, in exchange for free lessons. They tend to be teenagers," she explained, and Ryan remembered it had been the same back in his day.

"Were any of them here this morning?"

"Yes, they were. Saturday is our busiest day and most of them arrived around seven, in time for the early-bird lessons at eight o'clock. That gives them an hour to get the horses ready for the day ahead."

"I see," Ryan murmured, thinking of how he could frame his next question. "Could you let me have a list of their names, for completeness?"

"Sure, I don't see why not. Kielder isn't exactly a metropolis; I'm sure you'll get around to meeting them anyway."

She rattled off a short list of names and Craig Hunter was one of them. Ryan took his time asking sufficient questions about the others and then worked the conversation back around to Craig.

"Has Mr Hunter worked here for long?"

"Yes, Craig's been a part-timer for a few years now," Kate said, polishing off her tea. "He's a bit rough around the edges but he's a hard worker and the horses don't seem to mind him."

Ryan decided not to pass comment about animals being dumb.

"Craig was here at seven?"

"Oh, yes. I saw his truck coming up the hill just before then."

"You saw nobody unusual crossing your land during the morning?"

"No, not at all. Tourists come and go all the time, but they're mostly accounted for. We had a couple of walk-ins but we have a list of their details and they all came after nine o'clock."

Ryan shut his notebook and set a business card on the table in front of her.

"Thank you for your time, Ms Robson. If you remember anything you think might be useful to our investigation, please contact me on this number or ring the Control Room who will transfer you through."

She clutched the little rectangular card in her hand, reading the plain black lettering on the front.

"Chief inspector, should I be worried? I mean, if someone died so near here, does that mean there's a killer on the loose?"

His response was enigmatic.

"It's advisable to remain vigilant at all times, Ms Robson."

CHAPTER 14

Ryan pulled into the car park at Kielder Waterside and found the place deserted, a far cry from the hustle and bustle wrought by the full-scale search party earlier in the day. Aside from his own, there were only a few cars remaining, including a single police squad car, the little Golf belonging to Melanie Yates and Anna's university minibus, which looked as if it may finally have rusted itself onto the tarmac. The playground and Birds of Prey Centre were empty and a quick glance told him the gift shop was closed for the day. He spotted Mitch Fenwick and Freddie Milburn on the water in their bright blue jackets, but there were no paying customers with them and the passenger ferry that operated between several stopping points on the reservoir was nowhere to be seen.

He found Anna standing on the small shingle beach overlooking the water, wrapped up in a cream knitted scarf with her dark hair blowing loose in the breeze. She was alone, which gave him a sharp stab of concern.

"Anna?"

When she turned, her eyes were red-rimmed and swollen.

"Oh, hello."

Protectiveness washed over him when she walked into his arms and rested her head against his chest without a word. He wrapped his arms around her and tucked his chin against the top of her head, wishing there was something he could say to relieve the aching sadness.

"The police are interviewing the rest of the students now. Melanie Yates is in there with them, so I came out to get some air," Anna said quietly. "I've already contacted their parents to explain the situation and there's a grief counsellor lined up, once they're back in student accommodation at the university. Melanie says she'll arrange for a couple of squad cars to drive them home after they're done."

Ryan nodded his approval at that.

"You've done all you can," he reassured her.

"I should never have stayed," she said wretchedly. "Not after that boy's body was found in the water. I should have driven them home and then none of this would have happened."

Ryan spoke carefully.

"Firstly, there was nothing to suggest Duncan Gray was killed recently, so there was no imminent threat. This place was full of families and other tourists who weren't put off either, so don't start second-guessing yourself on that score."

"But—"

"Secondly," he interrupted, "it isn't your fault that Guy Sullivan died. The only person to blame for that is the person who killed him."

"But if I'd only stayed with them through the night," she muttered.

"Your students are grown men and women," he reminded her. "They live independently while they're at university, they survive each day without a chaperone and they can certainly drink if they want to. Short of enforcing some kind of prohibition on alcohol—which they'd ignore, anyway—and babysitting them all hours of the day and night, there's no way you could have prevented what happened to Guy."

"I just can't understand why he'd leave the lodge."

"It's never the victim's fault," he said gently. "Regardless of whether Sullivan was right or wrong to leave his front door or to drink himself into a stupor, it didn't give anybody the right to kill him."

She nodded wearily.

"I know that," she said. "It's just, sometimes, I feel like I carry bad luck around with me. Why here? Why now?"

Ryan gave a short, mirthless laugh.

"Why *anytime*? Duncan Gray's body had been gradually rising from the reservoir bed for years until Lisa Hope gave it the final push. Who could have predicted she'd be there, at exactly the right spot, at the right time?"

He stepped forward to cup her face in his hands.

"You didn't kill that boy, Anna."

A single tear leaked from the corner of her eye.

"I heard it was brutal," she said in a choked voice. "That they'd mutilated his face—"

"Whoever it was, they'll pay for what they did. Believe me."

* * *

Back at CID Headquarters, Denise MacKenzie lifted a hand to rub a sudden cramp in her leg and was convulsed with pain as her nerves contracted around the thick scar tissue left over from the knife wound a few months earlier. She bore down, taking several deep breaths while her hand kneaded the skin as the physiotherapist had shown her. Not that it made much difference, but it made her feel useful in the face of a crippling reminder that she was forever changed, thanks to the actions of a monster.

When the pain receded, she blew out a shaky breath and rose carefully, hobbling around her desk to get the blood circulating again. The open-plan office assigned to the Cold Cases Team was smaller than she was used to and it appeared she had it all to herself. The clock on the wall told her it was quarter-to-five and she guessed the other staff must have taken themselves off for a cup of tea to kill the last fifteen minutes of what had, admittedly, been a long and uneventful weekend shift.

MacKenzie had spent the day trying to re-familiarise herself with the list of priority cases that had been identified as such because they continued to crop up in the media or the victims' families continued to shout the loudest. It was belittling to know that something as fickle as public opinion could mean the difference between extra resources or a lack thereof, but that was reality. It was more likely that an attractive missing person would gain traction with the press and drum up public sympathy than an unattractive one would; just as a woman with a blonde, curly-haired young child stood more chance of achieving justice than a woman of the same age with a history of drug abuse and prostitution.

People were prejudiced.

Including herself, MacKenzie admitted. She'd seen plenty of things over the years to make her hair stand on end and it was hard not to develop stereotypes. Though she worked hard for every victim, she was as human as the next person and therefore fallible.

And that just wasn't good enough. Not in her line of work.

Guilt pricked at her conscience and she dismissed the notion of heading home just yet. There was time for one more case file and, this time, the case concerned a woman who was neither attractive nor squeaky clean.

MacKenzie gave it her full attention.

Jade Tan.

The image of a nineteen-year-old girl filled the computer screen and MacKenzie felt her heart contract at the picture that followed, taken after she'd been found in a farmer's field. In life, Jade worked as a prostitute in Newcastle to fund a long-term drug habit and had a sheet for solicitation and shoplifting. Yet her body had been found miles away from the city, on the way to Cumbria.

Time slipped by as she clicked through the pages of the digital files, reading and re-reading statements to see if there was something they had missed and, by the end of the day, there were six faces pinned to the wall to greet her new team on Monday morning.

* * *

The nearest police station had recently shut its doors and transferred operations further afield to Hexham, a cool two-hour round trip from the crime scene at Kielder. Ryan supposed it was a testament to the low crime rates in the area that the Constabulary felt it was no longer necessary to keep an office within easy reach of a major tourist destination, but it posed an immediate problem from a logistical perspective.

Where to set up an Incident Room?

There were conference facilities attached to the inn overlooking the reservoir at Kielder Waterside, with access to high-speed broadband that would enable his staff to access the police mainframe from their secure laptops. The room could be locked and, therefore, its contents secured overnight. It was the sensible choice all round and he'd taken it.

However, it would require him to approve a non-regulation building as the Incident Room for the duration of their investigation. To top it off, fate had chosen to put his wife within a stone's throw of the investigation once again, through no fault of her own.

He could only imagine what Lucas would have to say about that.

"Sir?"

Ryan turned to find Yates standing a few feet away carrying a file beneath her arm. He glanced at his watch and saw that it was almost five o'clock and officers attached to the aptly-named 'OPERATION STARGAZER' would soon begin to file through the doors.

"Phillips asked me to pass on the message that he's running five minutes late but he'll get back as quickly as he can."

Ryan nodded and returned to his task of setting up the murder board ahead of the briefing.

"Fabulous, isn't it?"

For a moment, he thought she was referring to the unsightly 'before and after' images of Duncan Gray and Guy Sullivan tacked to the wall. Then he realised she was talking about the view. The conference room overlooked the reservoir, where the late afternoon sun burnished the water so it rippled like liquid gold. The forest backdrop was picture-perfect and it was tempting to stand and watch out for the first stars to appear.

Instead, Ryan made a mental note to tweak the blinds so there would be no distractions once the briefing began. He wanted the full attention of his staff so they would focus their minds and hearts on the task ahead.

The stars weren't going anywhere, after all.

"It's not hard on the eyes," he agreed. "But that view also represents thousands of acres of land and water, twenty-seven miles of shoreline scattered with houses and tumbled down shacks; campers, hikers, forestry staff…it's a minefield for the investigation, Yates."

She dragged her eyes away from the window as the enormity of it hit home. For a certain breed of killer, it was an ideal hunting ground and a perfect place to conceal themselves.

"Do you think it's one of the locals?"

Ryan continued to tack up images.

"I don't know," he admitted. "There's such a transient population. If somebody owns a holiday cottage or is just renting one, they could come and go as they please. It doesn't have to be someone living in the area permanently."

"It looked like a frenzy killing," she remarked. "It could be someone with existing mental health issues."

Ryan smiled to himself and thought that his newest recruit was learning fast.

"Good thinking. Only problem is, surgeries and outpatient centres won't give out sensitive data about their patients without a warrant, which we're unlikely to secure at this point without further evidence against a specific suspect. It would be great if that weren't the case but, on the other hand, there needs to be checks and balances."

She nodded, only slightly disheartened.

"Speaking of data, all five of the remaining students volunteered to give a DNA sample, so we've sent those off to the lab straight away."

"That's good," Ryan said. "The sooner we can rule out their involvement, the better—let's just hope the killer's left us some trace evidence to work with."

Before they had a chance to say anything further, members of the local police and forest rangers began to file into the room. Bringing up the rear, Tom Faulkner joined them with a tray of steaming coffees.

"Thought we might need sustenance," he explained.

"I always said you were a good bloke, Tom," Phillips said, completing their number. "Got any biscuits?"

"Is the Pope Catholic?"

Faulkner retrieved a packet of custard creams from his back pocket and jiggled them proudly.

"If we've all finished settling in, I thought we might talk about murder," Ryan said, with an air of sufferance.

"Aye, keep your hair on," Phillips said, gesturing with a half-chewed biscuit as he made his way across the room. "Have a swig of this cuppa."

Ryan snatched up the cup Phillips offered him, downing a few mouthfuls straight off the bat.

"Thanks, I needed that."

Phillips grunted, cast his eye around the small crowd of men and women who had assembled, and noted immediately that one person was absent.

"Where's Lowerson?"

Ryan downed the rest of the liquid in his cup, scalding his tongue in the process.

"Not here."

"Aye, I can see that," Phillips turned his all-seeing eyes on Ryan and berated himself for failing to notice before now that there was something badly wrong. Their colleagues continued to chatter, going through the usual niceties of hand-shaking and back-slapping before they got down to the serious business of policing, so he lowered his voice and prodded for answers.

"What's happened?"

Ryan stuck his hands in the pockets of his jeans in a gesture Phillips had come to realise was a sign of stress. Well disguised to the casual onlooker, but stress all the same.

"He's taken a job with Lucas, who says she'll promote him to sergeant," Ryan said, trying valiantly to keep the disappointment from his voice. "It's a good opportunity for him."

But Phillips hadn't been born yesterday.

"That sounds like a load of old hogwash to me. Lowerson is a good lad but I wouldn't have thought he was ready—"

"Yeah, well, Jack doesn't want to hear it," Ryan said. "In fact, as it turns out, I'm the last person he wants to get any advice from."

There it was, Phillips thought.

"He's only young," he said. "You know as well as I do, Jack thinks you walk on air. Probably thinks you shit gold nuggets, n' all."

Ryan smiled at that.

"Young people say things they don't mean and then regret it later. I was the same, myself, and so were you," Phillips continued.

"That's exactly the point. I was the same as him, once upon a time. Naïve, idealist, ready to think the world consisted of good people who just did bad things from time to time. Now, I know better. There is evil out there, Frank, and it takes many forms."

"I can speak to him—"

"You can try, but he's on a crusade to prove himself." *And to prove me wrong,* Ryan added silently.

He thought of Lowerson's earnest young face and swore softly.

"Tell him—tell him whatever you have to, just make sure he's alright."

Phillips patted his shoulder.

"Leave it to Uncle Frank."

CHAPTER 15

"This is Guy Sullivan."

Ryan looked at the young man as he'd been in life, smiling out of a blown-up photograph taken recently at a party. He looked relaxed and slightly cocky, safe in the knowledge that he would live to be an old man, never thinking anything would remove that privilege without warning. And it had not been cancer or some other debilitating terminal disease, but the will of another person who extinguished his life for no reason other than because they could.

Ryan turned and cast watchful grey eyes around the room, compelling them to listen.

"I want you to remember his face. Think of him when you're tired or hungry or when you think you've come to a dead end. Think of him when you're frustrated or angry; channel it to find the animal who did *this*."

He held up an image of Guy Sullivan in death and heard shocked murmurs from those who had not yet seen the aftermath of such violence. Sometimes, shock could be motivating.

Ryan set the image aside and moved further along to where a photograph of Duncan Gray had also been tacked to the wall. It was an enlargement of a polaroid taken back in 1981, the same year Duncan died, and it had the grainy quality people tried to replicate nowadays to be artsy on social media.

"This is Duncan Gray," he said, looking at a boy of sixteen who could have passed for eighteen. "He went missing on 21st October 1981, when he disappeared from his home without a trace sometime during the night. His body was found yesterday morning by a scuba diver and recovered by the Marine Unit."

Ryan nodded towards a second image of Duncan, showing his mummified remains.

"He was well preserved, thanks to the uniquely anaerobic peat conditions in sub-strata levels of the reservoir, deep beneath the bed. If you're interested in the science, it's all in the report in Appendix C of your packs."

There were a few rustles.

"Sir? Are the two deaths being treated as linked?" This from one of the local constables.

"No, for the moment we are not treating them as linked given the timescales and different MOs. However, we'll be running the two investigations from this room and under the same umbrella for the sake of convenience. Whilst you should remember that the cause of death is different in each case and, obviously, there is a significant gap in time, it would be prudent to bear in mind that there may be a connection between these two deaths and if any facts come to light that would support a connection, you should flag it up."

There were more nods around the room.

"Alright, let's turn to Guy Sullivan first," Ryan said, hitching his hip onto the edge of a table. "Twenty-two-year-old postgraduate history student, originally from York. His parents were informed this morning and they'll be taking the first available flight back from where they've been holidaying in the Canary Islands."

Ryan thought back to what had been a very difficult conversation. It never got any easier with practice and he knew he would have to do it all over again when the Sullivan family arrived the next day, demanding answers.

"As far as we can tell from the statements given by his friends and fellow students, Guy and his five companions stayed up in their lodge drinking and chatting into the early hours. At around four in the morning, they called time and went to their respective bedrooms. Sometime after then, Guy decided to take an early-morning walk. He took nothing with him except the clothes he was wearing, a mobile phone and his wallet, which we recovered at the scene."

"Not a botched theft, then," Phillips surmised.

Ryan gave a slight shake of his head.

"There's no suggestion of drugs, either. His mates were honest enough to admit they smoked some weed before stumbling into bed, but that's as heavy as it got."

"Unlikely to have been meeting a dealer, then?"

Ryan turned to look at Yates.

"No, it doesn't look that way. There were no text messages or calls from unknown numbers to suggest the interlude was planned. Guy left his lodge without any maps or means of navigating his way around the forest. However, his supervisor, Doctor Anna Taylor, states that the students were all informed of safety procedures whilst staying in the area and were provided with maps and compasses in case of emergency, which has been corroborated by the other students."

It felt strange to talk about his wife in such impersonal terms, he thought, but it was best not to muddy the waters.

"Guy probably thought he could use the GPS on his phone," Yates reflected. "It's an easy mistake to make these days."

Ryan nodded.

"Our best guess is that he found himself lost in the woods and ended up in the wrong place at the wrong time. Then again, not all those who wander are lost." He gave a slight shrug. "If there isn't any apparent motivation for why Guy was killed, that's a worry because it means—"

"Fruitcake," Phillips said baldly.

Ryan sent him a frustrated glare and there were a couple of guffaws around the room.

"I was going to say, *it was an unprovoked attack.*"

"Aye, well, if there's no logical reason for it, that means we've got someone on our hands who's a few chips short of a butty, haven't we?"

Ryan opened his mouth then snapped it shut again. Call it what you like, the man had a point.

"If our killer is *disorganised*," Ryan said, with emphasis, "there is a chance he'll strike again, without warning. That being the case, we've already taken steps to ring-fence the area and record everybody entering and leaving."

Ryan walked over to a large map pinned to the adjacent wall and chair legs scraped against the carpet as his audience shuffled themselves around to get a better look.

"There's only one major road giving access into and out of Kielder Forest and Water Park. That's the C200, otherwise known as 'Shilling Pot'," he said, tapping a biro against the map. "It runs northwest from the A68 motorway and is the most direct route for anybody wanting to get to or from Newcastle, or to connect with the road north to Scotland or south to—well, almost anywhere."

He pointed at a cluster of red pins stuck into the map.

"The first major checkpoint has been set up at Stannersburn. It's not much bigger than a hamlet but the road runs directly through it, parallel to the River North Tyne which is fed by Kielder Water."

Ryan waited for them to find the spot on their own smaller maps before continuing.

"After Stannersburn, the main road continues west and curves around the south side of the reservoir, passing the turn-offs for Kielder Waterside—where we are now—until it reaches Kielder Village at the north-western tip. The village has a ferry stopping point, a castle which is now used as a visitor's centre and some other amenities. The C200 runs through it and continues north towards Jedburgh and the Scottish border. So that's where we've set up a second cordon," he said, tapping another cluster of red pins on the map. "We've also set up a smaller cordon at the entrance of the Forest Drive, but that still leaves a lot of unbeaten track."

"What's the Forest Drive?" Faulkner enquired.

"It's an unsurfaced road out of Kielder Village. It gives access to some outstanding views of the valley but you'd need an all-terrain vehicle, especially at this time of year."

Ryan tapped his pen against the map to locate the Forest Drive and then straightened up again.

"There's a secondary checkpoint there, but it's a toll road and the traffic will probably be lighter than via the other surfaced roads. We're waiting to see whether the CCTV cameras at the toll booth by the castle can give us any useful footage. I'm grateful to all of you for your hard work in putting these cordons in place but as soon as possible, I want us to set up additional cordons on the north side of the reservoir, which has a minor road running parallel to the shoreline known as 'Lakeside Way'. I'd like one on either side of the dam road, too, which runs along the top of the dam at the eastern tip of the reservoir and which gives access to both sides of the water."

"That's a lot of manpower," Phillips cautioned.

"I want this case shut down by Monday or Tuesday, so we can stretch to it for a couple of days."

Ryan let those words hang in the air and watched some of the local police shuffle in their seats, clearly surprised by the speed at which they would be required to work.

"The first few hours are the most important to a murder investigation," he told them. "Now, I know it's unfamiliar territory for some of you, but we're not dealing with your average criminal; we're dealing with an unknown quantity who has the upper hand because we're on the back foot. It's our job to turn that situation around as quickly as possible.

"Frank? Give us the lowdown on where we stand with preliminary enquiries."

Phillips pushed up from his chair and moved to the front of the room.

"Thanks to all the local officers drafted in from Hexham, we covered a lot of ground this afternoon. PC Yates took care of liaison with the victim's classmates, who have all given statements and consented to DNA buccal swabbing which has already been done and sent for testing. As for the rest, we've been covering every building in expanding circles from the crime scene and we've interviewed thirty-eight people so far, including Craig Hunter, who is the closest resident to where the search party found Guy this morning."

"His alibi checks out from seven o'clock," Ryan put in. "I visited his employer, Kate Robson, at the *Hot Trots Equestrian Centre* who confirmed he was on the premises from that time onwards."

"That's handy, because we hadn't got around to talking to her yet," Phillips remarked. "Still doesn't cover what Hunter was doing before seven o'clock."

Ryan nodded.

"What about CCTV footage around the Waterside area?"

Phillips let out a blustery sigh.

"There aren't any cameras outside the holiday lodges, only outside the main visitor's facilities, which we've already checked and we know that Guy didn't wander down there. There's a couple of cameras on the main C200 road and we've requested the footage but we're unlikely to get that before Monday. Bearing in mind the general direction of the tracks, I'd say our first conclusion was right: Guy walked through the trees rather than following the path of the road."

Phillips reclaimed his seat and one of the local constables stuck a hand in the air.

"Excuse me, sir? Given the size of the search area, how are we going to narrow it down?"

"Process of elimination," Ryan replied. "DS Phillips and PC Yates are supervising the house to house interviews up to a radius of five miles from the crime scene. That sounds like a lot of turf but, in this landscape, it's peanuts. While that's going on, we're going to look at the statements we have already and see who has an alibi between four and seven o'clock this morning, which is the timeframe when Guy Sullivan died. We focus our attention on the people who cannot account for their whereabouts."

"But what if they all say they were in bed, sleeping?"

Ryan smiled.

"That's where solid forensics comes in," he said, and gestured to Faulkner across the room. "Tom? Tell us what your search turned up today."

Faulkner cleared his throat.

"It's good news," he said. "We isolated a hair sample from the victim's clothing that doesn't match his own, so we should have an excellent basis for comparison with any DNA samples we receive from individual suspects."

"Can't we just swab everybody and get to the bottom of it that way?" Yates asked, innocently enough.

"I wish we could," Faulkner said, with feeling. "It would make everybody's job much easier, but it would also diminish a fundamental right to privacy."

"But, surely, when there's been a murder?"

"We can seek voluntary consent, to begin with," Ryan interjected. "Most people are happy to help because most people have nothing to hide. I'm sorry to tell you that it comes down to the same old chestnut once again: resources. The department won't spring for mass DNA-testing, even if the subjects agreed to it, because it would be costly and time-consuming."

"So, what do we do?" Yates asked.

"Our jobs," Ryan said, shortly. "We look at these people and we look *hard* to see who had the means and opportunity to be on that bridleway to kill Guy Sullivan and who lived close enough to make a hasty retreat afterwards without being seen. We prioritise those people and swab them first. If that doesn't work, we expand the net."

"What happens if they refuse consent?" Yates wondered.

"Then, if we have solid grounds for suspicion, we arrest them and use our powers to obtain a sample anyway. They can do it the easy way or the hard way, Yates, but *whichever* way they decide, the killer will find themselves behind bars."

* * *

As the sun fell off the edge of the world and night reigned once more, they met at their usual spot overlooking the water. They could just make out the lights shining from the conference room on the other side of the lake where Ryan and his team continued their briefing, plotting how they would find the person responsible for taking a life.

"The police came around today."

"Yes, I saw them. You brought this to our door. If you had only let things lie, they would have consigned Duncan to the pile of unsolved cases in their archive room and everything would have carried on as before."

"I-I didn't think—"

"You seldom do."

"I'm sorry. I'll try to be better, next time, I'll…"

The other listened with half an ear while planning how to dispose of the childhood friend who had been a constant, oppressive burden for the last thirty-three years. It had never been possible to relax, not knowing that Roly could crack at any time or get drunk and start frothing at the mouth about poor Duncan Gray lying dead at the bottom of the lake.

This was a course of action that was long overdue.

"…do you think?"

"What's that?"

"I was asking whether you think I should go away for a while, just till everything blows over?"

"It's too late for that. They've set up traffic cordons."

"They have? That means we're trapped—"

"*You're* trapped."

"Okay, alright, I could still use one of the smaller roads and go cross-country. I could head for Scotland—"

"If you leave now, your absence will be noted immediately and they'll set up a full-scale manhunt. Now, listen to me, *trust* me."

"I've always trusted you."

Poor, stupid Roly.

"Good. I want you to keep your head. Stay calm and, if the police come around again, I want you to stick to the story we agreed. Above all, you must remain in control. Can you manage that?"

Roly watched the shadows in the trees around them and fancied there was a boy lurking in there, somewhere.

"Y-yes, I'll try."

* * *

After a short break, Ryan turned to the other young man whose innocent, open face was forever captured in time like his wasted body now lying on an impersonal slab at the mortuary.

"Duncan Gray," he said. "Aged sixteen when he went missing back in 1981. Yates?"

Melanie jerked in her seat.

"Sir?"

Ryan gestured for her to come to the front of the room.

"You and Phillips worked the case yesterday," he said. "Give us a run-down of your progress so far."

Ryan had learned over the years that the best way to deal with fear was to channel it into productivity. In this case, Yates needed to overcome her fear of public speaking so she could move forward and meet her own potential.

"Just the key points," he said. "We won't bite."

Melanie could feel her palms growing sweaty. Why hadn't she noticed before how cramped and claustrophobic the conference room was?

"Um—"

The faces of the local police swam before her eyes and her stomach churned, then her gaze locked with Phillips, who gave her an encouraging nod.

"We, ah, after the body was recovered yesterday morning, DS Phillips and I went about the usual searches with Missing Persons and with the help of local police we obtained preliminary statements from everybody who was present at the marina. We also visited and spoke with Lisa Hope, the diver who first discovered Duncan Gray's body in the reservoir, and confirmed the sequence of events. Later in the day, we spoke with the police pathologist and a forensic anthropologist who confirmed the cause of death and approximate age of the body, which is supported by a bus pass found on his person and the facts now in our possession following identification."

"How did he die?" Ryan asked.

"There was a major fracture to the skull and a series of shallow knife wounds to the chest, any of which might have led to asphyxiation or cardiac arrest. The pathologist is of the opinion these were not self-inflicted."

When no further questions were forthcoming, she continued.

"We were able to identify Duncan Gray thanks to an existing profile on the Missing Persons Database and his dental records, which were already on file. His mother was informed first thing this morning."

Ryan folded his arms comfortably.

"What's your game plan?"

"Sir?"

"If you were managing the case, what would you do next, Yates?"

Melanie thought of the next logical steps and was surprised to find she was no longer in fear of her audience, who looked on with professional curiosity.

"I would review the original investigation," she said, tentatively. "It was a Missing Persons case in 1981 and it doesn't look like the police took matters very seriously. It seems there was a widespread feeling that Duncan Gray left of his own accord and the sergeant in charge at the time accepted that without too much rigour. It's a murder investigation now, and we need to re-interview all relevant parties and use any evidence at our disposal with the advantage of thirty-three years' worth of advancements in forensic science."

Ryan was impressed.

"Who was it? The sergeant in charge of the case, I mean."

"Arthur Gregson."

The room fell completely silent at the mention of a man whose name was now notorious throughout the echelons of the Northumbria Police Constabulary; their former superintendent who had risen so high and fallen so far.

"I might have known," Ryan muttered.

CHAPTER 16

Jack Lowerson rubbed a tired hand across his eyes and leaned back in his chair. He was seated at his new desk in a cubicle beside DCS Lucas's personal assistant, who had busied herself for the remainder of the afternoon before leaving on the dot of five o'clock without saying 'goodbye'. He tried not to mind; after all, he had a serious job to do and had been offered a pathway to promotion.

He should be happy.

Shouldn't he?

It was hard not to miss the camaraderie of the office he'd shared with the other detectives of CID on the first floor, where there was always somebody to talk to and share a joke with, or a pint after work. It softened the blow of heading home to an empty house. By now, they would have heard about his transfer and were probably wondering why he hadn't been down to tell them all about it.

The truth was, he was embarrassed.

Lowerson thought back to his argument with Ryan and cringed at the memory. He'd admired the man for years and had hardly been able to believe his luck when Ryan had plucked him from the quagmire of obscurity as a young constable and helped him along the pathway to becoming a detective three years ago. Ryan had taught him so much during that time; how to read people, how to lead people and, perhaps most of all, how to believe in himself. They'd become more than work colleagues, they'd become friends and he'd always felt included, right down to being invited to Ryan and Anna's wedding three weeks earlier.

And how had he repaid their kindness?

He'd bitten the hand that fed him and, worse still, used his friend to vent all his paltry frustrations at life.

There was only one thing to be done.

Apologise.

Galvanised, Lowerson shut down his computer and shrugged into his blue blazer, slapping his hands against the pockets to make sure he had his wallet and car keys. He secured the paperwork back in his filing unit and was about to make for the exit when it struck him that, really, he ought to bid his new boss farewell for the evening.

He turned back and knocked on her office door.

"Come in!"

When he stepped into the room, Lowerson couldn't help but marvel at how pristine she still looked, even after a full day's work. He'd been mildly surprised to find she wasn't required to be at work this weekend, so it was obviously dedication to her job that led her to put in the overtime and bring herself up to speed with her new environment.

"Ma'am? I'm sorry to disturb you but I wanted to let you know I'm heading off now."

Jennifer Lucas laid her pen down at a perfect right-angle to the paperwork on her desk and then glanced at the clock across the room. Clocks were usually the same design in whichever public service building you went—round, white plastic wall-mounted monstrosities— but hers was an antique walnut affair with gold dials and it gave her much pleasure to know it was a cut above the ordinary.

"You've stayed well past the hours you're obliged to work," she said, in a tone that held both approval and reproof. "Are you heading home now?"

Lowerson reddened slightly and thought it best not to mention his fall-out with Ryan, or the reason for it in the first place.

"Ah, yes, ma'am."

"Oh, but it's not even eight o'clock," she purred. "What do you say we have a quick drink to celebrate our new jobs?"

He hesitated, feeling torn.

"I'd like to, but—"

She looked at him and he was suddenly convinced that she would see through any lie he might tell. Perhaps it would be easier to have a friendly glass of wine at the local drinking hole, then go their separate ways.

"Okay, thanks. That would be nice."

She smiled.

"I'll see you in the car park in five minutes."

"Oh, but the pub we usually go to is within walking distance," he told her. "Just a couple of minutes around the corner, so you can keep your car parked here if you like."

She looked at him indulgently, wondering if he had any idea what fate had in store.

"The place I have in mind is on the way home," she told him. "Not far from where you live."

Lowerson shrugged and agreed to meet her downstairs. Only later did he wonder how she knew his address but he assumed she had reviewed his HR file before offering him a promotion.

That must have been where she'd seen it.

* * *

It was nearly nine o'clock by the time Phillips let himself into the little three-bedroom semi he owned in Kingston Park, a suburban area on the western fringes of Newcastle. The cul-de-sac was occupied mainly by young families, most of whom would already be in bed, and the street was quiet except for the faint glare of his neighbour's television.

The lamps were on in the hallway when he stepped inside the house and toed out of the comfortable brown leather loafers he invariably wore for work. When he spotted MacKenzie's smart navy woollen coat hanging over the newel post, he knew his fiancée must be around somewhere.

"Denise?"

The house remained quiet and he cursed himself for feeling the old dread rise again, the remembered anguish of a time months ago when he'd come home to find her gone.

Taken.

"*Denise?*"

He moved swiftly from room to room and was ready to heave himself up the stairs two at a time when he heard an odd sound coming from the direction of the garage. It was attached to the house through a door via the kitchen and when he cocked his ear against the wood he thought he heard fists hitting flesh, followed by the grunts and moans of a woman in pain.

"*Denise!*"

He grabbed the nearest thing to hand, which happened to be the kettle, and threw back the adjoining door to face whichever thug was attacking the woman he loved.

* * *

Denise MacKenzie had spent half an hour setting up her new, top-of-the-range punchbag. It hung from the ceiling in a heavy sack of black and red leather, to match the training gloves and mat she'd bought as a multi-save deal. Obviously, the sales assistant had seen her coming, but she didn't mind. The long strip light flickered its energy-saving white light around the concrete walls of the garage, spotlighting the imaginary ring she'd created in the centre of it all.

When she threw her first punch, it reverberated up her arm and along her funny bone eliciting a few choice words in response.

She stared at the bag and then closed her eyes, meditating until she found the anger she needed to expel.

His face. The knife. His eyes.

His eyes. His eyes.

Her own flew open again and, this time, she pounded the hell out of that leather bag. She pummelled out her rage in the empty garage and felt no pain as she danced on tiptoes against the plain rubber mat. There might be bruises the next day but it would be worth it, if only to get rid of the bubbling anger she carried.

"Sick. Bastard." She spat the words, punctuating them with a fresh blow.

MacKenzie was so far gone that she didn't hear Phillips call for her and was only vaguely aware of his presence when the door burst open.

But when she turned, half-distracted, the anger drained away at the sight of him standing there like an avenging angel brandishing the kettle—its cord flapped against the side of his leg and he looked as if he could easily have strangled somebody with it.

"Where—Denise?" He looked around the garage as if he were expecting to find an intruder lurking in the shadows behind the boxes of junk. "Are you alright? What're you doing?"

She sucked in a deep breath and then let it whoosh out again, feeling her pulse rate gradually return to normal.

"What does it look like? I'm letting off a bit of steam," she said. "Remember, you promised to teach me to box."

"Aye, I know, but—"

"Now's as good a time as any, Frank."

Phillips looked on in admiration. She was one hell of a woman standing there challenging him to box, given that he'd been knocking around since he was seven years old.

"Unless you're too tired, that is," she said, folding her arms across her chest.

Phillips set the kettle back down on the kitchen bench and grinned.

"Never heard you complain about me being too tired before," he said.

"You're not as young as you used to be," she sniffed, enjoying herself wholeheartedly. "I would hate you to put your back out."

"Worry about that later," he said, and rolled up his shirtsleeves to the sound of her delighted laughter.

* * *

After the briefing concluded and Ryan waved off the staff attached to 'OPERATION STARGAZER' until the next morning, he became acutely aware of how isolated it was for those who called Kielder their home. Unlike the cities which suffered from light pollution, the skies above the forest and water were so clear they had been awarded the gold standard for stargazing. Professional astronomers gathered alongside photographers and curious amateurs to witness the infinite cosmos on a nightly basis at the nearby observatory, but where Ryan stood on the banks of the reservoir it was eerily quiet and devoid of any human life, let alone astronomical enthusiasts.

Quickly, he jogged along to the holiday lodge where he knew there was at least one other living person to be found; the one whose company he preferred above all others.

"Anna?"

There was work to be done ahead of lectures the following week but it lay untouched next to the small stack of undergraduate essays she needed to mark on the plain pine table in the kitchen. Her mind would not allow Anna to focus, not when she thought of how Guy Sullivan would never again turn up to tutorials ten minutes late, as had been his habit. He would never live to fulfil his dreams or travel to see the historical artefacts he'd only read about in textbooks. He'd never fall in love or have his heart broken. He would never experience life in all its wonderful glory.

Ryan said her name again and she looked up from where she'd been staring at the fruit bowl. He understood the situation immediately.

"Why don't we go out and see the stars?"

Her eyebrows shot up and she looked out of the window.

"I can already see them," she reminded him.

"Yeah, but not like this," he said softly. "Come on, wrap up warm. Our lives are about to be put into perspective."

She gave a half laugh.

"Are you going to show me Uranus?"

"Only if you ask nicely."

This time, her laugh was genuine.

* * *

The observatory was situated on a stretch of high ground known as 'Black Fell' and, though it was only a ten-minute drive from the small complex at Kielder Waterside, it perched on a remote outcrop of land without any other visible signs of civilisation. The building was of ecologically-friendly wood; a long, low futuristic design built on a series of reinforced stilts that made Ryan think incongruously of beach piers on the east coast of America, although the terrain couldn't have been more different. During the daytime, the panorama of the valley below would be incomparable, but those who came to the observatory after dark had more celestial views in mind.

They had not passed any other vehicles on their short journey from the lodge but they found several cars and campervans parked outside the observatory.

"This is obviously where the cool kids hang out," Ryan said, with a rakish grin for his wife.

"I think I can understand why," Anna murmured.

Ryan turned his face upward and felt the breath catch in his throat.

Meteors burst and shattered across the night sky like fireballs, five or six at a time, flashing like the bulb of an old-fashioned camera from the twenties or thirties. He hadn't thought it possible to be so enthralled, but then, he'd never seen anything like it in his life.

"It would have always been like this before the Industrial Revolution," Anna whispered. "No matter where you lived, you could look up at the sky and wonder."

Ryan reached across to take her hand.

"Let's go inside," she said, eyes dancing with excitement. "We'll get an even better view from the telescope."

As if it had heard them, the observatory's timber frame began to rotate and long shutters slid open to provide a clear viewing platform for the two telescopes housed within. They hurried up a long, accessible ramp to the entrance of the building and followed the crowd into a warm room with a projector screen and seating set out for a welcome presentation.

"I'll be back in a minute," Ryan muttered. "Grab us a couple of seats in the back."

He flashed a smile and then went off in search of the facilities, leaving Anna to settle near the end of a row as the lights dimmed. A woman introduced herself as one of the astronomers attached to the observatory and Anna was drawn in by the easy, conversational style that appealed to the children in the audience as much as the adults. A girl of around twelve stuck her hand up to ask the first question and when Anna spotted Mitch Fenwick sitting in front of her, she assumed correctly that the girl was his daughter. Further along, there were younger children sitting on their parent's knees and they, too, were familiar faces from around Kielder Waterside.

When the screen filled with live-stream video images of the meteor shower outside, Anna was hypnotised.

* * *

He'd seen her as soon as she entered the room.

Of course he had; she stood out like a precious, botanical flower amid a garden of overgrown weeds. Tall and slender, with long dark hair falling in waves down her back, half-concealed by a ridiculous green woollen bobble hat. Her face was like fine bone china, all cheekbones and big brown eyes.

He'd watched her hands when her gloves came off and felt a shiver in response.

Perfect.

Long and shapely; artistic but without artifice. It was impossible not to imagine them trailing over his skin.

A man hovered behind her, exuding the subtle, proprietary air that developed between couples. Usually, that didn't concern him overmuch, but there was something about the man's face that struck a chord, reminding him of someone, like an actor or a musician he'd seen on the television sometime. He moved unhurriedly but his eyes tracked the room as if it were a habit, scoping out the exits and the level of threat. For a moment, their eyes locked, then the man's silvery-grey gaze passed on, dismissing him.

That was just as well. It might have been novel to be recognised—truly *recognised*—for what he was; for everything he had seen and done, for the power he wielded and could use whenever he chose. But that would be vainglorious and short-sighted. He'd cultivated exceptional levels of self-denial over the years, delaying the instant gratification so the pleasure would be all the sweeter when it came.

His eyes strayed back to the woman.

* * *

"Quite something, isn't it? Just like you."

Anna heard the deep timbre of a man's well-spoken voice whisper in her ear and assumed it was Ryan, so she turned with a smile automatically in place.

"You took your time—oh! Sorry, I thought you were somebody else."

The man who had spoken stood just behind her chair alongside a few other stragglers who'd arrived late to the astronomy session. He was tall and blonde, somewhere in his late forties, but it was his eyes that made her shiver. They were very dark and trained directly on her rather than the projector screen.

He smiled at her astonished face.

"Shh," he joked, tapping a finger to his lips. "You're distracting me."

Anna spun back to the screen, feeling irritated. He'd made her feel, well, as if she'd been *flirting*, whereas she'd only mistaken him for her husband when he'd loomed over her shoulder. What did he mean by telling her she was 'quite something' and practically nuzzling her neck?

Arrogant so-and-so.

Anna sat stiffly for the remainder of the talk feeling oddly vulnerable and increasingly annoyed by the fact Ryan hadn't returned. What on earth could be keeping him? She could sense that man was still standing somewhere nearby and it made her hair stand on end.

Ryan finally snuck into the room as the lights went up and the talk ended, sliding into the chair beside her.

"Did I miss much?"

Anna kept her voice lowered.

"Only the whole talk," she said, testily. "Did you get lost or something?"

"I had to take a call from the office. Is everything alright?"

He knew his wife well enough to know when something was bothering her.

"It's nothing really, just a man—"

Ryan's brows drew together and he eyeballed the man sitting on Anna's other side, who happened to be at least eighty.

"Not *him*," Anna couldn't help but chuckle. "Don't look now, but he's standing behind us."

Ryan ignored her edict and looked openly around the room, finding it half empty now that people were moving through to one of the observation turrets to try out the telescope.

"He must have gone."

Anna shrugged it off.

"I'm sure it was nothing. He probably didn't notice I was with someone and thought he'd try his luck."

"Can't blame him, I suppose," Ryan said, but even the thought of it brought a surprising rush of jealousy flooding through his veins. "All the same, he'd better watch himself."

Anna laughed and gave him a playful nudge in the ribs.

"Let's go and find out some more about these Orionid meteors."

"What's that?"

She merely smiled and tugged him through to the next room.

* * *

"The Orionid meteor shower happens every October, when Earth's orbit intersects with the stream of debris left by Halley's Comet. It burns up inside our atmosphere, usually at a speed of around sixty-six kilometres per second."

Ryan was the last to take his turn peering through the enormous telescope in the larger turret room of the observatory while the rest of the group began to make their way out, and found he could hardly tear himself away from the lens.

So much to see.

"What kind of telescope is this?" Ryan found himself asking the enthusiastic astronomer currently guiding the machine to the best position.

"This is a manual twenty-inch, split-ring equatorial telescope."

"Right."

"There's a computer-operated Meade twenty-four-inch in the smaller turret room," she continued, mistaking his silence for comprehension. "We hold events in both areas, so you could come back and see how that works another time, if you're staying in the area."

Ryan straightened up again.

"Thank you for a very informative evening," he said, and meant every word. It was a fine, rare thing to be able to read the stars and he was disposed to admire anyone who devoted themselves to a subject until it became second nature. He supposed he could make the same claim around the subject matter of murder and serious crimes, but that was nothing to brag about.

When the lights came up, the astronomer moved across to some sort of rack and piston device, winding it quickly so that the slatted wooden shutters began to close again for the evening. Anna waited patiently and he decided to make a few off-balance-sheet enquiries, since he was there.

"I'm sorry, I didn't catch your name?"

The astronomer looked up from her task, pushing thick curly brown hair away from a rounded face that gave the impression of a jovial personality.

"Michaela Collingwood," she replied. "Most people call me, 'Mikey'. Are you and your wife here for a day trip?"

Anna smiled politely but guessed that Ryan was trying to wheedle information, so left him to do the talking.

"No, we're staying over the weekend," he told her. "Unfortunately, I'm here on business."

"Oh? What kind of business are you in?"

"I'm with the police," he replied.

Her face fell instantly.

"Oh, my goodness. You must be investigating the death of that poor lad down at Adderburn," she said, looking between them with over-bright eyes. Ryan wasn't sure whether to attribute that to excitement, or tiredness.

"Do you live in the area?"

"All my life," she said. "I went to university in Newcastle but I just didn't like living in the city. I think all this big sky gets into your veins and makes it hard to settle for less."

Ryan smiled.

"Understandable," he said, then brought the conversation gently back around to recent events. "Ms Collingwood, it's likely that one of my colleagues will be knocking at your door to take down a statement but, since you grew up here, may I ask whether you knew a boy called Duncan Gray?"

"Poor, poor Dunc," she whispered.

"So you knew him?"

She nodded.

"Duncan was a friend," she explained. "There's only one school in the area, so all the kids knew one another. My parents only lived a couple of doors down from where Duncan used to live and where his mum, Angela, still lives in Kielder Village."

Ryan nodded.

"You and Duncan were the same age, then?"

"No, he was a couple of years older than me but they often mixed children of the same ability together since the school was so small. I was in the same group as Duncan for Maths and English."

"Then you must remember the events surrounding his disappearance?"

"Of course," she said. "Although, at the time, people thought he'd run away. I don't think things were great at home and he talked about running away a few times. When the search parties couldn't find anything of him and considering he'd taken a bag and some clothes with him, people naturally assumed…" She trailed off, with a helpless shrug. "It's terrible to think he's been lying down there, all these years, and we never knew."

Over her shoulder, Anna made a discreet gesture to let Ryan know the place would be closing soon, and he gave an imperceptible nod.

"Thanks for your time, Ms Collingwood. This must be an incredible place to work."

Ryan and Anna smiled their farewells and turned to leave.

"It was the same time of year," Mikey murmured, almost to herself. "I remember, the Orionids were falling around the same time Duncan went missing. They can last for weeks, you know, all the way through October and sometimes into November, but they're at their brightest every year around 21st October."

Ryan tried to put himself into the mind of a killer and wondered how he could be sure that people would not stumble across a murder in progress. How perfect it would have been if the residents of Kielder had gathered in some regular spot to view the meteors, leaving him free to act without fear of discovery.

"Before the observatory was built, where would people have gathered to see a meteor show like that?"

She turned to look at him with a dazed expression, her mind far away.

"It used to be an old tradition to hike up to Deadwater Fell," she said. "It's the highest summit around these parts and you get some of the best views of the valley. It's about six miles north-west of Kielder Village, a three-hour walk if you know the trail. People would often trek up there with a picnic around dusk to watch the stars, then use torches to hike back down again later, after dark. Still do, sometimes."

"Sounds a bit hairy," Anna couldn't help but remark.

Mikey smiled.

"Not if you know the land like we do. You get to know its nooks and crannies like the back of your hand."

She turned back to Ryan with sad eyes.

"I hope you find whoever you're looking for, chief inspector."

* * *

Fifty miles away in central Newcastle, Jack Lowerson polished off his fourth glass of expensive white wine and realised he was starting to feel a bit woozy. If he wasn't careful, he'd end up embarrassing himself in front of his new boss, which was the last thing he needed.

Time to go home.

Except, he was now over the legal alcohol limit and unable to drive himself home. He was wondering how he could get himself out of that sticky situation when his companion broke into his thoughts over the rim of the glass of soda water she'd told him was vodka-tonic.

"I think you may need to walk me home, Jack," she said, slurring slightly for effect. "My house is just around the corner but I don't think I should drive."

They were seated in a cosy wine bar in Jesmond, off the main road along a residential side street flanked by upscale restaurants, delis and posh barbershops. It was an upmarket area Jack aspired to live in one day but, for the moment, he had a little two-bed conversion half a mile further south, in an area called Heaton which was what his mother would have called 'perfectly respectable'.

"What about your car?" he asked, yawning widely.

"It'll be safe—so will yours," she added. "It's all free parking around here."

He yawned again and checked the time on his phone.

Ten-forty.

He could hardly believe how the time had flown. What had begun as a friendly drink between two new work colleagues had quickly escalated into easy, free-flowing conversation and one sociable drink had turned into two, then two into three.

It had been all too easy to forget that the woman seated opposite was his superintendent. She was funny and chatty—bubbly, even— with so many stories to tell about life in London. He'd laughed until his belly hurt, at times, and as she gathered up her coat and bag he couldn't understand the tension between her and Ryan at all.

She was incredibly likeable, not to mention attractive.

Very attractive.

Jen—she'd asked him to call her 'Jen' when they were outside of the office—had shown a genuine interest in his career, his thoughts, his politics and even his love life.

Her husband was a lucky man, he thought suddenly. At least, he'd heard she was married, but there had been no mention of a Mr Lucas during the evening and he thought it would be rude to ask.

When Lucas rose, he hurried to pull back her chair, delighted to be able to perform a small act of chivalry most women he knew would have mocked.

"Thank you," she said, and her eyes lingered a fraction too long on his mouth.

The cold air hit them as they exited the wine bar and Lowerson realised he was a lot drunker than he thought. Probably because he hadn't eaten, he thought with inebriated clarity.

"Come on," she murmured, tucking a hand through his arm. "This way, Jack."

They clattered through the darkened streets and, by the time they reached the front door of her palatial Edwardian terrace, Lowerson's face was flushed thanks to a combination of giddy pleasure and cold night air. He waited until she found her keys and turned up the thin collar of his flashy blue suit, wishing he'd brought an overcoat.

She opened the front door and he took that as his cue to leave.

"Thank you for a great evening," he said politely. "I'll see you on Monday morning."

She leaned against the doorframe and surveyed him with a hooded expression.

"Why don't you come in for a cup of coffee, before you head home? It'll help to sober you up."

She was so considerate, Lowerson thought.

Lucas didn't bother to wait for a response and turned to hang up her coat. A moment later, she heard the front door click softly shut behind him and smiled at her own reflection in the hallway mirror.

CHAPTER 17

Sunday, 2nd October

The sun had not yet risen before the media caught the scent of murder and began to arrive at Kielder Forest in their droves. Like a pack of ravenous wolves, they roamed the villages in search of a juicy, early-morning titbit to satisfy their readership and, by the time Ryan had kissed Anna goodbye and made the short journey from the lodge to his car, he found several reporters gathered around it.

"Chief Inspector! Is it true there's a serial killer at large?"

"No comment."

"Is it true another one of The Hacker's victims has been found?"

Ryan almost laughed. They'd do anything to milk that man's devastating legacy, even down to inventing new victims that bore no resemblance to his usual type.

"No comment."

"Is it true there's a mass grave lying beneath the surface of the reservoir? Is it true that the Kielder Ghost is responsible for these deaths?"

The *what?*

Ryan glared at the journalist who'd shouted those inane questions and at least he had the grace to look abashed. Clearly, pickings had been slim on the news desk lately.

"If you have any *intelligent* questions to ask, contact the Press Office," he said, witheringly.

"What about the traffic cordons, Inspector? People have a right to know if they should be on their guard!" another reporter shouted at him. *"They have a right to know!"*

Ryan's hand stilled on the car door and he turned to look at the journalist. Her face was earnest, seemingly passionate about uncovering the truth, and if he was feeling charitable he might have admired it. However, more important concerns weighed upon his mind, such as not being responsible for starting a widespread panic and finding justice for the dead according to proper procedures. It was true that the media could be useful to an investigation sometimes but he'd learned it was a double-edged sword that should be wielded lightly.

"At present, official advice remains the same," he said. "That is, to exercise common sense and avoid situations which may give rise to danger wherever possible. No further comment."

Their cries buzzed like flies in his ear and then muted as the car door slammed shut behind him. Ryan rested his hands on the steering wheel and then gave a brief toot of his horn, to clear a path on the road ahead. He could only imagine what Lucas would have to say about public relations if he mowed down a group of journalists in cold blood.

It was tempting, but he had to be satisfied with their shocked expressions as he fired the engine and missed them by inches.

* * *

While Phillips and Yates oversaw operations at Kielder, Ryan returned to the office to meet Guy Sullivan's parents who had returned from Lanzarote late the previous evening. He'd taken the trouble to wear a suit and tie and spent the long drive back to the city preparing himself for an emotional meeting. It was never going to be easy to face the parents of a young man whose life had been taken but there were coping strategies he tried to employ; methods of boxing away his own emotions which were completely superfluous to the situation. Words ran through his mind, hackneyed phrases he'd used over the years to convey sympathy and they sounded trite even before he'd spoken them aloud. Trite they may be, but it didn't make them any less true.

Green fields gave way to urban development and, before long, the uninspiring architecture of the new Police Headquarters came into view.

"Home, sweet home," Ryan muttered.

The duty sergeant at the desk told him Mary and Paul Sullivan had arrived very early, over an hour before they'd agreed to meet at eight-thirty and Ryan sighed, scrubbing a hand over his face. He didn't blame them for wanting to seek answers to the impossible question of why someone had murdered their son; he only wished he had the answers they were searching for.

He strode across the foyer and buzzed into a separate corridor containing a dedicated 'family room' on the ground floor. It bore a small red placard warning Ryan it was occupied and he paused on the threshold to check his tie and steel himself for the outpouring of grief and anger that awaited him beyond its closed door.

When he stepped inside, the first thing he noticed was Mary Sullivan. She had fallen into an exhausted sleep across a row of foamy visitor's chairs and her husband's jacket was draped across her huddled form, while Paul sat across from her with his hands clasped between his knees, staring down at the floor between his feet.

He looked up with bloodshot eyes when Ryan entered.

"Mr Sullivan?"

Ryan spoke quietly, careful not to disturb the sleeping figure, but Mary heard him anyway and her eyes flew open.

"Paul—Paul—"

The jacket slipped unheeded onto the floor as she forced herself upright, reaching out to clasp her husband's outstretched hand.

Ryan moved into the room, hating the neutral décor and cheap scented sticks on the window ledge for their vain attempt to create a calming environment for the bereaved. He hated the posters taped to the walls and the stacks of leaflets they insisted on leaving around the side tables, full of counsellors touting their services and 'healing' yoga classes which claimed to ease the burden of grief. No matter which police station or hospital you went to, the room was always the same and it couldn't fail to remind him of his sister's death and the numb, empty faces of his parents when he'd delivered the devastating news. Now, he saw the same look mirrored in the faces of the Sullivans.

Ryan reached across and pulled a chair in front of them so they were seated in a triangle, and settled himself so they were on eye level. What he needed to say deserved to be said face to face and at close quarters.

"Mr and Mrs Sullivan, I want to tell you how very sorry I am for the loss of your son."

Time was suspended for a moment while the words penetrated and then they both seemed to wilt, their bodies swaying against the weight of the news no parent should ever hear. Ryan sensed that, until that moment, there had been hope. On a subconscious level, they'd hoped he would tell them it was all a terrible mistake.

"What happened?" Mary whispered, and fixed him with a direct stare. "I don't understand this at all. My son went away on a history trip with his university and now you tell me he's—he's d-dead…"

Her chest rose and fell as she battled tears, all the while watching Ryan with fierce, unyielding eyes that demanded to know *why.*

"Was he attacked? Why? Was it drugs? Was it?"

Her body was shaking, Ryan thought, and bore down against his own reaction.

Later, he told himself. *Later, he could let go.*

"I'm very sorry, Mrs Sullivan," he repeated. "We're using all available resources to investigate your son's murder. There is no evidence to suggest his death was drug-related. Unfortunately, it bears the hallmarks of an unprovoked attack."

"What do you mean, 'unprovoked'?" Paul asked. "Are you saying there was no reason for it at *all?*"

Ryan watched the man's eyes fill with tears.

"We're working very hard to find out the answer to that question, Mr Sullivan," Ryan said, detesting how clipped and formal his voice sounded.

It was either that or break down completely. The latter would do little to inspire confidence in the minds of these people who had already lost so much and who needed to believe that their son's death would be avenged; there needed to be a price paid for what had been taken, to bring some small measure of closure in the empty void of time stretching before them.

Ryan watched the tears begin to spill down Paul Sullivan's face and forced himself to watch, to offer the box of tissues sitting handily on the table in front of them and not to look away.

"My boy," Paul said, brokenly. "My boy."

* * *

An hour later, Ryan ordered a squad car to deliver the Sullivans back to their hotel, accompanied by a family liaison officer who would be a point of contact for them during the remainder of the investigation. Ryan had given them his personal card, too, because nobody wanted to be fobbed off by a junior member of staff. They wanted to speak to the person in charge and, in this case, that responsibility fell squarely with him. They also wanted to see their son first thing tomorrow and no amount of cajoling or well-intentioned advice seemed to put them off. He had a feeling that, even if he'd told them the mortuary was closed on Mondays, they'd still turn up just to be sure.

He stood by the main entrance until the squad car left, then turned and marched back across the foyer and along the corridor to one of the smaller conference rooms at the far end of the interview suite. There were no cameras in there, no windows and the walls were sound-proofed.

Ryan locked himself inside.

He prowled around the four walls, then sank into one of the chairs and let his head fall into his hands. There, in an impersonal room without anybody to see or to comfort him, Ryan allowed himself a moment to process the emotions swirling through his mind.

Logically, he knew his grief was borrowed. What right did he have to grieve when the pain of those people ran so deeply? He wasn't the one who had lost a child.

Except, he grieved not only for their son but for so many more. Their faces swam before his eyes, the faces of the dead. They walked beside him every day, a procession of men, women and children who demanded that a toll be paid for their lives. And he was the ferryman, Ryan realised. He was the man who ensured their passage to safety, in the minds of those who lived on. They sat in the waiting area for hours for somebody to tell them they hadn't been forgotten and their loss was still important.

And it *was*, Ryan thought, vehemently.

Their loss was no less important because science and police methods had failed to equalise the scales. The press called it mismanagement; the executives blamed the politicians and the politicians blamed a broken society.

What did he believe?

It was a little of everything as well as something else that was more elusive and subtle. Something that they could not quantify or manage or try to control.

It was human nature.

But what should he do when the nature of a person was more animal than human? How should he explain the frenzied attack of one person against another when there was no defensive motive? There was only one explanation, Ryan thought. Perhaps, when a person lived in the wilderness, it was only a matter of time before they turned away from society's norms and reverted to a state of nature.

He lifted his head up again and his eyes were a hard, silver-grey. It was time to put down whichever predatory animal was roaming free, before another face was added to the reel.

* * *

Craig Hunter knew the police were coming even before their car entered the clearing outside his cottage at Adderburn. It got that way, in the country, when you were surrounded by trees and the only sounds you heard most days were the swaying of the leaves, the squawk of crows and the rustle of animals in the undergrowth. Your senses developed, just like Nature had intended.

Quickly, he threw another log onto the large bonfire burning in the small patch of garden at the back of his house, then walked around to head them off at the gate. The dog loped alongside him, tail quivering between its legs as it sensed the tension building in its master.

Finally, the car came around the bend.

The fat little sergeant was back, Hunter noticed. There was a man who looked like he could plant a fist in your face and not feel the difference. He had a different dogsbody with him this time and no sign of the pretty little brunette with the ponytail.

Pity.

She'd looked just the type who needed a real man to show her the facts of life. He'd seen her staring at him the other day, getting hot under the collar at the thought of him giving her a piece. Too many namby-pamby types waltzing around, in his opinion, worrying themselves sick about what was right and proper and whether they'd booked a tooth-whitening appointment, or some shit. Too much talk of 'don't say this' and 'don't touch that'. Far as he was concerned, if a woman was going to put it all on show, he was damn well going to have himself a slice. If he had anything to thank his father for, it was for teaching him how to handle a woman.

Hunter wheezed out a laugh and re-arranged himself as the two policemen walked across to meet him.

"Back again, are we?"

Phillips stopped at the gate.

"Mr Hunter? I'm DS Phillips, we met yesterday morning. This is PC Walton, from the local area police. As you've likely heard on the news, we're investigating the murder of Guy Sullivan and we're hoping to eliminate as many people as possible from our enquiries. We're asking local people to give a voluntary sample of their DNA and we're hoping you'll also agree."

Hunter looked between their bland, expressionless faces. Cop faces, with dead eyes.

"I thought you needed a warrant, or whatever you call it?"

"Would you like us to get a warrant, Mr Hunter?" Philips asked.

Hunter thought quickly.

Nothing to worry about.

"Nah, you're alreet. Nowt to hide. D' you want me to piss into a bucket?"

"That won't be necessary, Mr Hunter. We use a buccal swab, which looks like an ear-bud. It shouldn't take more than a minute to rub it around the inside of your cheek."

"Help yourself," Hunter shrugged, and opened his gob.

Phillips' nose wrinkled at the meaty scent of Hunter's breath and he wondered if halitosis was contagious. You could never be too careful, so he stepped aside and gestured for the constable to come forward.

"Walton? Howay, lad, this'll be good practice for you."

"Thank you, sir."

CHAPTER 18

Before he paid a visit to the mortuary, Ryan swallowed his pride and jogged upstairs to the executive suite in search of Jack Lowerson. There had been a sufficient cooling-off period since their argument the previous day and it was time to bury the hatchet. Life was just too short to hold a grudge, especially against a man who'd saved his life. Taking the time to gaze at the stars had achieved its objective the previous evening, which was to gain perspective on his trivial existence in the world and when he'd walked away with his wife by his side Ryan had realised one, very important thing:

He was a lucky son of a bitch.

He was alive. He was loved. That was a hell of a lot more than many could boast.

Could he blame Lowerson for being the one to remind him of his good fortune?

Of course not.

So Ryan went in search of peace with his friend. His long legs ate up the stairs until he emerged onto the first floor but he found most of the office cubicles empty aside from a skeleton weekend staff, since it was Sunday.

"Damn," he muttered and checked his watch.

Still early.

Time enough to make a short detour on his way to the mortuary.

But when he slowed his car and crawled along the curb alongside the entrance to Lowerson's garden flat fifteen minutes later, there was no sign of the man or his car. Ryan drummed his fingers against the steering wheel and then moved off again, telling himself Jack's private life was his own affair.

* * *

Half an hour later, Ryan walked into the chilled air of the basement mortuary.

At first glance, the place looked completely empty, but he knew Jeff Pinter would be lurking somewhere since he'd called the man at home and offered to pay him overtime if he got his bony arse back to work. There were few things in life that money couldn't buy, especially when the recipient had expensive tastes in opera and fine dining.

Ryan realised he must have become desensitized to the mortuary environment because he barely glanced at the bank of metal drawers lining the back wall, or the new immersion tank which oozed all manner of unpleasant smells. God only knew what festered inside its slimy interior.

He found Pinter in his office, his skeletal body draped over a metal wheelie-chair as he tapped away at his computer.

"Jeff?"

Pinter favoured Ryan with a haughty expression which Ryan met, stare for stare.

"I had plans today," the pathologist complained.

"Yeah, well, I had plans too but a little, itty-bitty thing called *murder* got in the way of my Sunday morning lie-in."

"Oh yeah? Well, I'm trying to work on having a Sunday morning lie-in which doesn't involve just me and the cryptic crossword," Pinter muttered. "I had a date last night and it was shaping up very nicely."

Ryan's lips twitched.

"What's she like?"

"Gorgeous," Pinter said, dreamily. "She's a curvaceous divorcee who doesn't mind real-life crime documentaries."

"What'd you tell her you do for a living?" Ryan asked, settling his long body against the doorframe. "Fitness instructor?"

Pinter guffawed and removed his glasses to polish the glass against the back of his lab coat.

"Doctor," he confessed. "I just didn't mention what kind…not yet, at least."

Ryan felt a moment's sympathy. Telling somebody you worked with dead bodies for a living was hardly an aphrodisiac.

He'd know.

"Well, once you tell her you helped to catch a killer, that'll make you sound a lot more heroic," Ryan offered.

Pinter perked up a bit at the thought of that new spin.

"Maybe," he agreed. "Although I hardly know what to tell you about this one, Ryan. The face was so badly mangled, it was difficult to—well, let's just say, it was bloody difficult."

"Just tell me what you can," Ryan urged. "And, Jeff, his parents came to see me today."

Pinter sighed, and this time there was no trace of the usual theatrics he sometimes employed.

"Hell."

"Yes," Ryan said. "Is there anything you can do for him before they have to see? I've told them to stay away but they won't listen."

Pinter looked away, obviously thinking of the body, then shook his head sadly.

"The face was completely destroyed. We've cleaned him up as best we can and I can stitch… I'll do what I can for them," he offered. "Otherwise, we'd need a specialist."

Ryan nodded his thanks and left it at that. He couldn't expect miracles.

"Let's start from the top," Jeff said briskly, and Ryan prepared to face another kind of horror.

* * *

Denise MacKenzie decided to spend her precious day off with her friend, Anna.

Ryan's wife was more than just her boss's spouse; she was a trusted friend, an intelligent professional and it had often been said she had the makings of an excellent murder detective—if she ever decided to swap her life as an academic historian. Denise had asked Anna to be Maid of Honour at her wedding and it provided an excellent excuse to go shopping and eat cake.

Anna needed no second bidding and the two women found themselves in the elegant town of Corbridge for the day, roughly halfway between Newcastle and Kielder. There were drinking holes aplenty and after a respectable time had been spent roaming the little shops filled with quaint knick-knacks, they took themselves off to a quiet corner with two large glasses of something fruity.

MacKenzie took a generous gulp and watched her friend from the corner of her eye.

"How'd you feel about apple green?"

Anna almost choked on her wine.

"In what context?"

"In the dress-wearing context. With a flower garland and bangles."

Anna searched MacKenzie's face and decided it was a fifty-fifty risk.

"I call bullshit," Anna said.

MacKenzie feigned offence.

"It's an old Irish tradition," she lied. "All the women of my family get married in green and the bridesmaids wear the same shade."

Anna snorted.

"Well, in that case, I'd better tell you it's an old Geordie tradition for the groom to wear a black and white Lycra onesie."

MacKenzie laughed, but Anna's smile slipped as she became aware of a strange creeping feeling, one she'd experienced before. Her skin tingled in reaction and she cast her eyes around the pub to see who was watching her.

She found the source of her discomfort immediately and her spine stiffened.

It was the same man from the observatory the previous evening. He was sitting at one of the bar stools, watching her.

Just watching.

Anna turned pointedly away.

"Is everything okay?" MacKenzie asked, noting that her friend had turned pale.

When Anna looked back, the stool was empty and a pint glass stood untouched beside it.

"It's probably nothing," she murmured.

* * *

It was early afternoon by the time Phillips and Yates paid a visit to the final address on their list of residents within a five-mile radius of the crime scene at Adderburn. The thriller writer Nathan Armstrong lived part of the year right on the banks of the reservoir, his residence accessible only by a footpath from the road or by private motorboat. The house nestled on a secluded bluff known locally as Scribe's End, thanks to its owner's literary exploits, and afforded complete privacy from the rest of the world.

"Storm brewin', I reckon," Phillips remarked.

Yates lowered her face against the wind.

"How far is it?"

"Can't be much further now," Phillips puffed.

The walk couldn't have been more than ten minutes over even ground that undulated gently towards the water until the trees parted and gave way to a view that stole their breath away. The water seemed to go on forever, shimmering in choppy waves against the short wooden jetty and the small red motorboat moored against it. The vista was so all-encompassing it was easy to miss the old stone hunting lodge that seemed to perch on the very edge of it all.

A far cry from the ordinary three-bed semi Yates still shared with her parents. She had dreams of her own little place but never in a million years could she afford this slice of heaven.

"Wow," she breathed.

"Looks like an insurance nightmare," Phillips said. "And I bet it's draughty in winter."

"I'd risk it," she muttered.

* * *

Craig Hunter had not been wrong about quiet places leading to heightened senses, but it didn't hurt to employ a little technology either. Nathan Armstrong knew he had police visitors long before they emerged from the trees to stare at his home, thanks to a series of top-end CCTV cameras fixed to high branches at intervals around the trees surrounding his property. The lenses tracked their bumbling journey and transmitted a live feed to Armstrong's computer screen so he could watch their progress from the comfort of his desk chair.

He had plenty of time to save his work and lock away his research materials, to turn off the grinding rock music playing through the linked speaker system running throughout the house and even to put on the kettle.

Police and tradespeople always wanted cups of tea or coffee, didn't they?

The doorbell rang and he padded along the hallway to answer it.

"Mr Armstrong? Detective Sergeant Phillips and Police Constable Yates. We're here in connection with the murder of Guy Sullivan," an astute-looking man in his mid-fifties made the introductions and showed off a tattered warrant card.

"Please, come in."

He led the way through to an enormous room with views out across the water, sumptuously furnished with objets d'art and an entire wall of books.

"Can I offer you something to drink?"

The sergeant declined politely and took stock of his surroundings with a pair of sharp brown eyes that gave the impression of missing very little. His companion seemed less guarded and stared openly around the room, as if the plain walls and antique furnishings would tell her something of the man who lived there.

"Mr Armstrong, we're conducting routine enquiries into Guy Sullivan's murder and we're hoping you'll be able to help us."

"Certainly, if I can."

He continued to make coffee, to give himself something to do.

"Could you start by telling us your movements between four and seven a.m., yesterday morning?"

"I was writing," he said. "It's what I do for a living."

"Yes, so we understand. That seems rather early to have been writing, doesn't it?"

Armstrong took a sip of his coffee and leaned back against the countertop, crossing long legs at the ankles.

"Does it? I assure you, that's the least unusual element of being a writer, sergeant. I'm often plagued by insomnia and, during those times, I find writing very cathartic."

"You didn't go riding?"

Phillips sighed inwardly and reminded himself to have a word with Yates about questioning techniques.

"Oh, yes," Armstrong turned to the woman and watched her pupils dilate. "I tend to go for an early morning hack every Saturday. It's one of my little habits. I have quite a few, I'm afraid."

He flashed a smile for Yates' benefit.

"What time was that?"

"Oh, around six o'clock. I left here about twenty minutes' beforehand."

"On foot?"

"No, I drove," he said. "I pay to park my car at one of the smaller visitor's centres down the road so I have the option if I want it. As you can see, there's not much in the way of parking around here."

Phillips prepared to ask a delicate question.

"Can anybody vouch for your whereabouts during the hours of four and six?"

"This is getting very intriguing, sergeant. Perhaps I'll find inspiration for one of my stories," he said, but found no answering smile on the faces of the two police officers who watched him.

"Murder is a very serious matter, Mr Armstrong. I'm sure you can appreciate the difference between fictional crime and the real situations we're faced with."

Armstrong held his hands up.

"I apologise, sergeant. In my business, it's easy to get caught up in the world you create for others and to forget the real world that exists out there. You wanted to know if anybody can vouch for me? I'm afraid not, but I think I have something better."

He sauntered across to his desk at the other end of the room, facing out towards the water. With a few clicks, he brought up the CCTV images and a rotating live feed jumped onto the screen.

"I record everything within the bounds of my property," he told them. "I can provide you with copies of the CCTV which will prove I never left the house until around five-forty, which is when I said I went up to the equestrian centre."

Yates was disposed to feel relief that this tall, charismatic man could be eliminated from their enquiries but Phillips was less easily pleased.

"That would be much appreciated, Mr Armstrong. There's just one more thing. We're asking all local residents for their consent to provide a DNA sample so we can eliminate as many people as possible. Would you be willing to provide us with a sample?"

"No, I'm afraid not."

There was a short, awkward silence.

"May we ask why?"

Armstrong pushed away from the countertop and he was no longer the relaxed writer at home; he was an authoritative man who knew the law and its limits.

"You have no reasonable grounds to request it in the first place. My whereabouts have been accounted for and should be sufficient to eliminate me from your enquiries without the need for any DNA. If you want it, you'll have to go through the proper legal channels and get a court order."

Phillips gave the man a good-humoured smile, as if the refusal made no difference to him whatsoever.

"Thanks for your time, Mr Armstrong. If you could forward the CCTV footage to the e-mail address on this card," he took one from his wallet and laid it on the countertop. "We'd be much obliged."

CHAPTER 19

The evening news was a regurgitation of the lunchtime news and the morning news before that. Ryan listened as he sent an e-mail summary to DCS Lucas—he would never be accused of failing to report to his commanding officer—detailing the progress of Operation Stargazer, as well as three others currently on the books which he had delegated to the other DIs in his wider team. He trusted them to do their jobs because they were all able men and women but that was a concept Lucas would never truly understand.

Trust.

His hands flew over the keyboard and then he clicked 'send' with a decisive stab of his index finger.

The noise of the television in the conference suite at the Inn filtered through and Ryan set aside his laptop to listen. The newscaster's sombre face filled the screen and then the report cut to old footage of himself during the first investigation into *The Hacker*. Some clever media graduate had overlaid the footage with dates and times so the viewing public would be reminded of the chronology of recent investigations in CID, following which the newscaster flew dangerously close to the wind by postulating that one of those killers might also have been responsible for the deaths of Guy Sullivan and Duncan Gray. The footage skipped to Arthur Gregson as he had once been; an imposing man who had possessed enough gravitas to run the Criminal Investigation Department but whose inherent weakness of character had led him to turn away from the very principles he fought to protect.

There seemed to be a never-ending stream of footage but Ryan couldn't bring himself to look away. It was all filler, but to Ryan it was more than just a showreel of names and faces, it was a reminder of everything he'd lived through.

He swore inwardly at the next segment.

"Sources close to the investigation tell us the initial investigation into Duncan Gray's disappearance was led by Detective Sergeant Arthur Gregson, who rose to prominence in later life as Detective Chief Superintendent of Northumbria CID. Following his arrest in 2015, he has been remanded in custody and is awaiting trial while the authorities continue to investigate what has amounted to over thirty years of corruption and criminality. The family of Duncan Gray told this programme in an exclusive interview that they are considering legal action against the Constabulary…"

Right on cue, Ryan's mobile phone began to ring.

"Ryan."

"Did you see the evening news?"

Chief Constable Morrison's voice barked down the line.

"Yes, ma'am."

"What is Phillips doing about it? I assume he's still the SIO on the investigation?"

"Phillips and I are acting as joint SIO," Ryan told her. "DCS Lucas and I came to an agreement about how to direct operations that was acceptable to both of us."

Back in her home office, Morrison wondered what that entailed but that was something to worry about another day.

"I'm pleased to hear it," she said cautiously. "But that still leaves the problem of how to manage the media. Ryan, we've worked bloody hard for over a year to repair the damage Gregson left behind. Now, they're hashing it all up again, then there's the talk of legal action—"

"I want to know who leaked the information about Gregson," Ryan interjected quietly.

He thought of the police staff attached to the investigation but dismissed them almost immediately. He had warned them in no uncertain terms about giving unauthorised information to the press and had been met with affronted faces that told him the thought had never even crossed their minds.

"Could have been the family," Morrison offered. "They must remember Gregson was the person in charge of the investigation back in '81."

Ryan acknowledged that was a possibility, but there were others much closer to home. As always, there was no way to prove that Lucas deliberately set out to put obstacles in their path.

"There's been no suggestion from Duncan Gray's parents that they're considering legal action," he said. "That sounds like speculation."

"All the same, I've spoken to Lucas who says she's ready to step in if you want her to do a press briefing."

"I'll handle it," he said firmly. "There's a better way of getting the message across."

Morrison felt an immediate sense of relief.

"Whatever you do, do it quickly," she muttered.

* * *

When Ryan chose to act, he fell like a lightning bolt.

Within half an hour, he had arranged a town meeting to be held that evening at Kielder Castle, which was a major visitor's centre with sufficient space to house the press and any local people who might choose to attend. As it turned out, Mitch Fenwick was the elected local councillor for the Kielder community in addition to his water-sporting exploits and he was only too happy to help organise and chair the meeting. With those arrangements safely in hand, Ryan put the word out that he would be briefing the locals at seven-thirty and the media were welcome to attend if they wished. That way, he could be satisfied that, to all intents and purposes, the town meeting had not been arranged specifically to meet the needs of the press.

Finally, he put a call through to Angela Gray to issue a personal invitation to the town meeting. Her voice seemed far away on the telephone, with the dreamy quality he associated with an anti-anxiety drugs prescription and Ryan did not hold out much hope for her attendance but at least she made no mention of any pending legal action.

Duncan's father could not be reached.

As he finished his last call, Ryan's staff began filing into the room in time for another five o'clock briefing.

"I could murder a cuppa," Phillips declared, then let out a long whistle of appreciation when he caught sight of the view. "Now, there's a sight for sore eyes."

As the sun set for another day, it left a canvas of pink and red clouds melting into one another in shades of scarlet and cerise. As a prelude to the dawn, it was spectacular.

"My granny used to say, 'Red sky at night, sailor's delight,' " Yates remarked. "Or was it, 'shepherd's'?"

"Either way, it means another day has nearly come and gone," Ryan said. "I've just had Morrison on the phone. I don't know if you caught the news?"

Their awkward faces told him the answer.

"Yeah, well, once again, we're to blame for all society's problems unless we bring this home soon. I've organised a town meeting for seven-thirty and I know we'd all much rather be doing other things but I want to show a united front."

There were nods around the room.

"Good. We couldn't hope to keep this investigation out of the public eye for long but it bears repeating that under no circumstances should any of you talk to the press or even the general public about matters pertaining to the investigation."

Phillips grunted.

"Have somebody's lips been flapping?"

"It's possible, but that doesn't really matter. What matters is that we're making progress to find this arsehole. Tell me some good news, Frank."

Phillips pursed his lips.

"I don't know if I'd say it was good news but, as of around four o'clock, we've now collected DNA swabs from everyone on our list of residents whose whereabouts couldn't be accounted for when Guy Sullivan died. Every one of them, including Craig Hunter, agreed to provide a sample except for Nathan Armstrong."

"The writer guy?" Ryan thought back to his conversation the previous day with Kate Robson, who said he liked to have an early riding lesson on Saturdays. "Is he alibied?"

"He says he has CCTV from his property that shows he never left the house, but we haven't verified that yet."

"And he refused to give a sample?"

"Point blank," Phillips said. "Looked me dead in the eye and told me we'd have to go after a court order if we wanted it."

Ryan leaned back against his desk and folded his arms across his chest.

"Interesting," he said. "I wonder why he's so precious about it?"

"That's exactly what we wondered, so I took the liberty of running a quick background check on Mr Armstrong. Sadly, he's a law-abiding citizen with nothing more than a pop for speeding a couple of years ago."

"Disappointing," Ryan agreed, without any irony. "Let's shelve him for now and turn to Craig Hunter. I'm shocked he agreed to provide a sample."

Phillips linked his fingers across his paunch.

"You and me both, son. That's why I took another liberty and asked Faulkner to expedite the testing of his sample when we sent it through."

Ryan's ears pricked up.

"And?"

"It's negative," Phillips said, and Ryan felt his stomach plummet. If ever a man looked the type to kill and maim, it was Craig Hunter, but it turned out there was no forensic evidence against him.

"What about previous convictions?"

Phillips shook his head.

"Craig Hunter is clean as a whistle," he replied. "Of course, some might say, *too clean*."

Ryan smiled slowly.

"There's no record?"

"Bingo," Phillips said. "There isn't so much as a permanent address listed for Craig Hunter and the bloke's already told us he works mostly cash-in-hand. Could be he's living off the grid."

Ryan nodded and turned to Yates.

"Mel? I want you to dig up whatever you can on Craig Hunter. He might not be connected to Guy Sullivan but…" Ryan gave a self-effacing shrug. "Hell, something just feels *off*. We can't store his DNA but I want you to run it through the system for possible matches. Do it now, please. You never know what skeletons might be rattling in Mr Hunter's wardrobe."

Yates nodded and moved to the back of the room, where she pulled up a chair and began to enter the data onto the system for a full check.

Ryan turned back to Phillips.

"If not Craig Hunter, who are we looking for? Has Faulkner been able to narrow down the search from the hair sample?"

"Ask him yourself," Phillips said, as Faulkner shouldered through the door looking like an Arctic explorer. His hair stuck out at odd angles, whether as a product of restless fingers or because of the blustery wind buffeting outside. His feet were encased in heavy-duty walking boots which shook the floor as he tramped across the room and he wore thick all-weather gloves that doubled the size of his actual handspan.

"Perfect timing," Ryan told him.

Faulkner threw off his heavy winter coat to reveal waterproof khakis, a fleece and a clipboard

"Trainspotters Anonymous is down the hall," Phillips joked.

"Ha bloody ha," Faulkner said. "I happen to be well versed in the ways of country life and I know it's better to come prepared for the worst."

"Still seein' that gardener lass, then?" Phillips enquired, before popping a stick of chewing gum into his mouth.

Faulkner shuffled in his seat but couldn't quite hide the grin.

"We went out for a walk along Hadrian's Wall last weekend," he admitted.

"Y' old hound dawg," Phillips hooted. "Hope you took her out for dinner afterwards. It's awful hungry work, hiking up those hills."

The last statement was followed by a suggestive wriggle of his bushy eyebrows while Faulkner made a show of taking off and folding his gloves.

"Ah, I'm working up to the full three-course meal."

"Good lad."

Ryan waited until their exchange wound up before bringing the conversation back to the point.

"Much as we're interested in your love life, Tom, what we really want to know is what you can tell us about the hair you found on Guy Sullivan's body. Phillips tells us there's no match with Craig Hunter."

Faulkner nodded.

"He's right. There's no match with Craig Hunter, or any man, in fact."

Ryan's brow furrowed.

"You mean the hair belongs to a woman?"

"Exactly."

"How sure can you be?"

Faulkner shoved his glasses further up his nose, to give himself a second to think about it.

"I'm never going to be able to say I'm 100% sure on any of the work that we do," he said, fairly. "The unique DNA found on this strand of hair didn't flag on any of our systems, so I can tell you I'm fairly certain it's new on our radar. The hair sample was contaminated with blood and other bodily fluids, but we isolated those belonging to the victim and separated them from the alien hair follicle. After that, we try to narrow down the search by identifying gender, but it's not as easy as it sounds. We look at the sex chromosome to see if there are two X chromosomes which would signify female but, to do that, we test for a negative. In other words, we tested for the presence of a Y-chromosome and as there wasn't one present, we have to assume the hair follicle belonged to a female."

Faulkner paused to rub his eyes. It had been a long day at the lab and he was starting to feel the effects of staring through a microscope for several hours at a time.

"There is always a margin of error," he admitted. "But I'm as sure as I can be. You need to look for a woman. I've got technicians working around the clock to process the samples sent through today and we should be in a position to rule out the students—"

Just then, his mobile began to shrill out a tinny rendition of *Smooth Criminal.*

"That's the lab," he muttered, and hurried from the room to take the call.

"While Faulkner's dealing with that, where are we at with the traffic cordons?"

Ryan turned to the local police sergeant, who gave him a rundown. All cars entering and leaving the checkpoints set up around the forest had been noted, including registration plates and times of entry or exit.

"Thanks. In light of what Faulkner's told us, do we have any women on the list of residents whose whereabouts are unaccounted for?"

Phillips opened his mouth to answer but swallowed his words as Faulkner walked back into the room looking thoroughly dejected.

Ryan noticed the man's facial expression immediately.

"Spit it out, Tom."

Faulkner gave him an apologetic look.

"We've found a match."

"But—"

Faulkner shook his head.

"The hair follicle belongs to Isabella Lombardo, one of Guy Sullivan's fellow students."

"And she's fully alibied," Phillips threw in.

Ryan said nothing but wished he could kick something. Hard.

Instead, he pinched the bridge of his nose and then stalked over to the murder board to look at the victims' faces. It was an odd thing, but their faces gave him the strength to carry on regardless.

"So our star piece of forensic evidence ain't so hot, after all," he said to the room at large. "Luckily, I like a challenge. Faulkner? What else have you got for me?"

"We're still analysing most of the samples we took—we're working flat out—but some initial findings have come back from the murder weapon. The rock we found not far from the body was covered in Sullivan's brain matter but we also found some tiny leather fibres. Best guess would be that our killer wore gloves. Brown ones," he added.

"And the tracks?"

"You're looking for a shoe size somewhere between a seven and a ten, although the imprints suggest a tracked sole that could denote a running shoe, a wellington boot or some other kind of boot. In that case, people sometimes buy a size bigger."

Ryan almost laughed.

"So, you're telling me our perp is either a woman with an above-average shoe size or a man with a small-to-average shoe size?"

"I'm afraid so."

Ryan ran a frustrated hand through his hair and thought of how he would tell the local population and regional press that they had absolutely no new leads. That was bound to inspire faith in their profession, he thought caustically.

He turned back to the room and looked around the faces of the police staff who waited for his next instruction.

"Alright, this is what we're going to do. Nobody has forgotten about Duncan Gray but, for the present, we need to prioritise finding Guy Sullivan's killer who may still be active. That won't wash well with the press, but we don't have another twenty pairs of hands and I can't pull any more money out of my arse," he said, eloquently. "We're stretched to the limit as it is, so, without a sample to work from, the DNA testing isn't strictly necessary any more. Let's keep the samples in storage until the end of the investigation, okay Tom?"

"Understood," he said. "That'll free up time to work on the trace evidence we found at the crime scene."

"Good. Let me know if anything new turns up. Phillips? I want every witness re-interviewed and deep background checks on every person in the vicinity—not just those within a five-mile radius and not just those without an alibi. Somebody could be covering for them and we need to flush them out."

Having completed the processes for entering Craig Hunter's DNA onto the mainframe to see if there was a match with any unsolved crimes, Yates resumed her seat at the front of the room.

"Sir? Are we expanding the net?"

"Damn right we are, Yates. Get ready to go fishing in a bloody big pond."

CHAPTER 20

At precisely the same moment MacKenzie reached for the bottle of chilled white wine sitting lonely in her fridge, an automated e-mail *pinged* on her smartphone. After returning from a very enjoyable day out with her friend, she had been toying with the idea of treating herself to a quiet night in with a good book until Frank came home.

But it was not to be.

She brought up the e-mail and read its contents, then re-read it a second time in case her eyes were deceiving her.

A match.

All thoughts of books and pyjamas disappeared as she grabbed her coat and scurried back to her car. There would be nobody in the office from the Cold Cases Team; they worked sociable, nine-to-five hours and the recent lack of new leads had lulled them into a state of apathy. But if the automated e-mail was correct, MacKenzie was about to shake them out of their self-imposed stupor with a vengeance.

Twenty minutes later, she burst through the main doors of Police Headquarters with barely an acknowledgement for the duty sergeant who was dealing with the usual motley assortment of D&Ds, assaults and mobile phone thefts that defined a regular Sunday evening. Motion-activated lighting flickered on as she made her way down the central corridor towards her office and MacKenzie threw her bag on the floor in her haste to fire up the computer.

"Come on, come on," she muttered, never having felt so impatient in her life.

Finally, the system finished loading and she brought up the internal database to see whose name had flagged as a match for two of the six priority cold cases she'd identified the previous day, as well as five or six more possible victims that were linked by similar MO.

MacKenzie's heart hammered as she clicked through the necessary steps until she was presented with a name.

Craig Hunter.

But it wasn't that which made MacKenzie's eyes widen.

It was the name of the police officer who had entered his DNA onto the system, less than an hour ago.

Police Constable Melanie Yates, CID.

"Gotcha," she breathed, and scrambled for her phone to put an urgent call through to her colleague.

* * *

Kielder Castle was a stately eighteenth-century former hunting lodge of the Duke of Northumberland which housed permanent exhibitions about the forest, birds and night sky for the benefit of visitors to the region from its central position in the middle of Kielder Village. The building sat atop an ancient burial ground dating back to 3000 BC and, to take advantage of such marvellous good fortune, the castle also ran ghost hunts where tourists could stay overnight and frighten themselves with the prospect of meeting a malevolent spirit. But as the sun slipped away and blood-red uplighters illuminated the castle walls, the crowds gathered to hear about another kind of malevolent force, one that was still very much alive.

Ryan stood inside the main exhibition space on a hastily-erected platform so that he might be seen and heard by the people who turned out. At best, he had anticipated fifty or sixty residents, but as the clock struck seven-thirty he estimated over a hundred and fifty people were in attendance, not including the row of journalists he recognised by sight. Standing beside him, Mitch Fenwick had left behind his usual cut-off shorts and bright blue work jacket in favour of a more serious uniform of grey suit and matching tie.

"Nearly there, I reckon," he murmured to Ryan. "Shall we get started?"

Ryan glanced over his shoulder to check his team were in place.

"We're ready," he said.

Fenwick stepped up to a microphone and tapped it with one broad finger, which resounded around the speaker system with a loud, electronic whine.

"Sorry folks, let me just fiddle with the volume... Okay, that's better." He gave them all a friendly smile and launched into an eloquent introduction that had Ryan swiftly re-evaluating the man.

While Fenwick spoke of the recent tragedies and thanked the police, forestry workers and other volunteers for their swift action, Ryan studied the faces of those who had arrived early enough to grab a front-row seat. The primary function of the meeting was to satisfy his Chief Constable, the local press and residents who may be living in fear, but there was an additional advantage to events such as these. It enabled Ryan to take note of those who turned up to bask in the spotlight or, conversely, those who took pains to avoid it. It was a well-established tenet of criminal psychology that killers could seldom resist the lure of their own crimes. Often, they returned to the scene of their crime, came along to press briefings or purported to help the police in other ways, to remain connected with their act of violence and continue to draw pleasure from it. And so, Ryan studied the faces looking up at him, taking a mental snapshot of the audience.

At the front of the room, journalists sat with hand-held tape recorders and notepads balanced precariously on their knees while their cameramen stood at the sides capturing every word on film. In the second row, Ryan spotted Angela Gray beside another woman of the same age who might have been her sister or a friend. A little further along, Freddie Milburn was seated amongst a crowd of locals. There were more faces Ryan didn't recognise but assumed belonged to the wider local population and he spotted Michaela Collingwood near the back of the room standing next to Anna, who gave him a knowing smile as his eyes tracked over her face and their eyes locked.

At the very end of the row, Nathan Armstrong stood with a takeaway coffee cup in his hand talking to another one of the locals. Just before Ryan was called forward to the mic, Kate Robson let herself into the room and managed to find a perch at the back.

Craig Hunter was nowhere to be seen.

"…I'll hand over to Detective Chief Inspector Ryan, who is going to give us an update on the investigation and, hopefully, put our minds at rest."

Ryan took a step forward but was diverted by the sound of Yates' mobile phone ringing loudly somewhere over his left shoulder and she fumbled to turn it off, blushing furiously until the sound cut out.

"Sorry," she mouthed.

The look of mortification on her face was so priceless, he almost laughed. Instead, he turned to face the crowd with an air of authority, eyes narrowing in the glare of four or five bright camera lights.

"Thank you to Councillor Fenwick for his introduction and for arranging this meeting at such short notice," Ryan began. "I'm grateful to all of you for your attendance and for your patience and support during our investigation, which remains ongoing."

He cast calm grey eyes around the room, making as many personal connections as possible in the circumstances.

"I want to express our heartfelt sadness and condolences to the families of Duncan Gray and Guy Sullivan." He sought Angela Gray's eyes and spoke directly to her. "I want to reassure them that we, the Northumbria Criminal Investigation Department, are doing everything in our power to find the person or persons responsible for such devastation."

There was complete silence in the room, punctuated by a few nodding heads. Angela gave him the merest hint of a smile, the kind of smile he recognised as a product of medication, and his heart contracted.

"As you will have noticed, traffic cordons have been in place for over twenty-four hours monitoring anybody entering or leaving the

Kielder Forest area. This is a safety measure and we ask for your continued patience. If you plan to leave the area, we would welcome advance notification whilst the cordons are in place so that your onward journey can be achieved as smoothly as possible."

Predictably, there were a few eye-rolls, which he ignored.

"Aye, but what's being done to catch the killer? My missus is too scared to leave the house!"

One of the locals in his late twenties interrupted Ryan's speech, clearly unfazed by the usual running order of a town meeting.

Ryan turned to answer him directly.

"All available evidence is being rigorously tested for forensic leads and we are in the process of checking statements provided by you and your neighbours," Ryan said. "At present, there is no reason to think the two murders are connected. We advise you to continue life as normal but not to go out walking alone. In addition, we are imposing a curfew until further notice."

That brought angry gasps from the local population.

"A *curfew*? We're not kids!"

"No," Ryan agreed. "You're not. Which is why I'm sure you will understand and appreciate the need for safety measures. The curfew will be in place for the next forty-eight hours, following which we will review the situation. Until that time, we ask you to return to your homes by ten-thirty and not to leave the house before five o'clock in the morning unless it is by prior arrangement."

"And, if we don't?"

Heads swivelled towards Nathan Armstrong and Ryan gave the man a hard, unyielding stare.

"You will be escorted home," he said flatly. "No exceptions. If you refuse to comply, you will be arrested on suspicion of obstructing the course of an investigation."

Armstrong raised his takeaway cup in the parody of a toast.

"Any other questions?"

* * *

After fielding a barrage of enquiries, Ryan stepped down from the podium and escaped into an adjoining room to catch his breath.

"Phew," Phillips exclaimed. "Good work out there, lad. Came across like a steady pair of hands."

Ryan lifted his hands and shook them wildly, for the laughs.

"I'm sorry about my phone going off," Yates said quietly. "I don't know how I could have forgotten to mute the sound."

Ryan gave her a friendly smile.

"Don't let it eat you up, there are worse things to happen in life. Who was it, anyway?"

She took out her phone and frowned at the caller list.

"Seven calls from Denise," she said.

"Aye, and I've got another five missed calls on mine," Phillips added, all trace of humour vanishing as his mind began to conjure up worst case scenarios.

Just then, Ryan's phone began to vibrate in the pocket of his coat.

"Denise? What—"

There was absolute silence in the room as they watched the changing emotions on Ryan's face.

"His name is Craig Hunter," Ryan said, and the others exchanged curious glances. "Address is Ivy Cottage, Adderburn." *Another pause.* "Do you want to do it tonight? Alright. Get your team together and meet us at the conference centre at Kielder Waterside as soon as you can."

Ryan ended the call and began to shrug back into his coat, already planning the next steps as he updated his team.

"Craig Hunter's DNA flagged as a match for two of MacKenzie's cold cases," he told them. "With a further five or six possible matches based on similar MO. She's on her way here now to make the arrest. In the meantime, let's get this place locked down."

Yates looked at Phillips with a mixture of excitement and shock.

"Told you Hunter was a wrong 'un," he muttered, and they hurried to keep up with Ryan's long strides.

CHAPTER 21

The roads were closed quickly and quietly, under cover of darkness.

Police were stationed at traffic checkpoints and additional numbers were temporarily drafted in from neighbouring police stations to ensure Hunter did not try to escape via one of the smaller country roads. Ryan insisted there be no flashing lights or howling sirens to alert their quarry and, once that was done, the police gathered in their temporary headquarters at Kielder Waterside to plan their approach.

"Craig Hunter is a major flight risk so the quicker we get this done, the better," Ryan began. "How do you want to run this, Mac?"

MacKenzie stepped forward to address the packed room.

"I agree we should make everything as quick and painless as possible," she said, and was pleased there was no hint of the nerves she felt jangling in her stomach. Earlier in the year, she had almost died in a forest like Kielder. She'd suffered months of traumatic flashbacks and night terrors and she suspected they would continue to blight her life for years to come.

But despite all that, she was standing in front of a crowded room of police staff doing the job she loved. It gave her strength to know that her ordeal had not cost her the thing she valued most: her identity.

"Ryan and I will make the approach with Support Team A in the wings," she said. "Phillips and Yates, I want you stationed here, ready to liaise with tactical support if that becomes necessary."

Phillips nodded his assent. On the one hand, he felt a deep and abiding admiration for the woman who had, miraculously, agreed to become his wife in a few short months. He loved every inch of her, from the top of her shining red hair to the toes of her scuffed boots and would always rather be at her side. But that was only half the story. At home, they were equals, but at work, Detective Inspector Denise MacKenzie was his superior officer.

"Is that all clear?" MacKenzie asked.

"Yes ma'am," Phillips said meekly.

* * *

Hunter heard a car engine approaching and fell onto his haunches at the edge of the trees, quietly offloading the string of pheasants he'd poached so that he could listen unencumbered. Their gamey scent rose from the earthen ground as he crouched at the edge of the clearing, poised to run. The dog snuffled beside him and he gave it a warning sound, low in his throat, which had it whimpering softly until its belly hit the floor.

The sound of the engine grew louder until the car emerged and, this time, he could see the pigs had brought a squad car.

They knew.

His eyes glistened in the moonlight as he watched them walk around the car and knock on the door to his cottage, shaking their heads and peering through the windows.

The dog made a small bark, impossibly loud in the silent evening, and Hunter's reaction was instant.

He took it by the neck and twisted until there was a sharp *snap*.

The animal didn't even put up a fight.

Stupid dog.

He turned back to see if the police had been alerted to his presence. The pig-man was walking around the side of the house, checking the perimeter to see if anybody was inside, while the pig-woman waited and looked around the clearing. For a moment, it seemed she might have seen him and he reached slowly for the shotgun hanging from a leather strap on his shoulder and trained it directly at her chest. His finger hovered above the trigger as he watched, and he had begun to squeeze it when the woman's eyes passed over him.

Hunter let out a shaky breath, lowered the shotgun and tried to think.

It was better not to kill them here because there would be swarms of police coming after him and he needed time to get away. That would be a problem; he couldn't take his truck and, even if he could, the roads were blocked. There were basic supplies in his backpack but very little money and no passport or driving licence. As a matter of fact, he hadn't owned an up-to-date driving licence or passport since he'd changed his name from Bobby Jepson to Craig Hunter, ten years earlier.

"He's not here," he heard Ryan say.

"Might be at the pub, or visiting someone," the redhead suggested. "We can put a surveillance detail on the house in case he comes back."

Time to go.

Hunter melted back into the forest, as silently as he had come.

* * *

Ryan and MacKenzie lingered beside the empty stone cottage, wishing the law allowed them to force entry without a search warrant. There was a sinister stillness to the trees as night rapidly descended and the sky was no longer a bold reddish-purple but a deep, ink blue speckled with stars.

Ryan turned to look over his shoulder, his ears detecting some small movement on the far side of the clearing.

"What is it?" MacKenzie whispered.

"I don't know," he replied. "I thought I heard something over there."

He reached for his torch and shone it against the trees lining the perimeter of the clearing, trying to peer through the darkness to see if his mind was playing tricks on him.

"Let's have a look," he murmured, then stopped short and turned to look searchingly at her face. "You alright, Mac?"

She didn't bother to ask what he meant. It was a reasonable question given recent history, and, if she was being completely honest, the woods were the last place she'd choose to be. But this was a matter of pride.

"I will be" she said, and let that be enough.

Ryan understood what she was working through and trusted her to know her own limitations, so he merely nodded and moved forward.

Together, they walked the perimeter of the clearing, shining their torches as they went.

"Here," Ryan said dully, and shone a light on the small graveyard of animals Hunter had left behind.

"Coward," she said, looking down at the pitiful remains.

Ryan took out his police radio and made an urgent order for tactical support, gave the ordnance map coordinates and warned non-tactical members of staff not to approach anyone matching Craig Hunter's description as he may be armed and dangerous.

Once that was done, Ryan stormed back across the clearing where he started rifling inside one of the tumbledown sheds to the side of Hunter's cottage.

MacKenzie joined him.

"What are you doing?"

Ryan found a shovel with a squeaky handle and closed a gloved fist around it.

"I'm burying the dog," he snapped, then stormed back across the clearing. MacKenzie watched him with an almost maternal affection, understanding very clearly that the small act of senseless cruelty represented something greater in Ryan's mind. Killing a dog was the act of someone who was no longer civilised; no longer someone to be reasoned with or answerable to man's laws. It was a watershed moment in their understanding of Craig Hunter's psychology and so, despite the urgency, she waited while Ryan finished digging the small grave with swift, capable hands.

A few minutes later, he returned with a face like thunder.

"Let's go," he said.

* * *

Four miles west of Adderburn, Kate Robson made her final checks of the stables before turning in for the evening. Thanks to a colicky mare, she'd spent much of the previous evening and most of the day consulting with the local vet and trying to soothe the poor animal. Then, there was the question of whether to loan out the Arabian—

There was a clattering sound across the yard and she paused with her hand on *Dodger*'s mane.

"Shh," she warned him. "Quiet, now, boy."

There it came again.

Carefully, she opened the stall gate and walked around the edge of the cobblestones, keeping to the side of the farmhouse wall. Over the years, she'd encountered the odd vagrant or young kid trying to lift a few pieces of expensive equipment or even to steal one of the horses and she'd dealt with it. Living alone had its benefits and usually with the horses for company she didn't feel too isolated.

But now, she was terrified.

Her eyes were wide as she felt her way towards the back door of the house and her hand grasped the handle as one of the stall doors swung open. She squinted through the darkness and saw a figure.

With a gasp, she twisted the handle and rushed inside the house.

* * *

When Ryan returned to the Incident Room, the place was a hive of activity. Groups of police officers scrutinized maps of the area and listened to a local Forestry Officer giving them a crash course on the complex network of non-public forestry roads and tracks running through the forest that might afford Craig Hunter another means of escape. Two analysts from the local station manned the telephones and sifted through the inevitable slush pile of nuisance calls that had been coming through in a steady stream following the day's press coverage.

Ryan spotted Phillips standing across the room barking down the telephone to some unlucky person or another.

"I don't give a monkey's if it's inconvenient! If you don't pull your finger out of your arse, there'll be hell to pay!"

With that, he slammed the phone down and caught Ryan watching him with the hint of a smile.

"Somebody trying to help you reclaim PPI insurance?" he asked sweetly.

"I'm tellin' you, that jobsworth couldn't organise a piss-up in a brewery," Phillips exploded, pointing an accusatory finger towards the inanimate plastic handset as if it were to blame. "I've just been on to some lad in the Border Police and he had the bloody *nerve* to tell me it was an inconvenient time for there to be a manhunt! I ask you, did you ever hear such a load of old bollocks?"

Ryan's lips twitched.

"*Then*, he tells me they're dealing with a lot of drink-related crime this evening and could I call back tomorrow morning," Phillips continued. "Craig Hunter'll be gone by the morning!"

"And you, of course, politely explained to him that he had failed to grasp the urgency of the situation," Ryan said.

"I told him he was a bloody moron and, if he didn't start behaving like a policeman, I'd be straight on to his senior officer and he'd find himself facing a disciplinary for incompetence!"

On that final note, Phillips took a deep, shuddering breath.

"Feel better?" Ryan enquired, after a couple of seconds passed.

"Aye," Phillips muttered, blinking around the room as if he'd just come out of a fugue state. "Where's Denise?"

"She's gone to find Anna," Ryan said. "It's unsafe for her to be alone in the lodge while Hunter is at large. I've spoken to the Forestry

Commission and they're going to help put the word out that people should stay inside and lock their doors, too."

But as Anna and MacKenzie entered the room, one of the telephone operatives waved him across.

Ryan took the receiver.

"This is DCI Ryan. Who am I speaking to?"

"Chief Inspector, it's Kate Robson," she said, trying to keep the wobble from her voice. "You said—you said I should call you if I had anything to report."

"And do you?"

"Y-yes," she said, telling herself to keep it together. "I think there's a prowler up here. I saw a figure in the yard outside and I'm scared—"

"When did this happen?" Ryan cut in, signalling for MacKenzie, who hurried across the room.

"About five minutes ago," she said. "I think he's still around and I'm frightened. Please hurry!"

"Alright, Kate, stay put and lock your doors. We'll be there as soon as we can."

"Yes, alright."

CHAPTER 22

"That was perfect."

Roly put the telephone down and put shaking hands to her face.

"The police are on their way," she muttered and wrung her hands as she stared down at the receiver. "What are you going to do?"

"What I always do," came the reply. "Take care of your mess. You did the right thing, calling me before the police."

"How? How does this help us?"

As she turned, the heavy underside of a copper pan smashed into her jaw with a sickening crack of bone. The force of it sent her crashing back against the kitchen table while blood began to gush from her nose and mouth.

"It doesn't really help you," her friend replied, conversationally, as her body slid from the table and fell to the floor like a rag doll.

The toe of a boot slid beneath her ribcage and flipped her over so she found herself looking into the face of a childhood friend, as Duncan Gray had done so many years before. But there were no stars to ease her passing, no promise of divine intervention to ease the pain of betrayal.

There was only the brief flash of metal as the pan raised again and crashed into her skull one final time.

* * *

Ryan blithely ignored the speed limit signs as he raced along the single-track lane towards *Hot Trots*, this time with MacKenzie riding shotgun and Phillips and Yates in the back. While they battled valiantly against motion sickness, a van followed behind with a team of four sniffer-dogs and a bag of clothing taken from Hunter's truck to help them pick up a scent.

Lights shone from the windows of the farmhouse up ahead and Ryan stopped the car just outside the yard. They made their way towards the back entrance, expecting to find Kate Robson ready to let them in, but instead they found the door standing wide open.

Ryan held up an arm to indicate that they should proceed with caution.

"Ms Robson! This is the police! We are entering the property now!"

Cautiously, he took a step inside the boot room and then made his way through to the kitchen, following his nose. Outside, the Canine Unit had caught the scent of blood, too, and began to whine and bark.

He found Kate Robson lying on her kitchen floor in a cruciform formation, her arms spread wide. One side of her face showed the evidence of blunt trauma and a heavy copper pan stood proudly on the kitchen table, advertising its exploits.

"Poor woman," MacKenzie breathed.

"We were too late," Ryan said quietly. "She called us for help and we were too late."

Before MacKenzie could offer any kind of platitude, Ryan stepped back to allow Phillips and Yates space to take in the scene while he called it in. He stood in the yard outside until his team re-joined him and they huddled around to wait for the CSIs to arrive while the dogs tried to detect Craig Hunter's scent amongst a multitude of others on the wind.

"One of the horses is missing," Ryan said, and they followed his line of sight towards the empty stall at the end of the row. "Hunter probably came here for transportation and petty cash."

"He's out of control," Phillips said. "If he'll kill a woman for a horse, there's no telling what else he might do."

"He's already wanted for several murders," MacKenzie pointed out. "It doesn't get much worse than that."

"They're not having any luck," Yates pointed out, looking across at the Canine Unit. "They've been trying for fifteen minutes now."

Ryan folded his arms and thought of Craig Hunter, who was putting more and more distance between himself and the police with every wasted moment.

"What's the quickest route to the Scottish border from here?"

Phillips pulled out his map and Yates shone her torch light so they could see.

"He knows he can't take the roads," MacKenzie said. "They're cordoned off at every major exit and there are patrol cars running back and forth. It'd be risky to take the forestry roads, too, because the rangers are patrolling those. He's smart enough to know that his best bet is to go cross-country."

"Here," Ryan said, tracing his finger along a red-dashed line. "What's this?"

"The Bloody Bush Trail," Phillips read out. "The guide here says it's a difficult mountain biking trail, but it's a trail nonetheless."

"It starts near the end of the lower field," Ryan said, pointing a finger out into the formidable darkness.

"We should tell the 4x4 team and let them know," Phillips said.

Ryan walked along the line of stalls until he found the one he was looking for. As if she'd been expecting him, the mare he'd seen the other day popped her head out and butted him gently in welcome.

"You do that, Frank, but they'll tell you the trail is inaccessible to vehicles. There are rock faces and narrow gorges that a 4x4 couldn't handle—but a well-trained horse certainly could."

"We could wait for the helicopters to track his heat," Phillips said, already having guessed what Ryan planned to do.

"There are thousands of acres of land to cover. With every passing minute, we're losing precious time and increasing the probability that Hunter will kill again. I don't want that on my conscience, Frank, not when I'm an experienced rider and we need somebody on the ground."

Even as he spoke the words, Ryan told himself that he would soon find out whether riding a horse was just like riding a bike. But before he began to saddle up the mare, he paused to look at MacKenzie. It remained unspoken, but this portion of the investigation belonged to her new Cold Cases Team just as much as it belonged to his.

"What do you say, Mac?"

She weighed up the pros and cons but, ultimately, agreed with the logic.

"It makes sense," MacKenzie pronounced. "I'll let the tactical team know. Stay in radio contact and don't approach."

"Yes, ma'am," Ryan said, with a grin.

MacKenzie's eyes narrowed and she nodded towards a powerful looking black stallion braying in a neighbouring stall.

"Don't you want to ride that one? He'll be faster."

Ryan looked across at the sleek black horse, then into the chocolate brown eyes of the Welsh cob standing beside him.

He must have a weakness for brown-eyed women.

A carved nameplate next to the stall told him her name was Mathilda. It was true that a thoroughbred would be faster across open ground but he needed a sure-footed, reliable horse that didn't mind cold weather.

"No, I think Mathilda and I will do just fine together."

A couple of minutes later, he'd saddled the horse and with one smooth motion, he propelled himself onto her back.

"Howay man, you can't go on your own," Phillips called out, and to their shared surprise began muttering endearments to another sturdy-looking horse in a neighbouring stall. "There, sweetheart, you don't mind if we go and see the stars, do you?"

He opened the stall doors to a chorus of *"No!"* and with a supreme effort, he used a nearby bench to boost himself up onto its bare back—before promptly sliding off the other side.

"For God's sake, Frank, stand aside before you do yourself an injury," MacKenzie muttered.

Phillips bristled as MacKenzie reached for a saddle and deftly began strapping it onto the horse's back.

"Do you know how—?"

The rest of the question died on his tongue as MacKenzie gave him a withering stare, took a fistful of the horse's mane and swung herself up.

The horses whinnied and they all turned at the sound of the dogs becoming restless, somewhere out in the fields.

"I think they've got something," Yates said, and handed them a couple of riding hats. "Safety first."

"Be careful," Phillips said.

MacKenzie leaned down in her saddle to bestow a quick kiss on Phillips' upturned face, then looked across at Ryan.

"You ready?"

As MacKenzie urged her horse out of the yard with a clatter of hooves, Ryan spared one last word for Phillips.

"You know, if I wasn't already married to the greatest woman on earth, I want you to know I'd be seriously considering making a play for Denise MacKenzie right now."

"Aye, and if I wasn't such a peace-loving man, I'd be seriously considering planting my fist in your pretty face, lad."

Ryan laughed and with a gentle flex of his thighs, he and Mathilda disappeared into the night.

* * *

That had been close.

Too close.

Only once the door was firmly locked and the curtains drawn was it possible to let out a long, self-satisfied laugh. The poetry of the situation was most pleasing of all; a collision of circumstances that provided the perfect opportunity to say farewell to an old friend who had long outstayed her welcome, like the dinner guest who never went home or the fungal infection that never quite cleared up.

The feeling of release was euphoric; the elation indescribable.

Free *at* *last.*

CHAPTER 23

The air in the forest was thick and heavily scented with pine as Hunter followed the narrow bike trail through the trees. His eyes had almost adjusted to the darkness and he seemed to have picked a decent horse because it trod carefully across the stony path and only skidded a couple of times when the trail dipped downhill. It was like being on a ghost train at the fairground, unable to see where the car was hurtling and feeling branches brush against his skin like cold fingers, but he knew these woods and felt no fear.

Plus, he hadn't come across a single living soul since he'd almost floored a pair of idiot cyclists who were bedding down for the night on a patch of ground near Little Burn. He couldn't be sure if they'd seen his face but it had been dark and he hadn't stopped to let them catch a better look.

Once he reached the main trail, Hunter dragged the horse by the bridle down the steep section towards the small burn and went upstream to make it look as though he was heading north, towards the observatory. Then, after a quarter-mile of forcing the horse through icy water, he turned around and retraced their steps.

That would confuse the dogs.

He wasn't stupid. There were bound to be dogs, maybe even helicopters, but he hadn't heard any choppers flying overhead so he guessed they weren't even close to knowing where he was. Hunter smiled to himself and gave the horse another nudge when it protested at the next incline.

* * *

Ryan and MacKenzie kept pace with the sniffer dogs for the first half-mile as they strained against their handlers' leads and shook with excitement. Now and then, they stopped to stick their noses inside a bag of Hunter's clothes to be reminded of his scent but they led the police to the far corner of Kate Robson's property without any trouble and then veered north until they reached the edge of Little Burn running through the valley below.

Ryan and MacKenzie dismounted and secured their horses, then used their torches to pick their way down through the trees until they reached the water's edge. There, a gap in the trees overhanging the burn allowed the moon to shine a pearly white light over their surroundings.

"Which way?" Ryan asked.

The sergeant from the Canine Unit shook his head.

"They've lost the scent," he replied, watching the dogs. "We'll split them up into pairs and check either side of the riverbank to see if it helps."

Ryan and MacKenzie waited while the handlers walked along the high reeds lining the banks of the burn, stopping regularly to allow the dogs to sniff Hunter's clothing.

But still, it was no good. One of the dogs barked and strained in one direction, only to stop and quiver then turn in a full circle and come back again.

"I think he was here, guv, but we don't know which direction he took," one of the handlers called out.

"He had to go through the water," MacKenzie murmured, watching the moon shimmering on the burn. "He probably doubled back on himself because he knew it would confuse the dogs."

"And waste our time, in the process," Ryan added, thinking of the surrounding geography. "This direction leads north, back towards civilisation. If Hunter has any sense, he'll head towards Scotland, which is west of here if you take the trail."

MacKenzie looked back up to where the horses waited on higher ground. Behind them, an open expanse of mossy fields connected to the Bloody Bush Trail skirting through the trees, up and over the hills until it met with the Scottish Border.

During the day, it was difficult terrain but at night, it was nothing short of treacherous.

"Let's go," she said.

* * *

Three miles west of their position, Hunter led his exhausted horse up another rocky incline and when the animal stumbled again he was forced to accept it was time to take a short break. He'd hoped to put more distance between himself and the police but, since he hadn't heard any helicopters yet, he began to think they hadn't even noticed he was missing.

He'd assumed Kate Robson would get straight onto the coppers after she'd seen him stealing the horse, but maybe she decided to cut him a break or else assumed he was only borrowing it.

She never had been the sharpest tool in the box.

Not to mention frigid. She'd turned him down several times, as if he wasn't good enough for her.

Bitch.

Just for that, he gave the horse another good kick and was angry when it came to a complete stop.

"Howay, man, y' lazy brute!"

But the horse would go no further.

For a moment, he was tempted to kill it but he managed to control the impulse. He would need the horse for the rest of his journey, so there was no sense in killing the animal.

Yet.

Hunter peered through the trees on either side of the trail and calculated roughly how far he had come. By his judgment, he was still around six miles shy of the border but he was making good progress.

He steered the horse off the trail and into the trees, out of sight.

* * *

Phillips and Yates returned to the incident room at Kielder Waterside to find a maelstrom of activity. Some thoughtful person—probably Anna—had made a mountain of sandwiches for the mixed group of forestry staff, local police, volunteers from mountain search and rescue, and tactical support teams who had fallen upon the stack of bread and cheese like wild animals. Now, they milled in their respective groups and there was a constant buzz of police chatter as they argued over the next steps.

Although there had been very little time in which to muster the full-scale resources they would usually deploy for a manhunt, Phillips had to admit that the local response had been exemplary. A dozen officers with specialist firearms training were on their way in armoured vehicles from Northumbria Police Headquarters but army officers from the nearby military training camp at Otterburn had beaten them to it and were closing in from the north, south and east while their cohorts across the border awaited Hunter to the west. There was a lot of ground to cover on foot but they were equipped with night-vision goggles and, cloaked by the forest, military-trained personnel would move like swift shadows.

Phillips shrugged out of his coat and made a grab for one of the sandwiches before they were all snaffled.

"Any word on air support?" he asked the tactical team leader, between bites.

The woman nodded.

"There's an RAF GR4 tornado jet on its way from the base at Marham. It's fitted with infrared cameras with heat-seeking technology. The helicopter would have to come from Humberside Airport, which would take too long."

Phillips nodded his approval.

"What about the residents? Have we had any more sightings?"

"None whatsoever. The local police have made house-to-house calls to warn people to remain indoors and have evacuated three houses within a five-mile radius of the Bloody Bush Trail, for safety.

There's a couple of officers stationed back at Hunter's cottage, just in case he's crafty and tries to double back home to collect his vehicle or supplies."

"Good to cover all bases," Phillips agreed. "Are the media aware?"

The team leader pulled a face.

"Somebody must have tipped them off," she said. "The regional news channels were reporting a manhunt less than thirty minutes after Kate Robson's body was discovered, and now the nationals have picked up the story about another murder and there being a manhunt underway."

Yates looked across at the wall-mounted television and watched the silent news broadcast.

"Will this hinder us?" she asked. "What if they tip him off?"

"Unlikely," Phillips said. "Hunter's out there in the wilderness, so he's not going to be getting news updates, even if they did have anything useful to report."

"That's a point," Yates said brightly. "Has anybody checked to see if Hunter's mobile phone is still transmitting?"

Phillips smiled.

"Now you're getting the hang of this, aren't you?" He called over one of the intelligence analysts, who darted across the room with an energy Phillips could only admire. "We need to run a search on Hunter's phone to see if it's still transmitting. He might have taken it apart and dumped it—that'd be the smart thing to do—but in the heat of the moment it's easy to forget the simple things. Let us know if you have any luck triangulating a signal."

The analyst nodded and raced back to his desk.

Anna spotted them both and wove through the crowded room, feeling oddly at home in an environment that would have seemed alien three years before.

"I heard you found another body at the equestrian centre and there's a man on the run. Where's Ryan? Is he in one of the 4x4s?"

Anna looked expectantly between them, then held up a hand as the silence became awkward.

"Don't tell me, let me guess. Ryan decided to go off into the woods on foot?"

Phillips pursed his lips.

"You're close."

"On a mountain bike?"

"Getting warmer."

"On…horseback?"

"Got it in one."

Anna folded her arms and adopted a matter-of-fact tone.

"Right, so, my husband is now pursuing a dangerous murderer across some of the most difficult physical terrain in the country, at night—and now it's starting to rain," she added, as raindrops began to patter against the windows. "I suppose I can't say he didn't warn me. It's been nothing but an adventure since I met Maxwell Charles Finlay-Ryan."

"If it makes you feel any better, love, my fiancée is out there with him," Phillips said.

"I almost feel sorry for Craig Hunter," Yates piped up. "He doesn't have a clue what's about to hit him."

Just then, there came the delayed roar of a jet engine as the sleek plane seemed to tear the sky in half. The roof shuddered over their heads and the tips of the trees outside swayed wildly in its wake.

"Reinforcements have arrived," Phillips pronounced, and scowled as one of the constables nabbed the last sandwich.

CHAPTER 24

Hunter was about to remount his horse when he heard a rumbling sound in the distance. At first, he assumed it was the police helicopter arriving but the sound was growing louder and louder and approaching at a much faster speed than he would have expected.

"Hold still!" he growled at the horse, which moved restlessly in a bid to escape its captor.

He hauled himself back up and steered it through the trees until he found the trail again. The skies were rumbling and when the trail gave way to a short stretch of forest road, he looked up and saw the jet circling around like a giant eagle.

"Come on! *Move!*"

The horse whinnied and shied at the deafening noise of the jet and Hunter began to panic. It was the heat, he realised. They had heat detectors on those jets and they'd found him, even amongst all the trees and rivers, the moors and fields of sheep and cattle.

They'd still found him.

He needed to think.

Think!

There might still be a way.

With a fierce kick of his heels, he spurred the horse onward as the rain began to fall.

* * *

A mile to the east, Ryan and MacKenzie soothed their horses as the sound of the jet plane scorched across the sky. They waited quietly, both absently stroking their horse and listening intently for the direction.

"It's circling back around," Ryan murmured after a few seconds.

MacKenzie closed her eyes and focused on the sound, trying to ignore the patter of rain against the leaves all around.

"You're right," she said. "It's sweeping the area up ahead. I'll radio in and ask for the location."

A moment later, Phillips' voice came over the airwaves to tell them the RAF had located a strong heat source approximately four miles south of the border, one mile west of their current position.

"He's close," Ryan muttered.

"There are teams surrounding him from all sides, but they know our position and they'll await our signal," MacKenzie said once the transmission ended. "Let's finish this."

"Ladies first," Ryan replied.

MacKenzie smiled fiercely and blazed a trail through the forest, vowing that she would never be afraid again.

* * *

Hunter was slick with rain by the time he reached a clearing section of the trail, where trees were being felled and harvested. Every year, another three and a half million trees were planted to replace the ones that were lost, but right now long pieces of timber had been stacked on one side of the clearing and enormous logging machines were parked and ready for use the following day.

The jet followed his progress and continued to make passes above him. The horse began to turn in erratic circles, terrified by the noise.

Hunter tried to think of the best thing to do as he stood there in the middle of the clearing, wondering whether he could shelter beneath one of the large iron machines so the jet would no longer be able to see his body heat. If he let the horse roam free, maybe they'd mistake it for him and go in pursuit of the dumb animal instead.

But they were so close now, they'd be able to see his every move.

Then he thought of the peat bogs.

If he could make his way to the moorland bogs a mile or so further along, he could wade through the bog and shield himself that way.

With one last, desperate push, he urged the horse onwards.

* * *

Barely five minutes behind him, Ryan and MacKenzie entered the clearing. The uppermost branches of the trees were still swaying from side to side, so even without the information being fed through on their radios, they would still have guessed that Hunter was not far ahead.

"That way!" MacKenzie called over to Ryan, holding the reins in one expert hand as she pointed the direction. "We've nearly got him!"

Ryan nudged his thighs and the mare picked up a surprising amount of speed now that they'd come to a bit of open ground. He lowered his body into position as the horse flew across the rain-slicked turf and MacKenzie followed somewhere not far behind. They covered the ground quickly with the cold night air whipping against their skin and the rain battering against their clothes.

Soon, they emerged onto an area of open moorland with a purpose-built slatted mountain biking trail cutting across it. The land inclined gently at first but then dropped without warning in parts as it gave way to sharp precipices.

A quarter of a mile up ahead, the jet made a series of fly-bys over the horse and rider. Hunter was riding like a madman, Ryan thought, watching him weave and seemingly trying to outrun the jet in his bid for freedom.

He would kill himself, at this rate.

Hunter must have sensed something, or heard the clatter of their horses' hooves against the wooden slats behind him, and he twisted around in his saddle.

Then, everything happened quickly.

Hunter gripped the reins in one shaking hand while he swung the shotgun off his shoulder with the other.

When he spotted the shotgun, Ryan reacted instantly and manoeuvred his horse in front of MacKenzie's so that she would not be in Hunter's direct line of fire.

"Don't be a fool, Hunter! You're surrounded!"

But his words were drowned out by the engine noise. The jet passed by again and Ryan found himself staring down the barrel of a shotgun.

* * *

As with all animals—human, domestic or wild—there is a level of tolerance which cannot be breached without consequence. Craig Hunter had forgotten that as he punished his horse again and again, tormenting it with noise, exhaustion, hunger, thirst and painful kicks.

He pushed the animal once too far, dragging its head around to face Ryan and MacKenzie as he prepared to pull the trigger.

Without warning, the horse reared up and Hunter's shotgun went off as he was thrown backwards onto the wooden trail, narrowly avoiding the bog that might have cushioned his fall. He fell badly, twisting his neck at an angle that would have ensured he would never be able to walk again.

But it always paid to be sure.

The horse bucked and kicked out at the explosive shotgun discharge beside its head, bringing its back legs crashing down against Hunter's chest, and then his neck and face, before it escaped into the night with a clatter of angry, blood-stained hooves.

There was no time to prevent it, Ryan and MacKenzie knew that much, but they could not help but feel the bitter sense of defeat. They would have preferred to see Craig Hunter behind bars and felt cheated; there was no sense of victory to be found in the man's death, for it robbed the families of his victims of their right to see him pay for his crimes.

And yet, being trampled by a horse was an ignominious, painful way to die, so perhaps that was retribution enough.

MacKenzie lifted her radio.

"All units stand down. I repeat. All units stand down."

CHAPTER 25

Monday, 2ⁿᵈ October

The lengthy process of retrieving Hunter's body, coordinating the withdrawal of tactical and service team personnel, and the small matter of retracing their steps along the Bloody Bush Trail meant that neither Ryan nor MacKenzie arrived back at Kielder Waterside until dawn. After a deluge of rain, the trail was slippery and the going was slow as they led their tired horses back on foot, but they were relieved to find a police horse trailer waiting for them at the first available access road.

Before Ryan handed over the mare into their capable hands, he raised a gentle hand to rub the horse's nose.

"Thanks, girl," he murmured. "Go and have a rest and I'll bring some carrots for you soon."

The horse lowered her head and nuzzled at his hand.

MacKenzie watched the exchange with a smile and realised that, just when she thought she knew the man, Ryan still had a habit of surprising her.

"You ready to go home now, Doctor Doolittle?"

"You're just jealous I can talk to the animals."

They sat side by side in the back of a squad car as they were driven back to the Waterside, surrounded by the potent smell of horses and sweat.

"You put yourself in danger out there," MacKenzie said, looking across at his strong profile.

"So did you," Ryan said with a yawn.

"No. When Hunter took out his shotgun, you protected me. I didn't ask you to do that."

Ryan gave in to temptation and closed his eyes.

"Would you rather I'd used you as a shield?"

MacKenzie rolled her eyes.

"I'm not handling this very well," she muttered, and tried again. "Ryan, I'm not trying to assert myself and I'm not complaining about your instinct to protect others. I'm trying to thank you."

His eyes opened again and he turned to look at her.

"You're welcome, Mac. The world would be a much sadder place without you in it."

"I could say the same of you."

Ryan cleared his throat.

"Do you want to hug it out?"

"Bring it in, big guy."

* * *

Ryan and MacKenzie found a welcome party waiting for them back at Kielder Waterside with food, fresh sheets and warm beds inside the rental lodge. Ryan was chilled to the bone, physically and mentally exhausted, and so he was pliant as a child while Anna led him to a warm shower, waited as he stood under its spray and nudged him when he fell asleep against the tiles, then towelled him off afterwards.

"I could get used to this," Ryan murmured sleepily.

"So could I," she said with a chuckle. "I've never known you to be so agreeable."

Anna tumbled him into bed and whipped the sheets over him before he had a chance to make a grab for her.

"Sleep," she whispered, placing a tender kiss on his lips.

By the time she'd drawn the thick curtains to blot out the bright sunshine outside, Ryan had fallen into a deep sleep.

Anna sat on the edge of the bed and watched him for a few minutes, brushing the wet hair back from his forehead with gentle fingers as she wondered what he had seen during the night and what fresh horrors his mind would be forced to bear. Her eyes traced the lines of his face, envying the thick sweep of black eyelashes that any woman would have paid good money for, then smiled at how mortified he would be if she ever told him that.

She leaned across the bed to brush her lips against his and then padded out of the room.

* * *

Four hours later, Ryan awoke to the smell of bacon.

He yawned and stretched, then rolled out of bed and straight down into a few quick press-ups to wake himself up. Another few hours' sleep would have been good for his body but his mind was too wired to sleep any longer, not while there was work still to do.

Downstairs, he found the rest of his team tucking into bacon and eggs.

"Morning, lad," Phillips greeted him. "How're you feeling?"

Ryan's thighs were aching but he wasn't about to admit that to a roomful of people.

"Fresh as a daisy," he replied. "How about you, Mac?"

MacKenzie thought her glutes would never recover, but she sipped daintily at her coffee and smiled.

"Never better."

"That's good," Phillips said innocently. "I thought your arses would be falling off, after all that riding yesterday."

Ryan burst out laughing.

"Frank, I can always rely on you to tell it like it is."

"Aye, lad, that you can. And since we're chatting, I should tell you Lucas has been on the phone. She wants an update."

Ryan nodded.

"I'll get around to it."

Anna walked across to hand him a cup of coffee and he pulled her in for a quick kiss.

"I seem to remember having a very pleasant dream about a dark-haired angel who looked after me earlier this morning. Was that you, by any chance?"

"Well, you did smell pretty bad," she told him.

"Ah, marital bliss," he joked, earning himself a jab in the ribs.

"Why don't you leave Lucas to me?" MacKenzie called out. "The cold cases are my remit, so I should update her on that side of things anyway."

Ryan wasn't fooled by his friend's nonchalant tone. She was offering him a reprieve from dealing with a woman he couldn't stand, and they both knew it.

"Thanks, Mac. I appreciate it."

She polished off her coffee and leaned across the table to give Frank a farewell kiss.

"Right, I'd better get cracking. The media have had a feeding frenzy after last night's drama and I need to make sure we jump through all the right hoops when we're dealing with Hunter's body. The last thing I want is some eejit picking holes in our case management."

Ryan nodded.

"Keep us in the loop."

MacKenzie paused with her hand on the door.

"I could have done with Lowerson helping me on this one, but I haven't heard from him at all. Anybody know what he's been up to?"

Ryan's jaw tightened and Phillips realised he hadn't yet had time to tell MacKenzie about the situation.

"Jack's working with Lucas now. She offered him a fast-track promotion," Phillips told her, and watched incredulity pass over her expressive face.

"That's…sudden," she said.

"It's a shame not to have him around," Yates chipped in, and then blushed furiously when four faces swivelled around to look at her. "I just mean it was nice working together, that's all."

Ryan walked over to the window to look out across the reservoir and saw that the little fishing boats were back on the water now that people thought the danger had passed. Normal business had resumed at the Inn and families were gathered once more beside the shoreline and in the picnic area. It was time to move forward.

"Jack saw an opportunity and he took it," he said quietly. "We should all wish him well."

"He's out of his depth working for Lucas," MacKenzie averred, with her usual insight. "I hope he knows what he's letting himself in for."

"If he doesn't, he'll find out soon enough."

* * *

Jack Lowerson walked into the office on Monday morning as if he were walking on air. He could hardly believe it, but he'd found somebody special after all.

And her name was *Jennifer*.

Jen.

Jenny.

Jen Lucas.

Jen *Lowerson?*

He laughed at his own imagination and reminded himself not to start getting too excited. He'd had plenty of relationships fizzle out after the first few days or weeks, so there was no point in getting his hopes up too soon.

All the same, it had been a wonderful weekend.

There had been no sign of any husband and she wore no ring on her finger, so he'd decided that must have been the office rumour mill going berserk again. He'd stayed the whole weekend at her home making love, making breakfast, making dinner…doing everything together. She'd wanted to know all about his life, his family and friends, the things that were important to him. When it came time to leave, it had felt like a real physical wrench.

He could picture her waving him off at the door with that shy smile on her face and he realised it was going to be difficult to remain professional in the office when she dominated his every waking thought.

She was so lovely.

Lowerson hummed to himself and hardly noticed when he turned the corner and almost barrelled into MacKenzie.

He looked up in surprise.

"Sorry, Mac, I wasn't watching where I was going. How're you doing?"

MacKenzie gave him a searching look and noticed with surprise that he'd undergone some sort of style overhaul. Usually, Jack was one of the sharpest dressers in the whole office and his attention to detail was the stuff of legend. But today, instead of his usual tailored silk suit and tie, he wore a plain cotton shirt and chinos with brown suede boots that reminded her of a similar pair owned by Ryan. His mid-brown hair had been left to dry naturally rather than being primped and gelled to within an inch of his life. It should have suited him but, instead, MacKenzie couldn't help but miss the old Jack.

"New boots?" she asked, and Lowerson looked down at his feet self-consciously.

"Oh, right. Yeah, I've had these a while."

He wondered why he'd felt it necessary to lie, but MacKenzie didn't seem to have noticed.

"I heard you got a new job," she said, and gave him an encouraging smile. "Congratulations."

Again, he looked embarrassed.

"Ah, thanks. Um, did Ryan tell you about it?"

"No, Frank mentioned it," she said. "But Ryan is pleased for you."

Lowerson's face fell into sulky lines of disbelief.

"I doubt it," he muttered.

He'd had several revealing discussions with Jen over the weekend and she'd told him all about Ryan's exploits during his younger years down at the Met.

MacKenzie frowned at his choice of words.

"Jack, is everything okay?" she said, reaching out to put a hand on his arm. "Look, I know we're working in different teams now, but I want you to know I'm always here if you need me." But Lowerson shrugged her off.

"Why does everybody always assume I need *help*? Do I have 'LOSER' stamped on my forehead or something?"

MacKenzie was startled by his tone of voice.

"No, Jack, I only meant—"

"It doesn't matter what you meant. I'm perfectly bloody fine as I am, thanks, and you can pass the message on to Ryan when you see him."

With that, he brushed past her and made his way up to the second floor where Jen would be waiting for him.

CHAPTER 26

As the lunch crowd bustled in the restaurant next door, the remaining staff attached to Operation Stargazer turned up to the conference suite at Kielder Waterside for what they imagined to be a final briefing. The sun was at its highest point in the sky, burning off the fog that clung to the shoreline. Light streamed through the windows and sent dust motes dancing on the air of the incident room and, aside from a few messy boot prints on the floor and some leftover markings on the whiteboard, it bore no evidence that it had been the hub of operations for a manhunt only hours before.

"Do you want us to start packing up?" Yates asked, once everyone had assembled.

Ryan hitched himself onto the desk at the front of the room and linked his hands.

"Why would you want to do that?"

Yates looked startled.

"Well, don't we need to tidy up, now that the investigation is over?"

"What makes you think it's over?" Ryan asked, patiently.

"But… I thought, now that Craig Hunter is dead, that would be the end of it? We know that he killed Kate Robson and Guy Sullivan—"

"We know nothing of the kind," Ryan interjected, and reminded himself that she was still learning. "In fact, I'm going to walk you through exactly why this investigation is very far from being over. Is everybody comfortable?"

Phillips raised his cup of milky tea in salute.

"Alright, let's work backwards and look at Craig Hunter. We know that he was born Robert Jepson and went by the name of 'Bobby' until around ten years ago, when he changed his name and went off-grid. He was paid in cash, didn't have a driving licence or a bank account and paid his rent on a weekly basis to a local family who own the cottage he's been living in. But when he was Bobby Jepson, the DNA evidence would suggest he was responsible for the murder of at least two sex workers, possibly more if we look at his MO."

"How sure are we that Hunter—or Jepson—is responsible?" Phillips queried.

"The DNA evidence on record includes blood and semen in large quantities," Ryan explained. "He was arrogant back then, just as he was arrogant before he died. It looks conclusive but the CSIs are doing a search of his cottage to see if anything turns up. It may be that he kept trophies of his victims, which would add even more weight."

"Doesn't that make it even *more* likely he killed Guy and Kate?" Yates asked, but Ryan shook his head.

"The MO is very important," Ryan explained. "Bobby Jepson snatched his victims from the street, assaulted them and then broke their necks with his hands. They tended to be young, very slim women who would be easy to overpower. Neither Guy Sullivan nor Kate Robson falls into that category."

"But surely it had to be Hunter who killed Kate Robson. He was the one who stole her horse," Yates argued.

"Yes, and he was also armed with a shotgun," Ryan reminded her. "Why would a man choose a copper pan as a murder weapon if he had a shotgun already strapped to his shoulder? It doesn't make sense and it doesn't match his style, either. He was more likely to have been in and out of there as quickly as he could."

Yates felt the penny drop.

"But if not Hunter—then who?"

"That's the million-dollar question, Yates. Let's continue working backwards and look at our next person of interest." He rose and walked across the room to retrieve a picture of Kate Robson, taken at a recent horse-riding event. "If we assume that Robson *wasn't* murdered by Craig Hunter, we have to ask ourselves what possible reason somebody might have to kill her. Ideas?"

"Money," Phillips said simply. "She had a few bob knocking around and that's enough motivation for some people. Maybe they thought they could see her off and set Hunter up for the fall."

"Precisely my thinking," Ryan said. "Which is why I've requested the details of Robson's next of kin and I want to know who benefits chiefly from her will."

"I'll get onto that," Phillips offered.

"Great. Any other ideas?"

Ryan looked at Yates.

"Ah—sex? Relationships?" she suggested.

"It's certainly possible but, as far as we know, Kate Robson had no romantic interests in her life. We'll get a clearer picture once we've had a chance to interview her friends and neighbours."

"And if it's neither of those things, I'll bet you another pint it's to do with some skeleton or other rattling around in her closet," Phillips declared.

"You still owe me a pint from your last round of betting," Ryan said drily. "But let's say for the sake of argument that you're right and Kate Robson died for some other reason. That means her killer took their chance to murder her while another suspicious man was on the run, to take advantage of the timing of it all. How could they have known Craig Hunter was running loose?"

"They'd have to be on good terms with Hunter, or Robson, or both."

"Precisely. One of them would have had to tell him, because it was much too soon for them to have got wind of the manhunt at that stage from us or the press. We hadn't notified the local population, so news wouldn't have travelled by word of mouth either."

"So we check Robson's phone records to see who else she called; we speak to her friends and colleagues to see who had the opportunity or the motive, and then we do the same for Hunter."

"Yep," Ryan said shortly. "But that still leaves Guy Sullivan, a young man with absolutely no connection to the area, no family or friends who live here, no personal relationship with Hunter or Robson. He died most brutally of all—and what do you notice about his injuries?"

"They're all concentrated on his face," Yates realised. "Guy's killer obliterated the face but didn't touch any other part of his body."

Ryan nodded.

"Pinter hasn't had a chance to finish the post-mortem but it's safe to say that Guy Sullivan sustained no injuries other than around his head and face. Doesn't that strike you as odd?"

"They didn't want to see his face," Phillips muttered, half to himself. "Whoever it was couldn't stand to see his face."

Ryan looked across at the picture of Guy Sullivan and nodded.

"That represents a different MO," he said. "Kate Robson suffered fatal head injuries but she wasn't attacked to the same degree and her features were still distinguishable. Whoever killed her had a different motivation."

"Does that mean Guy Sullivan's murder was a one-off? Unconnected to the others, I mean?" Yates asked.

Ryan ran an absentminded hand through his hair and moved to stand back from the murder board so he could look again at the faces on the wall.

"Everything about Guy Sullivan's murder seems unconnected," he said. "But look again and tell me what you see."

"I see a twenty-something man and a woman in her late forties—"

"No, what do you see when you look at Guy Sullivan and Duncan Gray?"

"But, sir, Duncan Gray's murder couldn't be connected. It happened over thirty years ago and the injuries aren't the same."

"They look similar, though," Phillips remarked. "The hair colour's slightly different—Duncan's is a bit of a darker blonde—but they've got a similar look about them."

"Yes, I don't think any of us saw it straight away because, taken individually, they don't share many characteristics. But look at the cut of the hair, the line of the jaw, the open expression to the eyes... There's enough of a similarity, if you were looking for it."

"And you think somebody might have been looking for it?" Phillips asked.

"It's one theory," Ryan said. "Until we know more, a theory is all it is."

Yates nodded, studying the pictures with a new-found understanding.

"What do we do in the meantime?"

Ryan smiled grimly.

"We did everything right beforehand, prioritising Guy Sullivan over Duncan Gray because we needed to extract as much fresh evidence as possible. The problem is, we assumed there was a reason to kill Sullivan—but what if there was no logical reason except that he bears a passing resemblance to a boy who died thirty-three years ago?" Ryan shook his head slightly. "If that's the case, we should have been prioritising Duncan Gray right from the start."

He looked up.

"Mel, you were right when you suggested that we re-work the original investigation and go back over the old files. It wasn't a proper job the first time around in 1981, so this time we make it a good one. I want to know the full circumstances of Duncan's disappearance, who his friends were, who his enemies were, his likes and dislikes. I want to know about the area where his body was found, what it was like before it was submerged in water, who used to live there. I want to know everything, because I think Duncan Gray could be the key to all this."

Phillips tugged at his ear in a nervous gesture.

"There's another possibility we haven't mentioned," he said, and when Ryan turned to him blankly he spelled it out. "The sergeant in charge of the case back in 1981 was Arthur Gregson and, knowing what we know now about his exploits over the past thirty years, that begs the question: was Duncan Gray one of The Circle's early victims?"

Ryan felt something twist in his stomach, roughly where he bore a scar along his abdomen. Gregson had been one of the senior, most influential members of The Circle cult and had lived a life of corruption and murder in his quest for personal glory. In its heyday, The Circle had far-reaching tentacles stretching throughout the North East and their preferred method of execution had been to use a small-bladed dagger to carve the shape of an inverted pentagram on their victims' bodies.

"There was none of the usual symbolism I'd expect to see from a ritual killing on Duncan's body but you're right, we need to rule it out even as a remote possibility."

"I'll go and speak to Gregson," Phillips offered, but Ryan gave a brief shake of his head.

"We'll go together. Make the calls, Frank."

CHAPTER 27

While Ryan and his team worked the case, Anna stopped by the visitor's centre to extend her lease on the holiday lodge until the end of the week. The university had advised her to take at least three days' special leave of absence after losing one of her students and, at first, she had resisted the Dean's edict. But much as it pained her to admit it, he was right—Guy Sullivan's murder had left her feeling thoroughly shaken up and a few days off work wouldn't be such a bad thing.

But what to do with the time?

There was always work to do but the phone call with her boss had left her feeling restless. Another possibility was to pay a visit to the site where their new home was in the process of being built just outside the charming village of Elsdon. The land had been a wedding present from Ryan and they'd planned the design together, poring over architectural magazines late into the night. The construction would take months to complete, especially as winter was fast approaching, but it would be well worth the wait.

Instead of going for a drive, she found herself wandering down to the shoreline where she spotted Freddie Milburn hanging up his wetsuit to dry outside the little kiosk where he worked. A radio blasted music from the seventies and he hummed in time to Neil Diamond as he brushed off his equipment.

"Morning, Mrs Ryan," he said, and gave her a friendly wave.

The name was still so new, it took her a moment to realise he was speaking to her.

"Morning, Freddie. Have you been out on the water?"

"Aye, I was out first thing. The lessons are winding down now since it's that bit colder, but I still like to go for a paddle when I can."

"Nice day for it," she remarked, looking up at the cloudless sky.

He grunted and stuck his hands in the pockets of his jacket.

"Weather's changeable in these parts," he said. "You could drive from one end of the reservoir to the other and find sunshine in the east and a rainstorm in the west. The storm last night cleared the sky a bit for us today."

"Have you lived at Kielder for long?"

He gave her a surprised look.

"My whole life," he said. "But I had a bit of fun when I was younger, travelled around the Mediterranean doing boat trips, skippered a few privately-owned yachts, that sort of thing."

"That sounds idyllic. What made you come back?"

His face twisted and he looked out across the water with a thoughtful expression.

"I s'pose there's no place like home, is there? It pulls you back in."

She nodded.

"Do you have family here?"

He looked back into her warm brown eyes and tried to see what lay hidden behind them. Was she asking these questions out of a sense of natural curiosity or had her husband sent her to snoop about? It was hard to tell.

"My parents are both gone," he said shortly. "I live with my sister, now. She needs constant care," he added.

Anna's face fell into lines of sympathy.

"I'm sorry to hear that," she said.

He scuffed a shoe against the shingle.

"Aye, well, that's the way of the world. There's a nurse who takes care of her while I'm at work and then one who comes in before bed to help her... you know, with all that. I keep her company the rest of the time."

Anna put a hand on his arm in silent support.

"It's hard."

He nodded and cleared his throat.

"There's folk worse off than us," he said. "But it's thanks to Mitch that I can afford a private nurse. When I came back home, he was the one who offered me a partnership in the business."

"He seems well respected in the community," she offered.

"Aye, he is. It was the same when we were nippers," Freddie added, with a smile. "Always had the lasses running after him and all the lads wanted to be his mate. Mitch has that way about him."

"Some people do," she agreed, and thought of her husband. "It can rub some people up the wrong way, though."

Freddie laughed shortly.

"You're not wrong there, love. Most people around here like him but there's one or two who'd gladly see him go down the pan."

"Oh?"

"It's because he's done so well for himself," Freddie explained. "Back in the day, Mitch's family didn't have two pennies to rub together and he always said he wanted to make something of himself so his kids wouldn't suffer like he did. Now, he has his fingers in all kinds of pies. He owns a load of holiday cottages around here, puts a bit into stocks and shares, and he owns one of the cycle centres on the other side of the reservoir. Then, he's got this place."

Anna listened with interest.

"And he's the local councillor," Freddie added. "That's a popularity contest in itself."

"Mitch grew up here too?"

"Oh, aye," Freddie said. "We grew up together, in the same class as—well, we were all in the same class together. Seems a long time ago now."

Anna had a flash memory of being thirteen or fourteen and learning basic trigonometry from a classroom with views of the North Sea.

"It reminds me of my childhood," she said. "I grew up on Holy Island and went to the tiny primary school there. All my friends were older because they mixed the kids in together, since there were so few of us. I suppose it's the same around here."

Freddie nodded.

"Lovely place, the island," he remarked. "Got some good sailing routes around there, although the water can be a bit rough. D' you ever get back to visit?"

A shadow passed over Anna's face.

"Not as often as I'd like," she replied, and soon after bade him a polite farewell.

Milburn watched her walk back towards her lodge and wondered again what lay buried behind those beautiful brown eyes.

* * *

A request had been made to the Police Archives to recall the boxed files pertaining to Duncan Gray's original investigation but, until they arrived, Ryan's team had to make do with the digital case summaries. As part of a separate police investigation into Arthur Gregson, every case he had ever directly worked on whilst he had been a police officer was in the process of being reviewed so that the Crown Prosecution Service could put together their strongest possible case against a man who put most criminals to shame. Unfortunately, that meant that many of Gregson's archived files were missing or in bad order, but they made do with what they had.

According to statements from his parents, Duncan Gray went missing sometime after one o'clock on the morning of October 21st, 1981 and they raised the alarm later that morning at around ten o'clock. It had been a half-term holiday from school and they'd assumed Duncan was spending longer in bed, but when they went in to check they found his bed untouched and his rucksack missing. At first, Angela and John Gray called upon the help of friends and neighbours on their street and in the local community, who rallied around to search Kielder Village and surrounding areas for any sign of him. When that failed, they called in the local police and a full-scale search was mounted with the help of the Forestry Commission and local mountain rescue teams on the same afternoon, although back in those days, there wouldn't have been helicopters and fancy 4x4s to help them.

As Ryan clicked through the various pages of reports, his anger grew. If there had been institutional failings in the handling of Duncan Gray's case it had clearly not been the fault of the local police. He could find no discrepancy in their management of the search operation and their preliminary records were in good order. However, when the digital record switched to the centralised Missing Persons team operating out of Police Headquarters, things changed dramatically.

Under the supervision of Detective Sergeant Arthur Gregson, the case of the missing boy at Kielder had dwindled to almost nothing. Statements had not been followed up, local transport staff had not been interviewed until almost three weeks after the event, and it was unclear whether Gregson's team had ever gone over the area of ground where Duncan's body had lain hidden and which was now submerged in water.

Why? Why hadn't they covered every inch of ground?

Ryan looked up from his laptop screen and saw Yates bent over her own screen on a separate table while Phillips spoke in firm tones to the staff of Her Majesty's Prison Frankland to arrange an urgent interview with one of their inmates. The local police had returned to their ordinary duties but promised their full support should it be needed and Ryan had thanked them; their response over the weekend had been invaluable but he knew better than most the juggling act that they must perform to meet their duties to the public.

"Yates?"

Melanie looked up and blinked to clear the glare from her screen. "Sir?"

"You don't have to call me 'sir' all the time. Unless you want to, of course," he said, flashing a brief smile. "Have you had any luck researching the old landscape before the reservoir was filled?"

She huffed out a frustrated sigh.

"I could tell you all about the vital statistics of the reservoir, about the general geography and geology, but when it comes to finding out about the physical buildings, I'm drawing a blank."

From the corner of his eye, Ryan spotted Anna chatting to Freddie Milburn through the window.

"Yates, if you're having trouble getting to grips with the local history, I think I know the perfect person to help you out."

"Oh? What's their name? I'll give them a call straight away."

"That won't be necessary. Doctor Taylor-Ryan is standing about thirty feet away and I'm reliably informed she can easily be bought with the promise of coffee and biscuits."

"For the record, I can also be bought with biscuits," Phillips chimed in from across the room.

"Tell us something we don't know," Ryan grinned. "Your relationship with the humble *Jammy Dodger* is going to bankrupt this department."

* * *

Five minutes later, Anna was comfortably established at the conference table with a cup of coffee and a plate of baked sugar within easy reach.

"I'm formally enlisting your services as a consultant," Ryan said, just in case Lucas had the room tapped.

"Oh yeah? What kind of fee are you offering?"

Anna took a sip of her coffee and her eyes danced over the rim.

"I'll write you an IOU," he replied. "You can redeem it later."

Phillips let out a hoot of laughter.

"Good to see married life hasn't dimmed your sense of humour," he said, and thought of how Denise would be getting on back at the office.

"Yates has been trying to build up a picture of what the landscape looked like around here before the dam and the reservoir," Ryan said.

"I've pinpointed the approximate location of where Duncan Gray's body was discovered by Lisa Hope beneath the water," Melanie said, pushing a map across the conference table to show Anna the spot marked with a bold red 'X'. "Freddie Milburn, Lisa Hope and Oliver Tate agree that it was very close to the remains of an old farmhouse. Comparing the coordinates Freddie gave us and those provided by the Underwater Search and Marine Unit, I'm as sure as I can be that this is the location."

Anna looked over the map and nodded.

"To make way for the reservoir, everything was cleared between the villages of Yarrow Moor to the east and Kielder to the west, so very little remains of what used to lie beneath the water. However, I think I can tell you exactly what this building used to be and probably even show you what it looked like," she said. "There's a standing exhibition in Bellingham of photographs taken by a man called WP Collier. He spent months living and working around Kielder, travelling around on a motorcycle in the 1930s capturing images of the area and writing a brief history of who lived there and so on. You can go down and see the exhibition, but I also have a copy of the photographs in a book back at the lodge—give me a minute and I'll get them."

While Anna dashed back to the lodge, Phillips updated them on his progress with Durham prison.

"I've spoken to the warden—that's the new bloke they installed since the last fiasco," he added. "He says we can go in this evening if we want, but the problem's going to be getting it past Lucas."

"Why's that?"

"Well, ah, technically speaking, we're both witnesses in the case against him."

Ryan snorted.

"Almost everyone in the department is part of the case against Gregson…" He trailed off as his eye fell on Yates. "Except you, Mel. You weren't a member of CID when Gregson was at the helm. You could question him, with supervision."

Yates almost choked on her coffee.

"*Me?*" It came out as a squeak, so she tried again. "Me? Sir, I don't have the experience to handle that kind of interview."

"Why not? You've had the training, haven't you?"

"Well, yes, but I haven't had any experience."

"How are you ever going to gain experience unless you practice? Here's an opportunity to use your new-found skills."

Yates looked to Phillips for divine intervention but he just took a loud slurp of his tea.

"Don't look at me! I'm with the boss on this one. You're a capable lass; you can handle an old duffer like Arthur Gregson."

"I can't go in alone," she protested.

"No, you won't be alone," Ryan reassured her. "Phillips and I will still go in with you, but it needs to be you asking the questions and running the interview."

Her shoulders relaxed a bit.

"Alright, I'll try."

"You'll succeed," Ryan corrected, and looked across as Anna re-entered the room. "Found what you were looking for?"

"Yes, here's the book I was telling you about," she said, taking a seat at the table. "Judging from the map, I think the stone ruins the divers described would have to be this one."

She flipped the pages and tapped a finger on a black and white photograph of a large farmhouse, not dissimilar to the one that had been owned by the late Kate Robson.

"Reedmere Farm." Ryan read out the name underneath the image.

"Who owned it back in 1975?" Phillips asked.

"I couldn't say," Anna replied. "But if you're investigating a death that happened in 1981 or thereabouts, the family would have been long gone from the property by then. They started flattening these buildings and felling the trees from 1975 and the site was officially opened by the Queen in 1982. It took until 1984 for the water to fill the reservoir completely but there would have been a good quantity by the time Her Majesty paid a visit."

"Were the demolition sites protected?" Yates asked.

Ryan pointed a finger to capture the thought.

"Good question. If the site was cordoned off, who was responsible for maintaining its security?"

"I can find that out," she said.

Ryan steepled his fingers together.

"Look up something else, while you're at it, Yates. When you find the name of the security company in charge of the site, let me know the name of its CEO back in 1981."

"Do you think one of the security guards killed Duncan?" she asked, struggling to follow his train of thought.

"No," Ryan said. "But I've got a wild hunch about why a young Detective Sergeant Gregson didn't bother to investigate that part of the land too thoroughly."

Yates nodded and went back to the other desk to begin searching for the information.

"It's a huge land mass," Phillips said. "Could be they didn't have the manpower to cover all the ground back then."

"Yeah," Ryan said. "Or it could be Gregson put his own financial gain above the life of a young man who meant nothing to him. Something stinks in all of this and it's coming from the general direction of HMP Frankland."

CHAPTER 28

MacKenzie's Cold Cases Team spent most of the day fielding press queries, managing the widespread forensic enquiry into Hunter's death and speaking with the families of those victims who were suspected to have died at the hands of Craig Hunter, formerly known as Bobby Jepson. It had been an arduous series of phone calls which would be followed by home visits as soon as possible but, in the case of two of the victims, there had been no next of kin on record.

Although she was no stranger to the realities of life, MacKenzie was still saddened to think that two women had died at the hands of Hunter's brutality and yet nobody had been there to mourn their passing or seek vengeance for their loss. It made her all the more grateful for the blessings she had in her own life. If she'd suffered setbacks, at least there were people surrounding her who cared enough to help her overcome them.

"Boss?"

MacKenzie looked up to find one of her constables waving at her from across the room.

"I've got the pathologist on Line 1."

"Put him through to my new number, Andy."

A moment later, Jeff Pinter's nasal voice came down the line.

"Denise?"

"Hi Jeff, good to hear from you. How can I help?"

"Well, hopefully I can help *you*," he said, with just a hint of the oily charm that MacKenzie had long since grown used to and forgave on the basis that he was socially inept. "One of my team has been working on the body you brought in early this morning—ah, Craig Hunter?"

"Yes, that's right. Have you got some news already?"

"I don't have a lot, but we've made some interesting preliminary findings. The most important is that there were no traces of human blood found on Hunter whatsoever, aside from his own. However, there were three types of animal blood on his hands and in his hair."

MacKenzie shifted the headset to her other ear and frowned into the distance.

"No human blood whatsoever? That's impossible."

"I can only tell you what our tests show. Faulkner can confirm— one of his team came over today to cross-check our findings."

She tapped a finger against the edge of the desk while she thought.

"What about Kate Robson's body? Do you have any idea when you'll be getting around to that?"

"I'm looking at it right now," he said, and MacKenzie pulled a face at the image in her mind. "Faulkner's team have swabbed the body and he says he'll get through it as quickly as he can."

"Alright, thanks Jeff. I appreciate you getting in touch. I'll let Ryan and Phillips know."

"Pleasure's all mine, as always."

MacKenzie rolled her eyes and replaced the receiver, before picking it up again to put a call through to Phillips.

* * *

Why were the police still there?

It would have been understandable for a small team of local police to remain at Kielder following the manhunt to take statements, liaise with other officials or whatever else they were supposed to do when they weren't eating steak bakes or doughnuts, but there was no need for Ryan and his team of flat-foots to be skulking around the reservoir now that Hunter had been killed.

Surely they had been able to connect the dots by now?

Hunter killed Guy Sullivan and then he killed Roly while he was making his escape. The man even had the good sense to die at the end of it all, so he couldn't defend himself. It was all tied up in a nice, pretty bow.

And yet, they lingered by the Waterside asking questions.

There was only one explanation.

Duncan.

The years had dimmed the memory of Duncan's face to such a degree it had been easy to forget what he looked like—until they'd found his body, and suddenly images of Duncan were everywhere: in the papers, on the television and pinned up on noticeboards at the newsagents. People remembered the boy he had been and laid flowers at the end of the jetty or outside his mother's door. They spoke of him and reminisced about the search, waxing lyrical about his immortal soul as if he'd been the patron saint of Kielder Forest.

Duncan Gray, who refused to be forgotten so long as his killer lived.

* * *

The original local police investigation into Duncan Gray's disappearance focused on those most likely to have known his hangouts, or to have known if he was planning to run away. His parents were completely in the dark and, whilst there had been some arguments at home, there had been nothing out of the ordinary to prompt such drastic action. Ryan highlighted the statements taken from five people who still lived in the area and had been Duncan Gray's friends at the time of his disappearance, in addition to a further eight people who no longer lived in the Kielder area but could be contacted if necessary.

Ryan walked to the end of the conference room and picked up a marker pen.

"Let's look at the first five people on the list," he said, and wrote their names in capital letters on the whiteboard. "According to reports at the time and corroborated by their own statements, these five people were Duncan's main friends and they were in most classes together at school."

Phillips and Yates studied the names on the list, Anna having returned to the lodge.

"In no particular order, we have Michaela or "Mikey" Collingwood, who was two years younger than Duncan when he died but was in some of the same classes at school."

"The astronomer?" Yates queried.

"Yes. At the time, her family lived a couple of doors down from Duncan's, on the same street. Michaela says she'd known Duncan her whole life and they'd grown up together. She didn't have a bad word to say about him and her statement dated 22nd October 1981 says that she first knew of his disappearance when she called around to his house at around ten o'clock, which prompted his mother to go in search of him. That's when they found him missing. She states that Duncan had spoken of running away once or twice before, but never seriously."

"She has no alibi for the night Kate Robson died," Phillips put in. "Michaela lives alone and her place is only a mile or so from *Hot Trots Equestrian Centre*. Easy enough to get to, on foot."

Ryan considered the woman he had met at the observatory and decided that, no matter how nice, anybody was capable of murder given the right conditions.

"Next up is Freddie Milburn," he continued, tapping the edge of his marker pen against the man's name. "He was also in Duncan's class and they were the same age. Freddie lived with his parents in Stonehaugh, which is at the other end of the reservoir but considering Duncan was found about halfway between the two sites, it's possible for them to have met in the middle, especially since they both had mountain bikes."

"What's his story?"

"He states that he had spent most of the previous day—20th October—with Duncan, along with a crowd of local kids, including Mitch Fenwick. However, he knew nothing about Duncan's disappearance until the word got out the following day and his mother raised the alarm. Freddie joined in the localised search with his parents, who are now deceased."

"He's another one who doesn't have a decent alibi. He says he was with his sister while Kate Robson was being murdered, but his sister has advanced multiple sclerosis and can no longer speak."

Ryan wished he could say that no criminal had ever used a disabled relative as cover for their own misdeeds, but unfortunately it wasn't the case.

"Since you mention Mitch Fenwick, we'll turn to him next. Mitch was a year older than Duncan and most accounts describe him as the leader of the pack. He lived down in Stonehaugh, same as Freddie, with his family including four siblings who no longer live in the area. Mitch was with Freddie and Duncan the day before his disappearance and went home to Stonehaugh with Freddie, who confirms the same. He also states he had no knowledge of Duncan's disappearance but, like Michaela, agrees that he had sometimes threatened to run away, so he was not worried until the police search began."

"Mitch's wife claims he was with her all night last night, and before then he was doing his councillor gig on stage with us," Phillips said.

"But we all know how reliable spousal evidence is," Yates argued, and both men turned to her with pride.

"Frank, I think she's becoming as cynical as you," Ryan said reverently.

"And as sarcastic as you," Phillips returned. "It's enough to warm the cockles of my heart."

"Yeah, yeah," Yates muttered. "Who is Mitch's wife, anyway?"

"A woman called Jacqueline," Ryan said. "Goes by 'Jackie'. You'll notice that she's also down on my list as 'Jacqueline Dodds', which was her maiden name when Duncan went missing. She was the same age as Michaela and the two women are still close. Jackie and Mitch were what you might call high school sweethearts—"

"Bless," Phillips muttered.

"—and they married pretty much straight after leaving school and started on a brood of kids. In Jackie's original statement to the police, she said she was with Mitch the previous evening, which is inconsistent with Freddie's statement."

"Maybe they were having a bit of nookie," Phillips said, in his usual forthright manner. "Could be Mitch was too embarrassed to tell the police, so Freddie covered for him."

"All the same, it's inconsistent," Yates said. "I presume Mitch says his wife was at home all night?"

"Yep," Ryan said, leaning against the edge of the board. "Which leaves our final name on the list, Kate Robson. She might be dead, but there's no reason to scratch her off the list for Duncan's murder, especially if we think about all those rattling skeletons in her closet."

"What was her version of events, back in 1981?" Phillips asked.

"She changed her statement twice," Ryan said, "which is interesting in itself. First, she said she hadn't seen him at all the previous day, but when the police put it to her that other people had mentioned her being there as part of the group of kids, she changed her story to say she had in fact been there for most of the day. She said she went home at around seven, which was confirmed by her parents at the time, and they said she never left the house all evening. The next bit is interesting too, because in her original statement she says she first knew about Duncan being missing the following morning as soon as she awakened."

"Which was when?" Phillips was a quick study.

"Around eight o'clock in the morning," Ryan replied. "Which is mighty strange when you consider that Duncan's own parents weren't aware of his disappearance until ten o'clock."

In the residual silence, Phillips' mobile phone began to shrill.

After a brief conversation with MacKenzie, he ended the call and turned to his colleagues.

"Denise says Pinter's been on the blower and there was no human blood found on Hunter's person—only animal blood. Faulkner's going over the samples from Kate Robson's body now."

"Tell him to put a rush on it," Ryan said, and started to feel the indistinct sensation that light was becoming visible at the end of a long, dark tunnel. "Any word on Robson's financial arrangements?"

"There was no sign of a will at the farmhouse, so I called around a few of the local solicitors firms until I hit lucky and found the right one. The partner is going over the warrant now and once he's signed that off he'll release the details of her will to us."

"Tell him to do it before the end of the day," Ryan snapped. "We haven't got all the time in the world to faff about with box-ticking."

On that note, he turned back to Yates.

"Mel? We've got three hours before you'll be interviewing the scum of humanity. Let's talk about how one should handle somebody of that calibre."

"Good cop, bad cop?" she offered. "Flattery? Maybe a few veiled threats?"

"All excellent ideas, but no. You shove a boot up his lying arse and remember that you have more integrity in your little finger than he has in his whole body."

"I like your idea better."

CHAPTER 29

Her Majesty's Prison Frankland rested on the outskirts of Durham, thirteen miles south of Newcastle upon Tyne. It was never going to win any architectural prizes, being an uninspiring collection of boxy, red-bricked buildings housing a mix of standard and high-risk Category A male prisoners inside its fortified walls. A large sign which read, 'HM PRISON FRANKLAND' greeted them as Ryan drove Phillips and Yates towards the main entrance along the driveway flanked with high-level cameras.

"Have you been here before, Yates?" Ryan asked, as he found a parking space.

"I visited as part of my initial training, then a couple of times after that."

"Ever been to the Westgate Unit?"

It was an area reserved for prisoners requiring more secure detention or segregation, normally consisting of the most dangerous men in the prison population.

"No," she replied. "Is that where Gregson is living?"

"You'd hardly call it living," Phillips said quietly. "He's been in permanent segregation for months."

"Why?" Yates asked, a bit naively.

Ryan secured the handbrake and turned to look at her.

"When he was a free man, Gregson put a lot of his fellow inmates behind bars. Because of his actions, a good chunk of them are now appealing their convictions, claiming the investigations were rife with corruption and open to abuse under his oversight. For the past year, we've been fighting fires just trying to keep dangerous men off the streets." He shook his head. "Frankly, it's a toss-up over who hates Gregson more; the prisoners or the police."

On that note, they headed towards the main entrance and waited to be buzzed inside, where they went through the lengthy rigmarole of completing and signing the necessary paperwork. When they stepped inside the Westgate Unit, Ryan swept a glance over the bright space and consciously emptied his mind of intrusive memories that flooded in and reminded him of all the other times he'd been forced to come here. Most notably, the time he'd been forced to sit opposite the man who had killed his sister and almost killed him not once, but twice. *The Hacker* had cast a long shadow over their lives and even death was not enough to fully eradicate his influence because it was still here, in these walls, and in the small space at the back of Ryan's mind wherever he went.

"This way," one of the guards said, and guided them to a private conference room. The soles of their shoes squeaked against the linoleum and when they stepped inside they found it had been modelled on a police interview suite with a table in the middle and long mirrored window along one wall.

"I'll go and fetch him," the guard said, leaving them inside the cramped space.

Ryan turned to Yates.

"I'm going to wait in the observation room," he told her. "Phillips will be in here with you, but my presence is more likely to be a hindrance than a help."

"Alright," she said. "I'll stick to what we agreed."

Ryan could hear the lingering traces of self-doubt and he smiled encouragingly.

"Believe in yourself, Mel—you're worth ten of Arthur Gregson. And remember, nothing is lost if you fumble your words or forget to say the right thing. He's already trussed up like a turkey in here and, besides, it's highly likely he'll tell us nothing whatsoever regardless of what you say or don't say."

That helped her to relax a bit, but as soon as Ryan left the room, sweat beaded her forehead under the glare of the overhead light.

"Remember what we talked about," Phillips told her, as they paced the room. "Gregson is in his late sixties but he thinks he's still in his prime. He likes to think of himself as a real Ladies Man, so he'll probably try a bit of flirtation. Dirty old goat," he added, to make her laugh.

"What did the prison say about his behaviour while he's been inside?"

"Unpredictable," Phillips replied. "He won't shy away from a fight but he's not a natural fighter. Some days he's got plenty to say for himself, other days he doesn't say 'boo' to a goose. You have to remember that Gregson might have been a Super in his day job but he was only a lieutenant when it came to The Circle's hierarchy. He was senior, but he was never the Top Dog."

"But he was a powerful man."

"Aye, he was, for a while. But try to get inside his head," Phillips advised. "Arthur Gregson's a man with a chip on his shoulder. His whole life, he resented the fact he'd been born poor; hated anybody who had more than he did. When little Arthur grew up, he wanted to be respected and feared but the problem was—and this is important— he never quite believed his own hype."

Before Yates had time to formulate a response, the door opened and two guards escorted Gregson into the room. Phillips and Yates stood on one side of a metal table whose legs had been drilled into the floor for safety and they were dressed in their best suits, not in deference to their former superintendent but to distinguish themselves from him.

Their eyes followed his progress across the room, trying to assess the man. The Arthur Gregson they knew had been tall and imposing, with a shock of silver-grey hair framing a chiselled face that looked good in greyscale print on the front cover of newspapers. Although he was still tall, there seemed to be a curvature to his spine and a general air of fragility they hadn't noticed before. Phillips couldn't say whether it was because Gregson had changed over the past months or whether his former position had lent him such gravitas that they had been blinded to his faults, at least for a while.

Whatever his physical deterioration, nothing had been lost mentally and he looked between them with a pair of sharp, calculating blue eyes.

"Take a seat, Arthur," Yates began, and from his position behind the observation screen, Ryan silently applauded. She had set the tone; not only by speaking first but by choosing to use Gregson's forename and by pointedly offering him a seat. That way, he knew from the outset she had the upper hand.

Good for her.

Unfortunately, Gregson was a master of human behaviour.

"Very good, sweetheart," he said, with a hint of condescension. "Keep using my first name, that'll put me at my ease. Then you could offer to have my handcuffs removed, to show you're willing to be reasonable in exchange for whatever information I might have."

He settled himself on a chair and rattled his handcuffs expectantly, but Yates shook her head as she took a seat opposite and looked him dead in the eye.

"No, I think we'll leave the handcuffs where they are," she said, and went through the preliminaries, stating the date, time and occupants of the room for the video record. "We are here in connection with our investigation into the murders of Duncan Gray, Guy Sullivan and Kate Robson. You do not have to say anything, but it may harm your defence if you do not mention when questioned something which you later rely on in court. Anything you do say may be given in evidence. Do you understand?"

Gregson laughed.

"I was a policeman before you were even born, love. Do you really need to ask?"

"In light of recent events, the years you spent on the police force have been called into question," she shot back. "Do you understand the caution?"

"Yes," he spat.

Gregson turned to Phillips, running his gaze over the man he'd known for more than thirty years.

"You look good, Frank. Must be that little Irish piece you've been banging," he said, hoping to get a rise out of him. "Always did like the look of Denise MacKenzie. Did I ever tell you there's a peephole in the gents locker room? You can see right into the ladies room next door. Spent many a pleasant afternoon down there, I can tell you."

But Phillips merely smiled.

"Oh? Guess you haven't heard we moved offices a while back. Had to, since we couldn't quite scrape your stench off the walls," he added.

Gregson's mouth hardened and he looked over their shoulders to the observation glass.

"Is he in there?"

They remained silent and he let out a short laugh.

"You don't need to say anything. Of course Ryan's in there. Wouldn't pass up the opportunity of seeing me, would you, Chief Inspector?" He tried to lift his hands but found them shackled to the steel hooks on top of the table and had to make do with rattling the metal. "How come you haven't visited me before now, eh, Ryan? Or have you had your hands full with your new boss?"

Behind the glass, Ryan frowned.

How did he know about Lucas?

"You were in charge of the investigation into the disappearance of Duncan Gray, aged sixteen, while you held the rank of detective sergeant on the Missing Persons team in 1981. Is that correct?"

Yates diverted her attention back to the matters at hand and opened the file on Duncan Gray to give herself a moment to collect her thoughts.

"That's what it says on the paperwork, darling."

"The management of the case was transferred to your team on 22nd October 1981—"

"Look, love, I don't have to answer any of your questions unless you make it worth my while."

Yates gave him a curious look.

"And what did you have in mind, Arthur?"

"Depends what you're offering," he said, and gave her a lewd wink. "They allow conjugal visits here."

"But sadly for you, they don't allow Viagra," she replied, in the tone of voice she might have used to pacify an elderly relative. "Let's stick to the facts, Arthur. You're going to be spending the rest of your life in prison. You can tell yourself that a good lawyer will have you out in a few years but that's pure fantasy. Now, you can answer a couple of questions and sleep better at night, or you can return to your lonely one-man cell and watch yourself grow older without any hope of redemption. It's up to you."

There was momentary silence in the room and then he parodied a bow and looked over at Phillips.

"This one's good," he said. "Plenty of authority while she delivered her moralising little speech. All in all, I'd give her a six out of ten. I'm deducting four points for inexperience and lack of bargaining position."

Yates closed the file again.

"That's where you're wrong, Arthur. First rule of a negotiation? Always be prepared to walk away."

A moment later, she was out of her seat and Phillips hurried to keep up as she dealt Gregson a final blow.

"You're facing untold charges of murder, attempted murder, conspiracy to defraud, fraud, perjury... the list goes on. A lifetime spent in solitude, with only your own miserable self for company. Do you think you hold any kind of bargaining power with me, Arthur? All I see is a sad old man who wants to feel important. Help us or don't, you'll still be going back to your cell as we walk out of here and breathe the fresh air."

Yates swept out of the room with Phillips at her heels, scrambling to keep up.

As soon as the door closed behind them, Yates let out a stream of expletives that would've made a sailor blush.

Phillips gave her an astonished look, since he'd never heard her utter anything close to a profanity.

"Well," he said, and tried to think of something encouraging to tell her.

Ryan didn't join them in the corridor outside but remained in the observation room watching the man who had been his superior officer for over a decade spent at the Northumbria Police Constabulary. Now, Gregson was a shell of a man grasping at the memory of who he used to be. Yates had gone completely off script and it had been entertaining to watch but now it remained to be seen whether her approach had been successful.

And it had.

A moment later, Gregson motioned one of the guards standing sentry beside him to bring the two detectives back into the room.

Yates was as surprised as Phillips but she didn't hurry back, instead waiting another two minutes to give the impression they had almost followed through on her threat. When she did re-enter the room, her head was held high.

"Trainee Detective Constable Melanie Yates and Detective Sergeant Frank Phillips re-entering interview under caution with Arthur Gregson at HM Prison Frankland, Interview Room 1C. Prison officers Phillip Menzies and Fran Foster both present. The time is 19:26. Mr Gregson, do you require a reminder of your rights and obligations?"

He said nothing.

"Do you require—"

"I don't need any bloody reminder!"

"Good, then let's stop wasting time. You called us back in here. Are you ready to talk?"

"I'll talk, on one condition."

"There are no conditions," Yates said, flatly, and Phillips swelled with pride. The girl was a natural.

"Listen to me," Gregson growled. "If you want to know anything about the Gray case, then you're going to grant my request. I'm not talking to any bloody trainee. I want Ryan in here, right now."

"No. DCI Ryan is a material witness in the ongoing case against you—"

"You brought in Doctor Watson here," he said, with a smirk for Phillips. "So, you can bring in the big man himself. I don't care if he doesn't say a word, I just want to look the bastard in the eye."

"Absolutely out of the question."

"Your call," he shrugged.

Now, it was Gregson's turn to leave, and Yates sent Phillips a look of mild panic. Just then, there was a knock on the outer door and one of the guards walked across to let in their visitor.

Ryan had seen enough to know the direction things were headed and he gave Yates enormous credit for her handling of the situation. However, things had come to a head and if it was a simple matter of letting Gregson see his face one last time in exchange for useful information that could help their investigation, it was a small enough price to pay.

He stepped into the room and the atmosphere became electric.

CHAPTER 30

"Well, well," Gregson breathed. "The Prodigal's returned."

Ryan gave his name for the record.

"Detective Chief Inspector Maxwell Finlay-Ryan entering Interview Room 1C to observe," he said. "The time is 19:42."

He moved across to a side wall and leaned against it, arms folded.

Gregson stared up at Ryan from his shackled position at the table, eyes spitting hatred for the man he held responsible for his current situation. Ryan stared back and thought it was a strange quirk of the criminal mind that it tended always to blame others for a lifetime of bad decision making.

"I heard you'd married her," Gregson said, with an eye for the shiny new wedding ring on Ryan's finger. "Congratulations. I hope she knows what she's let herself in for."

Ryan said nothing, even as memories of Anna drugged and bound rose to his mind. Under Gregson's orders, she might have been slaughtered alongside all the other men and women who had dared step into the pathway of the cult.

"Not even a word for your old pal?" Gregson continued, and there was a persuasive quality to his voice that hadn't been there before. "There were good times over the years, Ryan. Surely, that deserves a word of thanks."

Ryan's eyes turned glacial and Yates decided it was time to cut through the chit-chat before things got out of hand.

"Your condition has been met," she told Gregson. "Now, let's talk about Duncan Gray. Was his death associated in any way with The Circle?"

Gregson turned sly.

"I have no first-hand knowledge of any dealings with the cult known as The Circle," he lied, and Ryan barely held back a laugh.

"To the best of your *belief*, was Duncan Gray's death associated in any way with the cult known as The Circle?" Yates amended.

"I still wouldn't know," he replied, and looked between Ryan and Phillips as if to say, 'Is this the best you could do?'

But Yates wasn't finished yet.

"Duncan Gray's body was discovered near Reedsmere Farm, now demolished beneath Kielder Reservoir," she continued. "Yet there is no record in the case file of a police search team ever having completed a coordinated search in that part of the valley. Why was that?"

"We did search," he said. "It's a lot of ground to cover. Easy enough to miss a patch of earth somewhere or to forget to make a note."

"Did you enlist the services of the Canine Unit?"

"Of course."

"But not in that area?"

Gregson shrugged.

"Maybe you can have a word with the dogs and ask them why they didn't do a better job," he said, derisively.

"Maybe," Yates said, turning the pages of her notebook. "Or, perhaps I'll just ask Derek Slater why he transferred money into your personal account shortly after the case fell into your lap."

Yates was bluffing about any money being transferred into Gregson's account, but it was not outside the realms of possibility. For years, Gregson had taken bribes from local businessmen to ensure that the wheels of justice would turn in their favour and if Ryan's hunch was correct, this was just another instance of the same apple with a rotten core.

"Who?" Gregson asked, too casually. "I have no idea what you're talking about."

"Derek Slater is the former head of Slater's Security which was, at that time, responsible for securing the demolition sites throughout the valley earmarked as the new reservoir bed."

"So?"

"Several witnesses state that the fenced boundaries were in poor condition and that children were in the habit of slipping through the fence to play amongst the rubble. Duncan Gray might well have been one of them."

"Then it was his own look-out, wasn't it? He should have read the signs."

From his position by the wall, Ryan flinched, realising he was looking at a person who was entirely devoid of human compassion.

"That's just it, Arthur. There were no signs, no warnings, no proper barriers. If Duncan Gray's body had been discovered in 1981 bearing any signs of an accidental fall, Slater's firm could have come in for a lot of flak."

"You're reaching too far," Gregson blustered, thinking back to the night Derek Slater had turned up on his doorstep with a roll of cash, stinking of desperation. Poor old Slater; he'd gone the way of the Dodo now.

"We did everything we were supposed to do," he said. "And back then, Duncan Gray had been talking about leaving—plenty of people said so. Still, we kept the case active for a few months until his mother got the postcard from him. It made sense to call things off—"

Ryan went on full alert and thrust away from the wall.

"What postcard? There's no mention of a postcard in any of the files."

They all turned at the sound of his voice, especially Gregson, whose face broke into a smirk.

"Woken up, have you?"

"Answer the question," Ryan barked. "*What postcard?*"

Gregson chuckled.

"Did I forget to mention it in the inventory? Silly me."

"Where is the postcard now?" Yates asked urgently, but Gregson just smiled. He had the upper hand now, if only fleetingly, and he would feed off it for the coming months until his trial. Whenever his strength or resolve failed him, he would remember the look on each of their faces and it would tide him over the dark times.

"Go and play finders keepers, little girl."

Gregson signalled to the guards that he was ready to leave and they began to unshackle him from the table. He hadn't been charged with this crime, so there was no obligation for him to stay.

"You gave up on that boy and didn't even bother to investigate new evidence that came to light, did you?" Ryan's voice stopped him. "You let his mother believe he was alive all these years. She believed her son didn't love her, that he'd abandoned his family, and you allowed her to believe it."

Gregson looked at Ryan for a long, charged moment.

"I'm still a better man than you," he growled. "Say 'hi' to Jennifer Lucas from me. There's a woman who knows how to keep her men in check."

* * *

Ryan said absolutely nothing until they were well clear of the prison compound—not as he stormed down the corridors of the Westgate Unit, nor as he scribbled his signature in the log book to record the time they were leaving. Only when they were safely inside the confines of his car did he finally put his hands on the steering wheel and say what they were all thinking.

"He hasn't changed, much."

Phillips scratched his wiry, salt-and-pepper hair and wished for a cigarette. It had been more than two years since he'd last smoked one of those addictive little sticks of molten tar, but the old craving still surprised him in moments of stress. Without the overarching fear of what would happen to him should MacKenzie ever find out he'd slipped, Phillips might have succumbed long before now.

"Bastard had the nerve to talk about Denise," he said, thinking back to Gregson's comments about the ladies locker room. "Had a good mind to teach him a few manners."

"You'd have been wasting your breath," Ryan said wearily. "The man's a sociopath."

"Who said anything about talking?" Phillips muttered.

Yates slumped back against her seat and caught Ryan's eye in the rear-view mirror.

"I'm sorry, sir. I messed up."

"You did no such thing," he replied. "I thought you handled the situation like a pro."

Phillips roused himself enough to agree.

"Aye, well done, lass. You went a bit off-piste halfway through, but it paid off in the end."

"What do we do now?"

Ryan turned the ignition key and swung out of the car park with more haste than finesse, which woke them all up.

"Howay, man, I left m' lunch back there!" Phillips protested.

Ignoring him, Ryan turned back onto the motorway and thought about how to answer Yates' question.

"What do we do now?" he repeated, half to himself. "We search the archive boxes for that bloody postcard and hope that Gregson wasn't lying about its existence. We'll speak to Angela Gray and her ex-husband to see what they can tell us about it and we chase up Kate Robson's financials."

"And then?"

"We hope to God there's a postage stamp on that little rectangular card because somebody had to lick it and saliva contains DNA. We might not have been able to test it back in 1981, even *if* Gregson had done his job properly, but Faulkner can work his magic now."

"Then, we check it against the database and the samples we've taken from everyone locally?"

"You're damn right we do," Ryan said, and put his foot down on the accelerator. "And one more thing. I want the fraud team informed about Gregson's involvement in Duncan Gray's case. He might have covered up a lot in the intervening years but if there's anything to find, they'll find it. Every little helps when you're dealing with that kind of scumbag."

"Amen to that," Phillips said, and spent the remainder of the journey holding on to his stomach.

CHAPTER 31

The call came just before midnight.

Ryan was still wide awake and poring over a stack of old paperwork he'd retrieved from the Archive Room at Police Headquarters. He was seated at one of the sofas at the lodge, barefoot in jeans and a thick woollen jumper to stave off the cold that was seeping through the cracks in the walls. Anna had fallen asleep on one of the squishy armchairs opposite. There was no sound except the wind that howled through the chimney grate where a small fire burned and the crackle of paper as Ryan sifted through box after box of paperwork generated on Duncan Gray over the past thirty-three years.

But still, he could find no postcard.

When his phone vibrated against the wooden coffee table, they both jumped.

"This is Ryan."

Faulkner's excited voice came down the airwaves.

"Sorry to disturb you at this time of night," he rambled. "I wasn't sure whether to call—"

"It's no problem, Tom. What have you found?"

He leaned forward and the light from the fire turned his hair blue-black as he waited impatiently for the news.

"I did some testing on the samples we found on Kate Robson's body," Faulkner said. "And you need to know I found something interesting. Very interesting. There were traces of blood beneath her nails and inside her ears and it didn't belong to her."

"Who, then?"

Ryan held his breath.

"It matches Guy Sullivan's blood type and DNA."

Ryan slumped back against the sofa and closed his eyes.

"You're sure?"

"Absolutely," Faulkner said. "We had Sullivan's DNA and blood profile on the system and we ran an automatic check for matches. It came back positive."

"Do you know what this means?"

"That Kate Robson probably killed Guy Sullivan?"

"Not only that, Tom. It means there was more than one of them."

* * *

When Ryan rang off a short while later, Anna had awakened and was sitting upright in her chair.

"You should try to get some sleep," she said. "You've been working flat out."

He shook his head.

"I can't…not when we're so close."

"You need to stay strong," she argued. "It isn't over yet."

He simply nodded.

"Somebody's out there and they think they've pulled off the perfect murder. If I'm right—"

"You usually are, when it comes to these things."

"Well, if I'm right this time and Craig Hunter had nothing to do with killing Kate Robson, that means there's a third person who has been waiting for the opportunity to strike. It confirms what every instinct was telling me about the way Kate Robson died."

Ryan leaned forward again and tried to imagine the scenario, sliding effortlessly into the role of a killer in a way Anna might have found disturbing in other circumstances.

"Let's say Duncan Gray went out there, behind the demolition lines, with a couple of friends late on 21st October 1981. One of those friends was Kate Robson. She, or maybe she and the third friend, killed Duncan for some unknown reason and they kept quiet about it for over thirty years. But later, when his body is found, Kate Robson begins to crack. When she sees Guy Sullivan, she thinks Duncan has come back to life, or whatever the hell these crackpots think just before they murder someone," Ryan said mercilessly.

"Then what?" Anna prodded, tucking her feet up onto the chair so she could listen comfortably. "The third friend goes after Kate Robson and sets Craig Hunter up?"

Ryan nodded slowly.

"Whoever it is, they're an opportunist, because it's unlikely they knew about Craig Hunter's history. But they needed to figure out a way of getting rid of Robson before she got any worse and started saying the wrong things to the right people."

"They'd have killed her anyway, then," Anna surmised. "Craig Hunter was just a bonus."

"Yes, I think so. She was threatening their way of life."

"It must be somebody already known to you," Anna said, thinking of all the names and faces of the people she had met around Kielder, shivering slightly at the thought of having chatted to a killer.

Unaccountably, she thought of the man she'd seen at the observatory and at the pub in Corbridge and she wondered whether to mention it.

"We have a shortlist of people who were part of Duncan's circle," Ryan was saying, and the thought melted away again. "They're all friends from school who lived in the vicinity."

"How are you going to narrow them down? Presumably, they'll have stuck to the same lie for all these years."

"And if you tell a lie often enough, people start to believe it's true," Ryan said grimly. "There's a team going over Kate Robson's equestrian centre but the farmhouse alone could take days to search. I'm hoping to hear back from the solicitors firm where she held a copy of her will, so we can see who she left all her money to, and I've requested copies of the account records from her bank. Maybe there'll be something in it."

"Did she have a phone?"

Ryan nodded.

"Already looked at that and there's nothing out of the ordinary, although there are a couple of numbers we'll need to cross-check." He sighed and lifted a hand towards the mountain of paperwork spread out over the carpet and coffee table in front of them. "What I really want to find isn't amongst any of these papers but it could be the most vital piece of evidence in the whole case."

"What is it?"

Ryan warred with himself but decided to ignore Lucas's edicts on marital sharing. The woman was no pillar of the police community whereas his wife was like a vault when it came to confidential information.

"A postcard, apparently sent by Duncan Gray to his mother in the months following his disappearance."

Anna frowned, stepping through the chronology in her head.

"That doesn't make sense," she concluded. "If Duncan sent a postcard, which implies he was elsewhere, how come his body was buried at Kielder? Surely, he'd have been found far away from here."

"Unless he came back at some point later and was killed, which seems bizarre," Ryan muttered. "But it's not impossible, so I won't rule it out."

Anna uncurled her legs from the armchair and walked around the coffee table to join him on the sofa, shifting some of the papers aside to make room. He watched her progress with darkened eyes and felt instantly at ease when she curved herself into the side of his body and rested her head on his chest.

"Are you going to speak to his mother tomorrow morning?"

"First thing," he said, and began trailing his hand along her arm in a gesture that was as natural as breathing. "I hope she's up to having visitors; she was in a bad state the last time I saw her."

"She must be broken," Anna whispered, hardly able to imagine the pain of losing a child. "I hope, for her sake, you can find who did this."

Ryan rubbed his cheek against her soft hair and drew her more tightly against him as they watched the flames flickering inside the log burner.

"I will," he said. "Their time has almost run out."

* * *

From the shadows of the trees outside, the couple were perfectly centred in the window, as if it were a picture frame or a TV screen.

The woman lay with her head against Ryan's chest, her dark hair falling in a curtain down her back while his hand stroked her arm with the kind of intimacy that came when two people were supremely comfortable with one another.

What would that be like?

It didn't matter.

People were encumbrances; curiosities that could sometimes be diverting, at least for a while. But it was becoming harder and harder to speak to anyone and not wonder what their insides looked like, or how their eyes would change when they died, or what fixed expression their face would settle into. Sometimes, it was funny, like a pantomime. Other times, it was disappointing and anticlimactic.

It was becoming more difficult to put on the same mask each day, to pretend to be just like everybody else, when beneath the surface was a seething, decaying core which was perishing more by the day. It was surprising that people didn't notice the difference; the evidence was surely there for all to see.

Ryan and his wife embraced, but that didn't evoke any feeling in the person who stood watching, other than a passing interest in their small, humdrum lives.

Neither of them would ever know what it felt like to be great, all-powerful and consuming.

Like a supernova.

Perhaps it was time to show them a taste of paradise.

245

CHAPTER 32

Ryan was up early the next morning to make his first and most important call of the day. As Freddie Milburn had warned, the weather was mercurial and by the time he had driven the short distance from Kielder Waterside to the village at the tip of the reservoir, he had left the blue skies of the morning behind him. A steady drizzle layered the windscreen and covered the tree-lined road in a fine, blurry mist which gave the impression that he was travelling through an ethereal, otherworldly place as he wound through the avenue of trees.

On the stroke of nine, he pulled up outside Angela Gray's home. The little 1950s terrace had been painted a pale yellow and the other houses in the row were also a pretty mix of complementary pastel shades. Ryan happened to know that the houses had originally been built for the forestry workers but now many of those families had moved on. Those who stayed, stayed because they loved the life. There was a lot to be said for it, Ryan thought as he slammed out of his car. Ingrained habit led him to lock the doors, but he'd bet nobody bothered locking anything around here. They trusted their neighbours not to steal from them, which was a rare thing in the twenty-first century.

Angela Gray answered her front door after the third knock and Ryan's immediate thought was of how frail she had become. As a woman of nearly seventy, Angela had been fit and healthy, albeit intensely lonely. Her only regular occupation had been her work at the gift shop, but it had been closed since Friday and Ryan wondered if she would ever have the heart to open it up again.

"Mrs Gray? I wonder if I might have a few moments of your time."

She raised tired eyes, ringed by dark shadows.

"Come in," she said quietly.

A stack of letters and assorted junk mail had accumulated on the hallway floor and, as Angela didn't seem to notice, Ryan bent down to pick it up and set it on the small console table as he followed her through to the living room.

"I'm sorry to disturb you again, Mrs Gray—"

"Angela."

"Thank you. I'm sorry to disturb you, Angela. I wouldn't, if it weren't important that I speak with you."

She sank into an armchair and looked at him vacantly for a couple of seconds, then rushed to get up again.

"I didn't offer you anything to drink," she muttered. "Tea? Would you like some tea?"

Ryan urged her back into her seat.

"Why don't we sit comfortably for a few minutes?"

"I was planning to wash the windows," she said, plucking at the material of her skirt. "Then I need to make a start on the skirting boards."

"I won't keep you long," he promised.

"Heaven knows what state the gift shop is in since I've been away."

Her tone suggested that she had been mildly inconvenienced and that, soon, everything would return to normal. Ryan had thought she was coming around to a stage of acceptance about her son's death but that had obviously been premature and it made his job all the harder.

"Mrs Gray, do you have anyone who you could call to come and keep you company? A family member, perhaps?"

"I told my sister to go home," she said tiredly. "There's nothing she can do... nothing she can say."

"All the same, you might need her support over the coming days."

"There's nothing. Nobody."

Ryan heard a note in her voice that gave him cause for concern, over and above the grief he would expect to hear. He forgot the reason for his visit as concern for her welfare took precedence.

"Angela, have you spoken with your GP since the news on Friday?"

"Joan took me to see Doctor Rush on Saturday morning," she said. "She prescribed those pills over there."

He looked across to where a stack of small cardboard boxes rested on a side table.

"They're for depression," she told him, faintly. "Sera-something inhibitors."

"Serotonin," he murmured.

"I don't like them," she said, and her eyes dared him to argue. "I don't need anything. If everyone will just leave me alone, things will go back to normal."

No, Ryan thought. She needed to find a new normality, one in which she could come to accept that her son was gone and would never be coming back.

"Does your sister live nearby?"

She sighed.

"Not far. She lives in Falstone."

He gave her his most winning smile and, though she was old enough to be his mother, it had the required effect of holding her attention.

"Would you do me a favour, Angela? Would you call her, as soon as possible? It would be a great help for me to know you weren't alone, so I can concentrate on finding the person who killed Duncan."

She flinched, as if she wanted to put her hands over her ears, but it was too late.

"Will you do that for me?" he persisted.

"Yes—yes," she capitulated. All the same, he made a mental note to contact the police counsellor as soon as possible.

"Thank you," he said, and considered how to approach the next question. "Do you remember telling my colleagues that you wanted to help our investigation, to find who was responsible?"

Her fingers stilled against the fabric of her skirt and she looked up at him with blazing eyes.

"Yes," she said. "I want to help."

He nodded.

"Good. I have a question to ask of you and it's very important."

She levered herself up a bit and focused on his face.

"What is it?"

"Did you receive a postcard from Duncan, a couple of months after he went missing?"

Her face fell again.

"Yes, I did. It was in the January of 1982. I remember it clearly, it was so unexpected and…well, he said a lot of harsh things. But that's why I never believed he was missing, Inspector. How could he be dead and still be sending me a postcard? I thought he'd just gone away. It's why I didn't believe it was Duncan you found, not until I saw him for myself."

Her eyes closed briefly as she thought of her boy; her beautiful boy captured in clay like a statue. The man at the mortuary had tried to show her on a television screen but she'd needed to touch her son, to know he was real, just one last time.

Ryan kept his face and his voice studiously calm when he asked the most important question of all.

"Do you know where the postcard is now?"

She focused on him again and a fog seemed to lift from her eyes.

"Yes, I think I could find it. I keep Duncan's things in his room," she said. "In case—well, just in case he ever came back."

She gave him an embarrassed look, expecting to see pity but finding only compassion.

"That's very organised," he reassured her. "Do you mind if we look for it now?"

She searched his face, trying to read the answers in his eyes.

"It wasn't from Duncan at all, was it? Somebody sent it to me, so I would think—so I would hope—"

"Yes," he said softly. There were no words of comfort he could offer; nothing to explain the basic cruelty of giving a woman hope when there had been none.

Her body sagged for a moment, then Angela drew herself up and her hands gripped the edge of the chair. The knuckles were enlarged after a lifetime of hard work and the onset of arthritis, but they were still capable.

"It's this way," she said firmly.

* * *

Entering Duncan's room was like stepping into a time warp.

The walls were papered with posters of musicians and bands from the late seventies and early eighties, with a big picture of David Bowie as Ziggy Stardust dominating the wall above the single bed that was freshly made. There was no dust or cobwebs on any of the surfaces and Ryan could see at a glance that Angela had truly believed that her son might one day come back. She hovered in the doorway beside him and he wrapped an arm around her shoulder in silent support.

"You're doing better than you think, Angela," he said quietly. "And you're stronger than you know."

It had been a long time since anybody had told her she was strong, or offered her a shoulder to lean on. Tears sprang to her eyes.

"Thank you," she managed, leaning against him. "Your mother must be proud."

Ryan's arm tightened on her shoulder while his throat worked.

"I hope so."

A minute later, Angela knuckled tears away from her eyes with a brisk hand and gave him a watery smile.

"Let's find that postcard," she said, and walked across to a large built-in wardrobe. Inside, Duncan's clothes hung neatly on hangers and she inhaled their scent as she always did, hoping to catch a remnant of the past.

But there was nothing.

Shaking it off, Angela kneeled on the floor to retrieve a plastic clip-box of cards and mementos and pushed it across the floor to the centre of the room.

"If it's anywhere, it will be in there. I almost threw it out, but I didn't quite have the heart."

Ryan joined her on the floor in the centre of the room and gently lifted the lid to reveal a collection of greetings cards from Christmases and birthdays, letters, small drawings Duncan had gifted his mother as a child, and a lot of photographs. Because he was so intent on finding the postcard, Ryan almost didn't notice the pictures of Duncan with an assortment of other teenagers he assumed to be the men and women on his current list of prime suspects.

"When was this one taken?"

He paused in his search to pick out a group photograph of eight or nine kids gathered outside an adventure playground, some with bikes, some without. Duncan stood astride his bike and had the same open-hearted smile Ryan recognised from the police image tacked to the Murder Board.

Angela peered at the image.

"That must have been the summer before Duncan went missing," she murmured. "Yes, it must have been, because Kate was still carrying quite a lot of weight in this one, whereas she lost a lot of it the following year."

Ryan looked up in surprise.

"Which one did you say was Kate Robson?"

Angela pointed to a plump girl with braces and freckles, wearing flared jeans that were a little too tight and a self-conscious smile.

"That's her."

Ryan's eyebrows shot up. Judging by Robson's physical appearance before she died, he would never have guessed at such a transformation.

"It's amazing, how she turned herself around," Angela was saying. "I remember Duncan telling me that the kids had started calling her a nasty nickname… Oh, my goodness, what was it, now? Something like Roundy, or Roly. Yes, Roly Robson, that was it. Poor Kate."

Angela shook her head sadly.

"It's so tragic, the way she was killed. I just don't know what's going on any more. I feel as though I hardly know the people around me."

Ryan listened and thought that her sympathy for Roly might evaporate just as soon as he was able to tell her his suspicions about Kate Robson's involvement in her son's murder, and that of another innocent young man.

He turned back to the image and tried to pick out the others on his list.

In the centre of the image, a tall, broad-shouldered teenager of around sixteen or seventeen smiled boldly at the camera. He had a mop of dark, curly hair and was wearing ripped jeans with scuffed trainers.

"Mitchell Fenwick?"

Angela nodded.

"Yes, and that's Jackie beside him." She tapped a finger on the image of a reed-thin girl with a mane of blonde hair, clinging to Mitch's arm. "They were inseparable. Still are, really, although I hear—"

She clamped her lips together, unwilling to gossip.

"It's alright, Angela. I won't repeat anything you tell me unless it's directly relevant to the investigation."

She pulled a face.

"It was just me being an old gossip. I was about to say that I'd heard their marriage was a bit rocky at the moment because Mitch…

Well, he just can't seem to help himself, sometimes. Other women," she added, in a stage whisper.

Ryan nodded, trying to think of any circumstances in which he could betray his wife, but finding none. He'd sooner carve out his own heart than hurt hers.

He turned back to the photograph.

On Jackie's other side, there was a shorter girl with a mass of curly hair and a rounded face he recognised immediately as belonging to Michaela Collingwood. On the other side of Mitch, he recognised Freddie Milburn wearing stonewash jeans and a baseball cap pulled so low it almost concealed his face.

"Hard to believe they were once so young," Angela said to herself, and was about to move on to the next photo when Ryan thought of something.

"Who was taking the picture?" he asked, gathering up a stack of similar photos taken around the same time. "Who took all these pictures?"

Angela gave him a startled look.

"Oh, I never thought of that. Um, it could have been anyone, really, but the only person I can think of as having the money to afford a Polaroid camera back then would have to be Nathan."

Ryan's eyes flashed, but were quickly veiled.

"Nathan Armstrong? But I understood he didn't live here in 1981."

"Oh, no, he didn't. But his family used to come and visit during the school holidays," she explained, still blissfully ignorant of the impact of her words. "If this picture was taken in the summertime, he'd have been up here visiting. All the kids got to know him, since he came every year. I think he bought his place on the reservoir because he'd been so happy here, as a child."

"How touching," he said.

"Nathan grew up to be such a nice man," Angela continued. "Every time he comes to stay in the area, he always pops in to say 'hello'. I can't count the times he's sat and listened to me droning on about the gift shop or about Duncan, but he's always so patient."

Ryan watched as she smoothed the pages of a hand-drawn Mother's Day card and warred with himself. Now was not the time to tell her, he realised. That time would come soon enough, when all the evidence was in place.

He reached inside the box with a gloved hand for the next stack of mementos and something fluttered right onto his lap.

It was a faded, yellowing postcard with a picture of Big Ben on the front.

* * *

With extreme care, Ryan flipped over the postcard and read the message written in faded ink on the back:

Dear Mum and Dad,

Don't worry about me, I'm fine. Tell the police to stop looking for me. I couldn't stand listening to you both arguing anymore, so I decided to leave.

Duncan.

It was a short, blunt message designed to put a stop to the police search, Ryan realised. But the last line about John and Angela Gray arguing at home was pure malice from a killer who enjoyed twisting the knife.

"Are you sure somebody else wrote this?"

Lost in thought, he'd forgotten for a moment that Angela was sitting beside him, waiting for him to speak.

"I strongly believe this postcard was written by Duncan's killer, yes. But I can't prove it until it has been tested," he replied, pulling out a plastic evidence bag to keep the postcard safe. "As soon as the results come back, we'll know for sure."

Angela's lips wobbled and she pushed herself up, with a hand from Ryan.

"Can I get you a tissue?"

She waved him away and went over to stand beside the window, where rain still pattered lightly against the glass. A dream-catcher swung from the curtain pelmet, a souvenir from a family trip to Scotland one year.

"I feel terrible even thinking what I'm about to say," she whispered. "But, God help me, I'm glad Duncan didn't write it. When it came through the letterbox all those years ago, I cried for three days. I couldn't understand how my son, the boy we raised, could be so cold. But now I know—I know it wasn't him."

Ryan came to stand beside her.

"Thank you," she said, in a tear-clogged voice.

Ryan shook his head.

"For what?" He hadn't done much for the poor woman; he still hadn't found the person who killed her son and it was tearing him apart. What could she possibly be thanking him for?

Angela turned and wondered if he knew what people saw when they looked at him. He was a good-looking man, yes, but that was incidental and would fade over time. What shone from his sad, serious grey eyes was absolute dedication; an unwavering commitment to helping others, and that was something that didn't tend to fade, it only grew stronger.

"Don't you understand, lad? After that postcard arrived, I thought my son didn't love me. I've blamed myself all these years but, thanks to you, now I know that he did, and it wasn't my fault."

CHAPTER 33

Ryan entrusted the postcard into the capable hands of a local police sergeant to deliver it to Tom Faulkner, whose team of CSI technicians were waiting on stand-by to begin testing the saliva bound to the adhesive on the underside of the postage stamp. It was an old sample and it would be a tricky job but they would give it their best shot, which was all Ryan could ask for.

In the meantime, he made his way back to the Incident Room, where he found Phillips waiting with news from Kate Robson's solicitor.

"Where've you been—on your granny's yacht?"

He bustled around the desk to greet him and Ryan was momentarily distracted from thoughts of murder and mayhem by the sight of Phillips' lurid yellow tie, decorated in a series of embroidered bananas.

Ryan pointed a finger at the offensive garment.

"What the hell is *that*?"

Phillips smoothed a proud hand over the woven silk and struck a dashing pose.

"D' you like it? I got it from the shop at the art gallery on the Quayside."

"Don't tell me you paid good money for it?"

"It's an investment," Phillips said defensively. "The shop assistant said it was 'wearable art'."

"Sounds like they saw you coming," Ryan muttered, dumping his jacket on the back of a chair.

"Play your cards right and I'll get you one as a stocking filler for Christmas," Phillips said.

As a threat, it didn't get much worse and so Ryan held his hands up in defeat.

"Did you hear back from Kate Robson's solicitor?" he asked, changing the subject back to more important matters.

Phillips nodded.

"No joy there," he said miserably. "She left everything to the RSPCA."

"Shit," Ryan muttered, then belatedly realised how that sounded. "Not that I don't care about the animals, but it would have been nice to have had a name."

"Where's the fun in that?" Phillips said. "Did you have any luck finding the postcard?"

"I've just seen Angela Gray. We found the postcard and it's winging its way back to Faulkner as we speak. He's going to prioritise testing the stamp and see what he can find. But if he does find any DNA, the problem's going to be finding a match."

"Unless it matches with one of the samples we already have on record," Phillips said, with his usual optimism.

"And what if the one we're looking for hasn't provided a DNA sample?"

It took Phillips less than a second to follow the train of thought.

"Nathan Armstrong? But he wasn't living at Kielder when Duncan died and he's alibied for the nights Guy Sullivan and Kate Robson were murdered."

"Is he? We still haven't seen any of that CCTV footage he's been promising us," Ryan said. "And as for his whereabouts in 1981, Angela told me that Armstrong and his family used to visit Kielder almost every school holiday."

"And 21st October was a school holiday?" Phillips guessed.

"Nationwide," Ryan confirmed. "Which puts Nathan Armstrong back in the frame."

"He still won't give us a sample."

"He doesn't have to."

Phillips did a double take.

"What d' you mean?"

"I drove back to Kielder Castle this morning and had a fish around the bins. I found the takeaway coffee cup I saw Nathan Armstrong throw away last night, at the town meeting. There's a chance Faulkner can extract something, and if he can match it to the DNA on the postcard, it would give us reasonable grounds to make the arrest."

"You're a crafty bugger," Phillips breathed. "Makes me proud."

They stood in silence for a moment, letting the facts and dates crystallise in their minds as the rain continued to fall outside. It was heavier now, thundering against the windows and bouncing off the reservoir.

Ryan looked around the room, suddenly realising they were one short.

"Where's Yates?"

"She's at the office tracing the details of who used to own Reedmere Farm, just in case it's important."

"Alright, that's good. Tell her to check in with MacKenzie and see whether anything else has turned up at Hunter's place or on his body. We need to be sure there are no further connections from that angle."

While Phillips put a quick call through to their colleague, Ryan walked across to look at each of the faces on the board, studying them as if their features alone would give some clue about what lurked within their hearts.

"What kind of person kills a friend, then continues to live in the same area as his victim's mother?" he asked, when Phillips re-joined him.

"The kind with no remorse," Phillips said. "What the head-doctors would call a functioning psychopath."

Ryan nodded slowly.

"He doesn't kill in frenzy, like Kate Robson did, and he doesn't kill animals or vulnerable women for sexual gratification and control as far as we know. There's something else that gives him satisfaction, some other motivation to kill."

"Duncan might have been his first victim," Phillips said. "That changes things, gives them a sense of incredible power if they manage to get away with it."

"Manipulation is another key factor here, Frank. Somebody had enough charisma to keep Kate Robson submissive all these years, keeping their secret even though it drove her to madness. Who do we know who could command that kind of control over another person?"

"Armstrong is the only one without a proven alibi," Phillips said. "And he's got the temperament. It's nowhere near enough to charge him with murder, but it's enough for a shake-down until Faulkner comes back to us with something more solid."

"Let's take a drive out to Scribe's End."

"Never did like his books, anyway," Phillips muttered. "Always getting the police procedures wrong, misquoting Latin—"

"Now, now," Ryan interrupted. "Nobody likes a know-it-all, Frank."

* * *

The rain was like a monsoon by the time Ryan and Phillips pulled up on the main road next to the pathway that would lead them to Nathan Armstrong's hunting lodge. They had come prepared, dressed in full waterproofs and sturdy boots, but the ground was hazardous underfoot as they made their way through the trees. Phillips pointed out the cameras as they went, and Ryan counted at least five, which was more than he'd expect to see at most banks, let alone a private residence in the middle of nowhere. Crime rates in the area were almost non-existent, except for the odd siphoned tank of oil or stolen vehicle, and certainly not high enough to warrant the kind of security Armstrong had erected.

"He's either packing gold reserves to rival Fort Knox, or the man's a control freak," Ryan said.

"Could be both," Phillips panted, as he made a valiant effort to remain upright on the muddy pathway. "Tell him to invest a bit of his gold in a new pathway."

A moment later, they emerged from the trees and the hunting lodge appeared before them. Ryan hadn't visited before and he was forced to agree that the setting was something special, regardless of its owner. However, when they approached the front door, they found the place deserted. No lights shone from inside the windows and the doors were firmly locked. A heavy-duty alarm system glowed neon green, which presumably meant it had been activated against intruders while the master of the house was gone.

Ryan and Phillips circled the perimeter, checking all the windows and doors until they met at the back entrance, which stood beneath an attractive wooden canopy with a decking area and seating. Sheltered there from the rain, they looked out across the panoramic reservoir and could see Armstrong's little red boat still moored by the jetty.

"What now?" Phillips shouted above the loud patter of the rain against the canopy roof.

"We need to find out where the hell Nathan Armstrong is," Ryan replied. "You liaise with the local police and get a squad car out here to meet you at the main road and watch to see if Armstrong returns. Meanwhile, I'm going to see if I can track him down."

"What if he's already made a run for it?"

"Then we'll put out an APW and he won't get very far. If he killed those people, there's nowhere he'll be able to run to without always looking over his shoulder and seeing us right there behind him."

* * *

Nathan Armstrong congratulated himself on another resounding success.

The women in the audience were especially lapping it up, he thought, sending a cheeky wink out to one of the middle-aged biddies in the front row who blushed furiously and started wittering to the friend seated beside her. He knew what they were saying, too.

What a handsome brute he is!

There was an enormous banner with images of his forthcoming book splashed across it, but on the projector screen behind him there was an even bigger portrait of himself in moody black and white. It had been taken beside some grubby industrial unit or other to reflect the grit in his novels and he'd been bloody glad to get back inside the comfort of his car afterwards. Still, the photographer seemed to have caught his best side, which made the ordeal worthwhile.

"… and thank you *so* much once again to Mr Armstrong for joining us this evening," the woman in charge of the book-signing event gushed, sending him a deferential smile which he returned with just the right amount of condescension. "After this, he'll be going on a tour of Europe and North America, so we are honoured that he was able to find the time in his very busy schedule to come and talk to us."

A polite round of applause followed, and he held up a self-effacing hand.

Afterwards, a stack of smaller A5 copies of his portrait waited to be signed and he handed them out to each adoring fan, posing for selfies and demanding re-takes where the image was not up to his exacting standards.

When the queue began to dwindle, he reached inside the pocket of his tweed jacket to switch his phone back on.

Almost immediately, the cloud storage system linked to his security cameras back at the hunting lodge pinged with a series of alerts and he stepped aside to fumble with the app so he could see who had been to the house. Less than twenty seconds later, video images of Ryan and Phillips popped onto the screen and he watched them circling the house, knocking on the doors and peering through windows.

The rest of the queue forgotten, Armstrong hurried to collect his briefcase and overcoat.

"Mr Armstrong? I thought you were planning to stay and sign a few more copies of your book?"

The event organiser hurried to stop him, and he almost thrust her aside in his impatience to get away.

"Something's come up," he said, and made swiftly for the exit lobby.

But when he flung open the panelled doors, he came to a shuddering halt as he caught sight of who was standing there waiting to greet him.

Ryan turned at the same moment and smiled grimly at the surprised look on Nathan Armstrong's face.

"Mr Armstrong? I'd like to speak with you, please."

"I have a plane to catch this evening, so I'm in quite a hurry."

"I'm afraid you'll need to cancel."

"Get out of my way," Armstrong hissed, suddenly becoming aware that they were drawing a crowd as his audience began to file out of the event room.

"Mr Armstrong, this will be much simpler if you will come to the police station voluntarily to answer a few questions and provide a DNA swab."

"I've already told your sergeant, I won't be giving you anything without the appropriate order."

"Then I guess we'll do this the hard way," Ryan said, and he motioned forward a couple of local constables. "Nathan Armstrong, I'm arresting you on suspicion of the murder of Duncan Gray and Kate Robson. You do not have to say anything. But it may harm your defence if you do not mention when questioned something which you later rely on in court. Anything you do say may be given in evidence."

Armstrong's eyes bulged from his face as a crowd of horrified fans watched him being led away.

"I'll sue you for this."

"And I'll counter-sue, for crimes against literature."

While Armstrong was rendered momentarily speechless, Ryan took his opportunity and stuffed him into the back of a squad car.

CHAPTER 34

Wednesday, 5th October

I t had taken Faulkner's team the rest of the previous day and most of the morning to complete their testing of the postage stamp and takeaway cup. As time ticked away, Ryan had already begun preparations to make an application to the magistrates' court to hold Armstrong for a further twenty-four hours, in case the forensic results did not come back within the legal timeframe during which he could detain a suspect without charge.

Luckily, Faulkner came through long before the eleventh hour to confirm a match had been found and that had provided Ryan with reasonable grounds to compel a sample from Armstrong to confirm that his DNA matched that found on the cup and the stamp.

It did.

And yet, Nathan Armstrong appeared entirely unruffled by the news.

He was seated beside his solicitor at a table opposite Ryan and Phillips inside one of the smaller rooms in the basement interview suite at Police Headquarters. The room had been chosen deliberately to create a feeling of claustrophobia because, in their long experience, they had found a stuffy room could be remarkably conducive in drawing out an unresponsive subject.

Not so, in the case of Nathan Armstrong.

His only concession had been to remove his jacket, but otherwise he continued to sit comfortably on an uncomfortable metal-legged plastic chair while he churned out a series of 'no comment' answers.

Ryan watched him with interest.

"Mr Armstrong, forensic testing has proven that your DNA was found on a postage stamp used to send a postcard to Mrs Angela Gray. Can you provide any explanation for that?"

"No comment."

"Mr Armstrong, how did your DNA find its way onto a postcard supposedly sent from Duncan Gray to his mother in January of 1982?"

"No comment."

"Mr Armstrong, the postcard in question was stamped by a London mailing distribution centre. Can you tell us where you were in January of 1982?"

"No comment."

"Mr Armstrong, isn't it true that you lived with your family at an address in the Borough of Islington and attended school there during January of 1982?"

"No comment."

"Mr Armstrong, is Islington a borough in London?"

"No comment."

"Mr Armstrong, isn't the Mount Pleasant Royal Mail Distribution Centre located on the outskirts of Islington?"

"No comment."

Ryan paused to draw in a frustrated breath. He had encountered interviews like these before where the subject refused to be drawn out, but he had seldom come across a person who showed no indications of panic or self-preservation.

Not since…

Not since *The Hacker*.

He met Nathan Armstrong's eyes across the table and realised they were the same; not the colour or the shape, but what lay behind them.

Nothing. No remorse, no pity—just an empty chasm where his soul should have been. It was like staring into an abyss and Ryan was suddenly afraid that, if he didn't look away, it would consume him too.

He carried on with his line of questioning.

"Mr Armstrong, where were you on the night of 21st October 1981?"

"My client has already answered that question in full in his statement dated 22ⁿᵈ October of the same year, Chief Inspector. He was at a holiday cottage with his parents and did not leave at any point during the evening. Statements from his parents confirm the same."

Ryan looked at the solicitor and wondered whether it bothered her to know she was defending a killer. The law dictated that everyone was entitled to a defence; that was the way the system worked, and he respected it—if not all the people who benefited from it.

"Are your parents still living, Mr Armstrong?"

"It is a matter of public record that Mr Armstrong's parents are both deceased," the solicitor piped up again. "Any further questioning on that subject could be perceived as harassment."

"My condolences," Ryan said flatly. "Let me put this another way: did you tell your parents to provide false statements to the police, prior to their deaths?"

"Chief Inspector, that is provocative and, once again, we will not hesitate to make a complaint if this harassment continues."

Ryan switched course.

"Mr Armstrong, where were you on the evening of Sunday 2ⁿᵈ October this year?"

"No comment."

"Did you, at any time, go to visit the *Hot Trots Equestrian Centre*?"

A slight smile touched Armstrong's lips.

"No comment."

Ryan held his eyes for a moment longer and then closed his file. If forensics was not enough to make the man talk, perhaps there was another way.

"Duncan was good-looking, wasn't he, Nathan? And popular with the kids around Kielder."

Armstrong said nothing, but he unfolded and re-folded his legs in a gesture that could have signified irritation.

"Is that a question, Chief Inspector?" the eagle-eyed solicitor cut in.

"I'm getting to it." Ryan shooed her away. "You, on the other hand, were an awkward teenager, weren't you Nathan? Not quite the self-assured, bestselling author we see sitting before us today."

Not a muscle moved on Armstrong's face, but his eyes burned.

"Chief Inspector—"

"Must have been hard, growing up without many friends. Did it make you feel powerful when you killed him, Nathan? Did it make you feel better about yourself?"

A tiny muscle flickered at the side of Armstrong's face; the only visible sign that he had heard the question.

"Did you kill Duncan Gray?"

The two men locked eyes and, for a moment, Phillips and the solicitor were forgotten. Armstrong continued to stare across the table at Ryan, memorising his features, and then leaned forward to open his mouth for a final time.

"No comment."

* * *

They worked on him for another hour before they called it a day and, as they left the interview suite, they were met in the corridor by DCS Lucas and a man they recognised as belonging to the Crown Prosecution Service, the central body who would decide whether to prosecute Armstrong's case given the evidence in their possession.

Lucas swept her eyes over both detectives.

"In here. Now."

She pushed open one of the doors and they followed her into a small, windowless conference room. Once inside, she turned on them.

"You're making no progress with Armstrong," she said, straight off the bat.

"He's guilty as sin," Phillips replied. "Give us another pass at him and—"

"We're not in the business of badgering witnesses," she snapped.

"He's not a witness, except to his own crimes," Ryan said. "Phillips is right. We could see he was beginning to crack when we started picking apart his psychological motivations. If we try again later today, there's every chance he'll slip up."

"If, but, maybe," she said, cuttingly. "I've given you a free run at this because you assured me you would bring it home for the department. Instead, all you've found is a thirty-year-old postage stamp and a bit of spit on the edge of a takeaway cup. Do you really think that's sufficient to hold up in court?"

"The significance of those items is the DNA found on both."

"And it's purely circumstantial," she said.

"I'm sorry, but I must agree with DCS Lucas," the CPS man spoke up, although his voice was barely above a whisper. "Without a more specific causal link between Nathan Armstrong and the two murders, the CPS is unlikely to bring the case to trial."

Ryan turned to him with furious eyes.

"You've got to be kidding! How else would the man's saliva find its way onto the stamp, unless he was the one who forged the postcard to lead people away from the scent of Duncan Gray's disappearance? What other explanation is there?"

The man squirmed.

"His barrister will argue that licking a stamp is not tantamount to murder and no jury will convict where there is reasonable doubt. Besides, he's a public figure. People will assume he is innocent."

Ryan wished he could argue with that.

"Look," he said, trying to keep his temper on a leash. "We're executing a search and seizure order this evening to confiscate Armstrong's CCTV and whatever else we find of interest at his house. That's sure to turn up something," he told them.

But Lucas just smiled.

"CCTV can be doctored," she said. "And, if he's been clever enough to remain undetected for over thirty years, he's surely been careful enough to remove any incriminating evidence from his home.

Besides, the fact he visits so regularly will look like a positive thing in the eyes of the jury."

"Not necessarily," Ryan argued. "It could also look like him returning to the scene of his crime."

"Pure conjecture," she said. "Do you have anything else?"

"What the hell are you expecting? A signed confession?" Ryan burst out. "They don't come cap in bloodied hand, ready to admit guilt!"

"Unlucky for you, then."

Ryan looked into Lucas's sharp blue eyes and realised she was enjoying herself. She revelled in the power that came from seeing him fail, feeding off situations like these.

"Who called you down here?" He turned back to the CPS man, who looked uncomfortably between the three of them before answering.

"I received a call from DCS Lucas's office," he replied. "Although I hardly see how that's relevant to the situation."

Ryan smiled grimly at his superintendent, who didn't so much as flinch.

"It's relevant because, if we'd had a few more hours, your decision might have been very different."

"I'm sorry," he said. "My hands are tied."

* * *

Thirty minutes later, Ryan watched Lucas sign the paperwork to release Nathan Armstrong without charge. He had refused to sign the release papers himself, so she had overridden him and made the determination.

"He's threatening to sue the Department," she muttered. "That makes two in one week."

"It's a bluff, you know that. You're making a mistake."

She turned and stalked back to her office without another word.

Across the foyer, Nathan Armstrong emerged from a lift and walked over to retrieve his personal effects from the duty sergeant. His eyes swept over Ryan and something passed between them. In that moment, he knew that Ryan had seen him—really *seen* him—and yet he was being forced to let him walk free, unable to stop it.

The feeling of power was intoxicating.

He turned to pick up his briefcase and was outside the main doors when a firm hand swung him back around.

"This isn't over," Ryan growled. "Wherever you go, whatever you do, know that I'm watching you because you're on my radar now. You'll never know the same freedom again."

Armstrong shook him off and pushed his face close to Ryan's, so close they were almost touching.

"Oh, but I will. In fact, I'm catching a late flight out to Paris tonight. Who knows? Perhaps I'll send you a postcard."

He smiled slowly.

"Happy hunting, Chief Inspector."

CHAPTER 35

Ryan's hands were curled into tight fists as he watched Armstrong drive away from Police Headquarters, his eyes burning with unshed tears as a guilty man walked free. It went against everything he stood for, and the prospect of being unable to fulfil his promise to Duncan Gray's mother made him sick to his stomach.

Phillips found him there, standing in one of the empty conference rooms looking out of the window.

Ryan sensed his presence but didn't turn around.

"She let him go," he said simply. "After everything, all the man hours, all the effort, she let him walk free."

"I know," Phillips replied. "She'll spin it a different way."

He walked across the room to join Ryan beside the window and they both watched darkness fall over the city. There were fewer stars to be seen here than in the clear skies over Kielder, but the twinkling lights were beautiful all the same.

"There'll be more victims to find," Ryan said softly. "Armstrong was too cool, too calm under fire. He's spent a lifetime perfecting his craft, so there must have been others."

Phillips agreed.

"We'll find them, lad."

"Will we?" Ryan murmured. "I don't know. He's clever, that one. And conceited."

"Those ones tend to make mistakes," Phillips reminded him. "Their vanity trips them up, sooner or later."

"Armstrong travels all over the world," Ryan added. "This will be multi-jurisdictional. It's an enormous task."

Phillips put a hand on Ryan's shoulder.

"We can start tomorrow. D' you know what we need before then?"

Ryan turned.

"What?"

"We need a pint. Besides, I owe you one."

"You owe me a whole bloody barrel, if we're keeping count."

"Aye, but with you being such a lightweight I thought we'd better round the numbers down. The others are going to meet us at the pub and Anna's on her way back from Kielder."

Ryan nodded and turned away from the window, regret and disappointment etched into every line of his body.

"C' mon Frank, let's go and get drunk."

* * *

Jack Lowerson watched his old friends walk out of the office, a small tribe of people banded together by their shared beliefs. On days like these, they pulled together and, ordinarily, he'd be down there with them.

But not today.

He shivered as two fingers walked up his back.

"Everything alright?"

Jennifer's voice melted like warm honey and the rest of the world seemed to fade into the background. She was all he could see; all he wanted.

"Everything's fine," he told her.

"What do you have planned this evening?"

"I usually have dinner at my mum's house on Wednesdays," he said, nervously.

"It's late," she said softly. "And Priya's gone home."

"Oh, do you need me to put in some overtime?"

She gave a husky laugh and walked back over to her desk, leaning against it with her hands braced.

"Lock the door, Jack."

Lowerson did as she bade him, silently locking away the past, discarding his old friends and his old life. He couldn't know what awaited him; couldn't see the danger until it was too late. He turned the key and stepped willingly into the rabbit hole.

EPILOGUE

One week later

Nathan Armstrong sat inside the Café Laurent in Paris with a champagne cocktail and a copy of *Le Monde*. On the small stage of the famous jazz venue, a woman crooned softly about her lost love, while a man in a black trilby accompanied her on the antique Steinway grand.

Armstrong reached across to take a sip of the bubbling liquid as his eyes skim-read the newspaper, flipping each page until he found what he was looking for.

There was a small paragraph covering the story on page thirty-three.

A young waiter had gone missing after leaving work at one of the city's premier restaurants and police were appealing for any word on his whereabouts.

By tomorrow, the story would have disappeared altogether.

And by then, he would be in Vienna.

He set the newspaper aside and settled back to listen to the music, keeping one eye on the door and another on his fellow occupants in the room. They were a mixed crowd of locals and tourists who were staying at the hotel which housed the café, but they shared the muted, understated glamour of upmarket middle-class people, the kind of people he preferred to be around. Their scent was different, he thought; more cultivated and distinctive than elsewhere. One could almost detect the meat in their national diet, although that was no drawback. He was nothing, if not a carnivore.

A tall, dark-haired man entered the room and Armstrong's chest contracted at the thought it might be Ryan making good on his threat.

But, of course, it wasn't.

He relaxed against the cushions and thought back over the years. It was possible that he had left something of himself behind, as he had foolishly done with the postcard, but he forgave himself for that oversight. Duncan Gray had been his first and most memorable victim, and everything that followed had been shiny and new. There were bound to be little hiccups in the early days but there was nothing to connect him to his other victims, he was sure of that.

He raised his hands to applaud when the music ended, and wondered what delights Vienna would hold.

DCI Ryan will return in early 2018

If you would like to be kept up to date with new releases from LJ Ross, please complete an e-mail contact form on her Facebook page or website, www.ljrossauthor.com

AUTHOR'S NOTE

Kielder Water and Forest Park is a very special corner of the world. I remember first visiting the area as a child and have since visited many times, most recently on a research trip where my husband and four-year-old son joined me in exploring the pretty village of Stonehaugh. We followed the burn towards Low Roses Bower in search of the Long Drop, an extraordinary stone-built outdoor toilet reputed to be England's tallest 'netty' that sits at the top of a gorge high over the burn. I was very tempted to include this site as part of the story of *Dark Skies* but the opportunity never quite presented itself—perhaps another time!

There is a real sense of isolation when you visit a place like Kielder and the tranquillity is incredible, affording a writer of crime fiction so much inspiration. The forest is lush during the day and, thanks to the wonderful observatory, stargazing pavilions and other sites dotted across the landscape, you can look up at the stars and begin to discover your own place in the universe. We are so fortunate to have dedicated organisations and individuals who look after the area and nurture its wildlife and eco-systems, encouraging the next generation to explore the best of what the natural world can offer.

In my fictional story, I wanted to convey some of the enormity of sky, water and forest, although it is no substitute for visiting the area and seeing its beauty for yourself. I have tried to remain as faithful as possible to the friendly atmosphere of Kielder Waterside and the villages surrounding the reservoir. Whilst it is true that a number of farmhouses were demolished and submerged beneath the new reservoir back in the late seventies and early eighties, I should point out that 'Reedmere Farm' is a figment of my imagination and should not be confused with any farmhouse that existed at the time. Likewise, the hamlet of 'Adderburn' is a work of pure fiction and does not exist on any map; although, I'm sure there are many pretty woodland clearings where you may stumble across a gingerbread cottage or two if you feel like exploring, which I heartily recommend that you do!

LJ ROSS

November 2017

ABOUT THE AUTHOR

Born in Newcastle upon Tyne, LJ Ross moved to London where she graduated from King's College London with undergraduate and postgraduate degrees in Law. After working in the City as a regulatory lawyer for a number of years, she realised it was high time for a change. The catalyst was the birth of her son, which forced her to take a break from the legal world and find time for some of the detective stories that had been percolating for a while and finally demanded to be written.

She lives with her husband and young son in her beautiful home county of Northumberland.

If you enjoyed *Dark Skies*, please consider leaving a review online.

If you would like to be kept up to date with new releases from LJ Ross, please complete an e-mail contact form on her Facebook page or website, www.ljrossauthor.com

ACKNOWLEDGEMENTS

I can hardly believe that *Dark Skies* represents my seventh full-length novel in the DCI Ryan series. It has been a wonderful three years and I have been so fortunate to have found such a fantastic readership. Your e-mails and messages on social media have been so kind and have sustained me through difficult patches and times when the words haven't flowed as easily as others—thank you.

At the time of writing, *Dark Skies* has been a UK #1 bestseller on the Amazon Kindle chart for eleven days whilst only available to pre-order, for which I am incredibly grateful. Each time I write a book, I feel a very real sense of responsibility: to myself, to the characters I have grown to love and, most of all, to the readers who have shown such affection for them. For those of you who have read other books in the series, I hope you enjoy this latest adventure of DCI Ryan as much as the others. For those who are new to the books, I hope this has been a good introduction!

There are so many people I would like to thank. First and always, there is my husband, James. He is a constant rock in a sometimes stormy sea of creative ups and downs and I am so grateful for his unwavering positivity, love and support over the fourteen years we have known each other. In the hope that (one day, when he is much older) my son might read these words, I would like to tell him how much he is loved and to thank him for bringing such happiness to our lives. To my mother, father and sister, I would like to reiterate my love and gratitude to them for being my greatest champions; I feel very fortunate to have such a wonderful family. To my friends and to all the kind bloggers and bibliophiles who have supported me and my books over the past three years, I can't tell you how much your enthusiasm has meant to me—I am indebted to all of you. I should also thank the innovators—those people who dreamed up a concept where anybody, regardless of background or contacts, could write a story and see it published independently by the author. Without them, my first book, *Holy Island*, might never have seen the light of day and over 1.5 million people might never have read about Phillips' love of the humble bacon stottie.

Finally, special mention goes to the real-life Jennifer Lucas, who made a very kind donation to charity and whose name is now immortalised in print (though it goes without saying that she is much lovelier than her fictional counterpart!).

37249914R00167

Printed in Great Britain
by Amazon